Critical Praise for *Glazed Murder*

"The perfect comfort read: a delicious murder, a like-able heroine, quirky Southern characters—and donut recipes!"

—Rhys Bowen, Agatha and Anthony award–
winning author of the Molly Murphy
and Royal Spyness mysteries

"If you like donuts—and who doesn't?—you'll love this mystery. It's like a trip to your favorite coffee shop, but without the calories!"

—Leslie Meier, author of the Lucy Stone
mysteries *New Year's Eve Murder* and *Wedding
Day Murder*

"Jessica Beck's *Glazed Murder* is a delight. Suzanne Hart is a lovable amateur sleuth who has a hilariously protective mother *and* great donut recipes! Readers will have a blast with this book."

—Diane Mott Davidson, *New York Times*
bestselling author of *Fatally Flaky*

GLAZED *Murder*

Jessica Beck

St. Martin's Paperbacks

GLAZED MURDER

Copyright © 2010 by Jessica Beck.
Excerpt from *Fatally Frosted* copyright © 2010 by Jessica Beck.

For information address St. Martin's Press, 175 Fifth Avenue, New York, NY 10010.

EAN: 978-1-250-25047-6

St. Martin's Paperbacks edition / April 2010

St. Martin's Paperbacks are published by St. Martin's Press, 175 Fifth Avenue, New York, NY 10010.

P1

To Ruby Hall,
mother and artist extraordinaire.

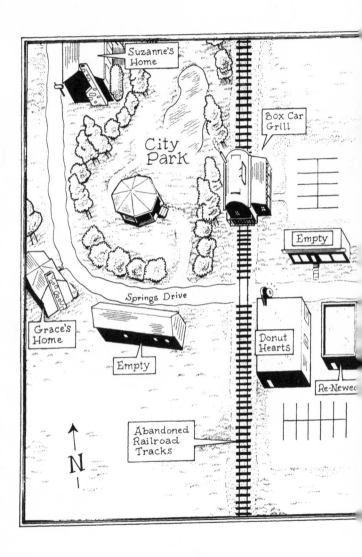

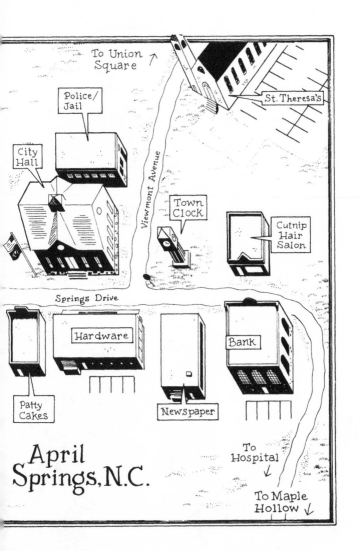

"Donuts. Is there anything they can't do?"

—Matt Groening,
creator of *The Simpsons*

GLAZED *Murder*

CHAPTER 1

Trust me when I say that I usually lead a pretty ordinary life. It's not every day that I stumble across
a body while I'm working at Donut Hearts, my
handmade-donut and premium-blend coffee shop
perched on the edge of the downtown district of
April Springs, North Carolina, population 5,001.

But this was anything but ordinary.

Someone had dumped a body in front of my shop
in the darkness of night as I watched, and then sped
off into the shadows before I could react to what I'd
seen.

I work the graveyard shift at the shop, there's no
other way to put it. My hours are off-kilter in rela-
tion to the rest of the world, from 2 A.M. when I mix
the first batch of dough until I sweep up and lock the
doors sometime around noon. It kills all possibilities
of dating after 8 P.M., but I haven't been all that interested in going out since my divorce from my ex-
husband, Max, the great impersonator. He's an actor,

and prides himself on his ability to fake his way through any role—including husband—something I found out much to my consternation. The man had been so smooth when he'd lied to me during our marriage that I doubted a polygraph could have picked up his deceit. He had an unsteady income doing nationally distributed commercials now and then, and I'd been urging him to try his luck in Hollywood, not because of his talent—of which there was little—but because it would get him out of my hair once and for all. No such luck. He refused to leave April Springs, the small town in the foothills of the Blue Ridge Mountains where we'd both grown up, and I wasn't about to budge, either.

Sorry, that's a tangent I'm in no mood to take. Let's get back to what happened. I watched in stunned silence as something heavy was dumped out of a speeding car just after I walked into the shop. As a matter of fact, my hand was on the switch to light the DONUT HEARTS sign when I heard the noise outside. At twelve past two in the morning, I was used to having the world to myself. Emma Blake—my assistant at the donut shop and my honorary niece—never made it in until two-thirty, and she wasn't coming in today at all, since it was her day off. On the one day of the week I was opening by myself and working in the shop all morning alone, the world had conspired to throw my life into turmoil.

The presence of the car itself had been enough to make me look up when I heard it outside. We don't get much traffic on Springs Drive that time of morning. Before I could grasp what I'd seen, I flipped the switch up, lighting the world just outside my shop and turning the shadowy lump lying on the street into what was clearly a body. All I'd really caught of the person dumping the body had been a face covered with a black ski mask, and the flash of a faded tiger embossed on a dark, hooded sweatshirt. The car door slammed the second I spotted him, and the killer drove off before I could manage to do much more than scream as it disappeared into the darkness.

"Did you check for a pulse when you found him, Mrs. Hart?" the young police officer asked as I finished brewing a pot of our specialty coffee blend. I usually need a jump start in the morning before I start on the dough, and today it was true, more than ever.

"I told you before, Officer Moore, it's 'miss,' and you should call me 'Suzanne'. I ran outside after I called you'all, but I'm not sure I could find a pulse if I had to." I shivered a little as I remembered my fingers probing the man's neck as he lay sprawled face-down on the pavement. When I'd rolled him over to try to help him, I'd nearly lost it when I realized it was Patrick Blaine. Patrick came by for donuts once a week since I'd taken over the shop, and I'd grown quite fond of him over the years. He didn't look peaceful at all now, like they sometimes show in the movies. I hadn't been all that surprised when there'd been no indications that he was still alive. His face grimaced in a death mask that nearly made him unrecognizable. He'd joked with me about being my honorary uncle, and now he lay dead in the street in front of my shop.

Officer Moore asked, "Did you catch a glimpse of the driver at all?"

I frowned, then finally admitted, "Not enough to identify who it was. It was dark out, and whoever was driving wore a ski mask and a hooded sweatshirt." I paused, and then added, "There was a faded tiger on the front of it; at least I think that's what it was. It could have been a dog. Or maybe even a race car. I don't know, I only saw it for a second."

Moore nodded, jotting again in his notebook. He was a hearty, robust young man, with jet-black hair and eyes that nearly matched. "And you don't know what kind of car you saw, is that right?"

I shrugged. "I'm sorry. It was dark, and it all happened so fast. Is there a chance Patrick is still alive?"

I fought the urge to look outside at the activity around the body. I'd seen the paramedics arrive just as the police cruiser pulled into the parking lot in front of the shop. Donut Hearts was now in the building that had once been the train depot, back when the tracks had run through the edge of town. They had long been abandoned, but the twin rails were still there, hiding sometimes beneath the brush. The only other remnant of their presence was across Springs Drive where the Boxcar grill sat, a converted train car that now served as a diner. My eyes drifted back to the street outside the shop. Honestly, I wasn't sure I wanted to see what the paramedics were doing, especially if they were zippering my friend into a black body bag.

Officer Moore, barely into his twenties, shook his head curtly. "No worries there. He was dead before he hit the ground."

His casual tone of voice struck me as a little too callous to be coming from someone ten years younger than me. "How can you be so sure? I knelt down in the street beside him and I couldn't tell."

The officer said slowly, "I know a gunshot trauma when I see it. The guy was practically a ghost, he was so white. He had to have bled out in the car. You must have noticed it yourself."

I gulped my coffee, then said, "I saw him, but I thought the lights might be playing tricks on my eyes." Officer Moore might be used to seeing dead bodies—though I doubted he'd been on the force long enough to run up against many of them—but it was a new and entirely unwelcome sight for me. I make donuts, plain and simple, and have ever since I bought the shop with my divorce settlement. Max had made a successful national commercial at exactly the wrong time, at least as far as our divorce was concerned. I'd caught him at one of the rare moments in his life when he'd been solvent, right after finding him in bed with Darlene Higgins, our once-upon-a-time prom queen and now a beautician at Wilma Gentry's Cutnip.

That's when I did three crazy things in the span of a month, after the official end of my marriage: I moved back in with my momma; I changed my last name to the one I'd been born with; and I bought the donut shop. It was a series of rash decisions that came when I needed to reestablish myself in the world as Suzanne Hart, not Max Thornburg's wife.

The young cop finally flipped his notebook closed and finished filling in a multicopy form. I glanced at it as he held it out to me, along with a pen.

"Just sign here and I'll give you a copy for your records."

I did as I was told, and shook my head at the man's precision. The time on the report was 2:37, not 2:40 or even 2:30. His seven would have looked like a one if it hadn't been for the bar he'd put through the middle of it. You'd think police officers would be required to have good penmanship, given how much writing they must do in the course of a day filling out paperwork and making reports. I signed the form and handed it back to him.

After he glanced at my signature, he pulled off a copy from the bottom and handed it to me. "That's all I need for now. Thanks for your cooperation."

"I did what anyone would do," I said as I walked him to the door.

"You're kidding, right? A lot of folks would have pretended they didn't see a thing and let someone else go through all of this."

"I can't imagine anyone in April Springs doing that."

He smiled, but there wasn't an ounce of humor in it. "Yeah, well, you don't exactly hang out with the wrong crowd, now do you? Thanks for the coffee."

"You're welcome," I said as I started to shut the door behind him. "Are you sure you don't want any donuts?"

If there was one thing I'd learned early on running Donut Hearts, it was that most police officers hated the association of their line of work with donut shops.

I don't know what I would have done if he'd said yes, since I hadn't even started on the dough yet, but he just shook his head as he walked back to his patrol car. I don't keep old donuts around the place overnight. If I have many extras at closing time, I box them up. What happens next depends on my mood. If I feel sociable, I take them around to businesses and offer them free of charge, in the hopes of drumming up more business down the line. If I'm dog tired and dead on my feet, which is more often than I care to admit, I give them to Father Pete at St. Theresa's, and he sees to it that they go to folks who don't have enough to eat.

I watched in silence as everyone finally drove away, and found myself once again alone in the darkness. It had been a traumatic way to start my day, but I had work to do, and I couldn't let what had happened stop me from making donuts. In a way, it was a good thing I had something to do that kept me busy. The last thing I needed was to keep replaying that scene in my head again and again, and feel that feathery touch of dead skin on my fingertips once more.

If I'm being honest about it, my favorite time of day in my routine is when no one is at the shop but me. As much as I love Emma—and need her help producing thirty-five or forty dozen donuts each morning—I relish the one day a week when I do it all by myself. Making dough and batter, working on glazes, and coming up with new creations is great fun, despite the appearance of drudgery to the outside world of doing the same thing day in and day out. I'd been working on a new pumpkin donut recipe for the past few weeks, and I believed that I had finally achieved nirvana with the perfect blend of pumpkin, cinnamon, nutmeg, and cloves in the recipe.

But there was only one way to find out. I dropped

a few of the donut-batter circles into the piping hot oil, flipped them with my beefy wooden sticks that resemble chopsticks on steroids more than anything else, and then pulled them from their hot bath when they were done. I tumbled the rounds onto the glazing grid, drizzled the donuts with a sugar glaze I'd made fresh that morning, and took my first bite. The sensation of the warm cake donut spiced just right burst in my mouth. Almost without awareness, I ate both samples and knew that this recipe was the one I'd been searching for. I caught a glimpse of myself as I opened my stainless steel fridge for some milk, and realized that I'd been sampling too many of my own wares lately. I was either going to have to learn to control myself, or start going to the gym again.

As I finished making the rest of the batch of pumpkin donuts and started on the plain cakes, I knew I'd have to start working out and cut back on my daily donut consumption. I have some willpower, but not that much. After the cake donuts were done—a selection of plain, blueberry, cherry, and more pumpkin today—I raised the heat of the oil from 350 degrees to 365 so I could make the yeast donuts sitting in the proofer waiting their turn in the hot oil fryer. "Proofer" is a fancy name for an insulated box with a lightbulb and a humidifier, and although the proofer is ancient, it works just fine. Besides, I don't have the money to replace it just because it's ugly.

The donuts need around half an hour to rest in the proofer once they are cut, but I'm never bored while I'm waiting. There's not a lot of downtime in the world of donut making, especially when I'm working by myself.

I managed to hold my snacking down to one more donut by the time I opened the shop at five-thirty, when the early morning was still shrouded in March's darkness. It hadn't been easy, but I was able to deal with what I'd witnessed.

At least I hoped so.

One of my regulars was waiting outside when I unlocked the front door.

George Morris, a balding man in his sixties who had retired from the police force a dozen years ago, said, "I heard what happened, Suzanne. Are you all right?"

"I'm fine, George. It didn't take long for the word to get out, did it?"

He shrugged. "I always sleep with my police scanner on. When I heard this location mentioned, I woke right up."

After he took his regular seat at the long counter in front, I asked, "Do you want your usual this morning?"

George nodded, and I grabbed two pumpkin donuts and a large glass of whole milk for him. I wasn't going to tell him about my new recipe. If he couldn't tell it was different, I had more work to do on it.

As I delivered his food, George said, "Come on, there's nobody else around right now. Tell me what really happened."

I frowned at the question, not wanting to relive what I'd witnessed, but also realizing that I wouldn't be able to get him off the subject until I did. "I was here at two, just like always, and I was getting ready to turn on the lights when I heard a car race by and a body hit the pavement." I shuddered involuntarily as I remembered the dull thud of the impact. I wondered if I'd ever be able to wipe it out of my mind.

George surprised me with an instant of tenderness as he lightly touched my hand. "It's okay; the memory will fade. Just give it some time."

"Thanks," I said. "I hope so."

He looked around the shop. "Where's Emma?"

"It's her day off," I said.

"I'm sorry you had to go through that alone."

I managed a smile for him. He was a sweetheart, and for some odd reason, I felt guilty about causing him sadness, which I know is ridiculous, but I can't help how I feel. If I could, I would have been able to save myself a bucketload of pain over the years, most especially from my ex-husband. Then again, if there hadn't been a Max once upon a time in my life, I wouldn't be running my own donut shop now, so maybe it was good I didn't have as much control over things as I would have liked.

I looked at George. "Did you hear who the victim was? It was Patrick Blaine."

He shook his head. "They didn't say over the scanner. That must make it twice as hard for you. You were fond of him, weren't you?"

"I was," I admitted. "I wonder if they know anything else about what happened."

George glanced at his watch. "Let's listen to the radio. Maybe Lester knows something about it."

I reached up to a shelf behind the register and

turned the radio on. It was permanently tuned to WAPS, and if there was any news about the murder, Lester Moorefield would have it in his morning report.

Lester's voice came on just as Toby Keith finished his latest song about cheating and retribution. It seemed to be a popular theme on the country music charts these days, one for which I had a great deal of sympathy myself. Lester said, "In local news, there was a homicide reported on Springs Drive in front of Donut Hearts this morning. The body has been identified as Patrick Blaine, a local banker and a resident of nearby Maple Hollow. The cause of death has yet to be released, but this reporter has learned that it was not a hit-and-run, as was first described, but a shooting."

I turned off the radio. "Nobody said it was a hit-and-run. What was Lester talking about?"

George shook his head. "The man loves to embellish the news, and one of these days it's going to bite him where the sun doesn't shine." The retired cop pushed his plate away as he stood. "Hate to eat and run, but I've got a few things I need to take care of before work. I'm filling in at the courthouse this morning."

George supplemented his retirement income by working as a substitute bailiff at the courthouse, which kept him in touch with his old pals, as well as new ones. He saluted me with two fingers to his forehead, then he said, "I'll touch base with you later."

I said, "You're not going to say anything to Lester, are you?"

George shook his head. "Why bother? It wouldn't do any good, would it?" He looked around the empty donut shop. "Are you going to be okay here by yourself?"

I nodded. "I'll be fine. Go on."

I'd miss him, but I wasn't about to admit it to him. Oftentimes George kept the place from feeling too lonely during some of the morning lulls I faced every day. If I'd looked into the razor-thin profit margin in the world of selling donuts before I bought the place, I never would have gone through with it. I was still glad I'd purchased the business, though. There were more profits to be made than those that could be shown on a spreadsheet, and I'd gained in immeasurable riches when it came to new friends. I had a nice sociable place where people could come to relax, enjoy a donut and a cup of coffee, and grab a few moments of sanctuary from a troubling world.

The first thing I'd done when I bought the shop was remodel the former train depot. The stiff booths and wobbly tables of the old donut shop went first, replaced by couches and comfortable chairs. As dingy beige paint on the walls was replaced with a plum faux finish—and the harsh concrete floor painted to match—the place transitioned from a utilitarian space to one where people liked to congregate. At least that had been my plan when I'd spent the last dime, literally, of my divorce settlement making Donut Hearts into the kind of place where I would like to hang out myself.

George said, "I'm going to nose around the precinct before I'm due to report and see if I can find out anything else about Patrick Blaine. There's got to be some reason he ended up dead in front of your shop."

"Is Chief Martin going to let you walk right in there and start investigating the case? You're retired, remember?"

"He cuts me a little slack most days," George said. "As long as I stay out of his way, it works out fine. Don't tell me you two are still having problems."

I shrugged as I wiped his section of counter down with a clean cloth. "I don't think he's ever forgiven me for being my father's daughter." The police chief had dated my mother back in high school before my dad had come onto the scene, and there were rumors that Chief Martin had never been able to let her go. He was clearly unhappy in his current marriage, and seeing my mother around town didn't make life any easier for him, I was sure. Dad had been dead and buried for six years, but he might as well have still been alive. My mother had mated for life, and she wasn't interested in anyone else, something she made sure the chief knew whenever the opportunity to tell him arose. I fully realized why he was so unhappy, but did he have to take it out on me?

George was nearly out the door when I called out, "Let me know what you find out, okay?"

He shot me with his finger, then grinned. "You betcha." He stopped out front and talked to a man in uniform, not Officer Moore or the chief, but another young cop named Stephen Grant who came in occasionally to get donuts on his days off. Officer Grant was slim, despite his love for donuts, and was barely over five feet eight, the height minimum for the force, he'd once told me.

"Good morning," I said, as he walked in. "Are you here for professional reasons, or personal?"

"Would you believe a little of both?" he asked. "If I could get a bear claw and a coffee to go, that would be great."

As I poured him a cup and grabbed one of the fried cinnamon treats I'd just finished making, I asked, "What part of your visit is professional?"

"I just wanted to ask you about what happened this morning. The chief's got everybody keeping their eyes open, so I thought I'd see if you might have remembered something else."

I frowned. "Nothing I didn't tell Officer Moore."

He slid money across the counter and grabbed his breakfast. "Then I guess this stop wasn't a total loss, was it? See you later."

"Come back any time," I said.

My mother came bursting in through the front door of the donut shop ten minutes later. "I'm going to horsewhip Lester Moorefield and then hang him up on the Patriot's Tree for everyone to see."

She had always been overprotective of me, and that had only intensified since the divorce. Though my mother was six inches shorter than me—barely five feet tall—she was a force to be reckoned with. I couldn't have her flying off the handle, though.

"Calm down, Momma. It's all right."

"The blasted fool might as well have said you witnessed the whole thing," she said. "He even mentioned your shop's name in his broadcast. Did you hear him?"

This wasn't going well, and I didn't even want to think about what she might say next. It would be best if I could make light of it. "Who knows, maybe the publicity will do me some good. We could always use the business."

She frowned at me, which was not an entirely unexpected reaction from her. "Suzanne Marie Hart, this is serious. Are you all right?"

"I'm fine, Momma. I didn't see a thing. There's nothing to worry about."

My mother had a strength of will that few in town could match. "You'd better be, or Lester is going to meet the back of my horsewhip."

After she had a cup of coffee and one of the wheat donuts she preferred, Momma left to take care of some pressing business. I had no idea what that might be, but I wasn't about to ask. It had been a tough transition moving back in with her, and even now—a full year after my divorce—we were both still trying to figure out how to live together without killing each other. Maybe that was a little harsh. Most of the time we got along just fine, but she had a way of pushing my buttons sometimes that even Max hadn't managed in our years together. I suppose it made sense. After all, she was the one who had installed them in the first place.

I was nearly back to normal when something happened that made my blood pressure jump two dozen points. My ex-husband Max showed up.

"Speak of the devil, and he appears," I said, wondering what was important enough to bring him back into my life.

A GOOD BEGINNING DONUT

This donut is a good place to start your morning, or your donut-making career. It's a fairly simple recipe that yields good results, and with a little practice, it can be your go-to recipe when you need a quick fix.

INGREDIENTS
4–5 cups bread flour
1 cup granulated sugar
1 teaspoon baking soda
½ teaspoon nutmeg
½ teaspoon cinnamon
2 dashes of salt
½ cup sour cream
1 egg, beaten
1 cup buttermilk

DIRECTIONS
Combine the flour, sugar, baking soda, nutmeg, cinnamon, and salt in a bowl and sift it into another bowl. Add the beaten egg to the dry mix, then add the sour cream and the buttermilk to the mixture and stir it all in lightly. You may need more buttermilk or flour to get the dough to a workable mix. This varies based on temperature and humidity, and the dough should resemble bread dough when you're finished. That is, it shouldn't stick to your hands when you touch it, but it should be moist enough to remain flexible. Don't worry, you'll get the hang of it soon enough. Knead this mix lightly, then roll it out to about ¼ of an inch. Then, take your donut hole cutter—a simple

circle with a removable center—and press out your donut shapes, reserving the holes for a later frying. The cutters are inexpensive, and worth having on hand.

Set your fryer for 375 degrees, and when the oil is ready, put 4 to 6 donuts in the basket, depending on the size of your equipment. This can also be done in a deep pot, but I find the precision of the fryer worth the money, especially if you're going to make donuts fairly often.

Let the donuts cook for about two minutes on one side, then check one. If it's golden brown, the shade I prefer, flip it over with a large chopstick or wooden skewer, and let that side cook another two minutes.

Once the donuts are finished, remove them to a cooling rack or a plate lined with paper towels, being sure to drain them thoroughly before serving. You can coat the top with butter and then sprinkle them with powdered sugar, cinnamon, or eat them plain.

Makes approximately 1 dozen donuts.

CHAPTER 2

Max gave me that beautiful smile of his, and I felt my knees weaken, despite our sordid history together. "Now is that any way to talk to me? I just heard about what happened this morning. I'm worried about you, Suze."

"Get in line," I said, intentionally keeping my voice firm with him. Max was gorgeous, too handsome for his own good, with wavy brown hair and the deepest brown eyes I'd ever seen in my life. What was worse was that he knew how good he looked, and took full advantage of it. Suze had been his pet name for me during our marriage, though I'd never cared for it.

"My name's Suzanne, remember," I said as I stared into his eyes.

He nodded slightly. "All right then. Suzanne, I miss you, and I don't care who knows it. I want to be a part of your life again."

It might have worked on someone who didn't know him better, but I fully realized that I couldn't believe this confession was the whole truth, or any part of it. Frankly, there was no way I was ever going to let him off the hook for his infidelity. "I bet you said the same thing to the prom queen after I divorced you."

He shook his head sadly. "Darlene was a mistake. I strayed one time in the entire course of our marriage. You have to forgive me."

I studied him closely. Was it possible he was telling the truth? I'd be lying if I said there was nothing about him that still got to me, but that didn't mean I'd lost every last shred of my dignity and respect. "Okay, I'm calling your bluff. You say you've changed. Let's see you prove it."

He looked startled by the challenge. "How do I do that—not sleep with Darlene again? Consider it done."

"You're not getting off that easily," I said, "and you know it."

"Tell me what to do, and I'll do it."

I frowned at him. "Don't be like this, Max. Not today."

"Like what? What am I doing that's so wrong? I love you, and I want to be a part of your life. Help me out here, Suzanne."

I didn't even know how to answer that at first, but suddenly, I knew what to say. "Go away, Max. That's all I want from you right now."

I expected a fight, but he just nodded, walked to the door, and then turned toward me before he left. "I'm going to respect your wishes for the moment, but I'm not giving up, Suzanne."

After he was gone, I stared after him, thinking

about my ex much longer than I should have. Did Max really want me back? It wasn't for my money; that was certain. Could I find it in my heart to ever forgive him?

If I was being honest about it, I just wasn't sure.

An hour later, Terri Milner and Sandy White came in and stood at the register looking over the day's offerings in the two large glass cases behind the counter. Terri was the mother of eight-year-old twin girls, and Sandy had a nine-year-old son who caused more havoc than both twins combined.

"Glad you two could make it this morning," I said.

Terri grinned. "Are you kidding? This place is so nice; we might just leave our husbands and move in here full-time."

Sandy matched her smile with one of her own. "I love the way you decorated this place. Most donut shops have those awful benches and hard plastic seats. You have these soft couches. It's like being at home."

Terri added, "If there weren't any children there."

"Not that we don't love our kids," Sandy added quickly.

"We just need a break sometimes." She looked up into the air. "I love the CD playing. Is it new?"

"I thought a little light classical music would be nice," I admitted.

"Delightful, as always," they said. I got them their donuts and coffees, and they settled onto one of the couches where they could relax and watch the world go past. It had been my goal to make the place somewhere local folks—and women in particular—would like to come to relax, and so far, I'd managed to garner quite a crowd of regulars. Not that I didn't welcome the men who came in, as well.

As I finished bussing a few tables after some customers that had left, Grace Gauge came into the shop. She worked as a corporate sales rep for a national cosmetics company, and more importantly, Grace was without doubt my best friend in April Springs.

"I just heard what happened," she said. "I looked outside, but I didn't see any chalk outlines of the body on the road." Grace is blonde whereas I'm a brunette, and she is as trim as I dream I'll be again someday, but I don't hold any of that against her. She works out more than any one woman in her right mind should, and eats dried and tasteless things I wouldn't touch on my worst day. If it comes right down to it, I'd rather have a few more curves and a bright smile than be as skinny as she is. Not that Grace is ever grumpy—her regime seems to fit her—but I would be a snarling bear if I ever tried to live a moment of her life, especially if I only got to eat what she ate.

"They took pictures before they left," I said. "Do they even make those outlines anymore?"

She rolled her eyes. "When are you going to start watching CSI and catch up with the rest of us?"

I smiled at her. "I guess I'll start watching when they show it right after the network news at seven. I'm not even awake when most shows come on now."

"There are reruns on cable at all hours of the day and night, you know."

I laughed. "Momma doesn't want cable television in the house, and honestly, it doesn't bother me, since I'm in bed by seven or eight most every night, anyway."

"I truly don't know how you do it," Grace said. "How on earth are you ever going to find a boyfriend with hours like that?"

I shrugged. I wasn't going to tell her about Max's recent declaration, at least not until I'd had a chance to mull over his words. "There's always third shift, and if I get desperate enough for male companionship, I could check to see if Jack Long has any friends at the hospital." Jack was a male nurse I went out with sometimes, though the relationship wasn't the least bit romantic for either of us. We were good company for each other, and that was it. Still, it was nice to be able to call him when I felt the need for some testosterone in my life, and if he was free, he was always interested in a movie and some popcorn at the Westbridge Theater. If they ever stopped having matinees there, I don't know what I would do for a social life.

Grace shook her head. "You are hopeless, you know that, don't you?"

I smiled. "Said the kettle to the pot. Now that we've talked about me, should we spend some time discussing your love life?"

She blew out a hearty puff of air. "I'd rather not, if you don't mind."

"A change of subject it is, then. Where are you off to this morning?"

"I've got a store reset in Charlotte," she said. "The good news is that I get to wear jeans, but the downside is that I have to handle dusty things all day."

"Somehow I'm sure you'll manage. Have fun," I said as I grabbed a paper coffee cup and filled it for her with fresh brew. I'd tried a handful of new low-fat donut recipes for her since I took over the store, but I still hadn't come up with anything that didn't taste faintly of cardboard, though I wasn't ready to give up yet. She would settle for whole wheat if it came to that, but I was afraid even that recipe wasn't healthy enough for her. In my opinion, donuts are meant to be a hedonistic experience—at least they are if they're done properly—but I wasn't licked yet in my search for something Grace would enjoy.

By the time I shooed the last of my customers out the door and locked up, I glanced back at the display case and saw that it was almost empty. I'd had a steady stream of customers all morning long, and I couldn't help wondering if Lester's on-air plug had revved up my business, at least temporarily. I wasn't happy about what I'd seen earlier, but then again, a full cash register was never a bad thing. I cleaned the place up, boxed the donuts that were left, got the bank deposit ready, and was just locking up when Gabby Williams from next door knocked on the glass. Gabby is a trim woman in her fifties who always looks nice, but there was an edge beneath the surface of her smile today, and I knew from talk around town that her teeth could be razor sharp. Gabby ran ReNewed, a second-hand clothing store that featured some of the better preworn clothes in the area, as Gabby liked to call her wares.

"Good morning," I said, wondering what she wanted as I unlocked the front door for her. Gabby knew everyone in April Springs, and consequently had a map of exactly where all the bodies were buried. She was a good woman to have on your side, and a bad one to have as an enemy. We'd danced that fine line since I'd bought the shop—neighboring storekeepers, but nothing more—and I was going to do my best to stay on her good side without making my personal life any concern of hers. Gabby prided herself on her figure, and loved to wear some of the nicer things that came into her shop. Consequently, she always appeared to be mingling below her station in life when she chatted with me, an impression she did nothing to dispel. Today she was wearing a gray wool suit that was topped off by a prim pillbox hat. I half expected her to be wearing matching gloves, but none must have come in, or she would have surely been sporting them. I always felt terribly underdressed in my blue jeans whenever she was around, and today was no exception.

"It must have been dreadful for you, dear," she said.

"It was just another day," I said, fighting to suppress my sigh.

Her eyebrows arched. There wasn't a soul left on earth who remembered their original shape. For some odd reason, Gabby had tweezed her brows into oblivion, carefully redrawing them every morning with a heavy eyebrow pencil that fooled no one.

She asked archly, "Do you mean to stand there and tell me that you find bodies outside your shop every morning?"

"Oh, that. It happened so quickly, I'd nearly forgotten about it." I only wished that were true. Unfortunately, I wondered if the image would ever fade, though George's words of encouragement gave me hope that someday it would.

"Come to my shop and tell me all about it," she said.

I considered making my excuses, but if I did that, I'd end up in Gabby's daily gossip report as a likely suspect, I just knew it.

"I've only got a minute," I said as I let myself be led into her shop after bolting my front door closed. With all of those old clothes in her inventory, I always expected the place to be a bit musty, but I had to give Gabby credit. She ran a tight shop, though the lavender scent ever-present in the air was a little strong for my taste.

We walked through aisles of clothing to the back register where she had a teapot staying warm on a fancy little hot plate. "Care for some Earl Grey?"

"Just a smidge," I said, putting my bank deposit on my seat.

Gabby poured a full cup, then she handed it to me. It appeared that I was going to be there for some time. I'd just recounted what had happened for the third time when my cell phone laughed at me. I'd changed the ring tone on a whim, and instead of a proper summons, it now laughed maniacally whenever I had a call. I was questioning that choice now—and vowing to change it at the next possible opportunity—when I answered it before it could laugh again.

"Hello?"

"It's George. Where are you? I'm at your shop and you're not here."

"I'm next door at Gabby's. What is it? Is something wrong?"

He hesitated, then said, "Don't say anything in front of that gossipmonger, but make your excuses and meet me in front of your place. It's important."

"I understand. I'll be right there."

I hung up and told Gabby, "I'm really sorry, but I've got to go."

"Was it the police?" she asked as she gestured to my phone.

"No, it's about the donut shop." It wasn't entirely a lie, since George was retired and not an official member of law enforcement anymore. And honestly, anything that affected me included my shop. At least it might let me get away from Gabby unscathed.

"Go, I understand. I'm a businesswoman, too, and we need to stick together."

"Thanks for the tea," I said as I started for the door.

"Aren't you forgetting something?" Gabby called out to me.

What did I have to do, rinse out my cup before I was allowed to leave? "I don't think so."

She held up my deposit bag. "It feels rather full. Should I take care of it for you myself?"

"No, thanks," I said sheepishly as I retrieved the day's receipts. "I'll see you later."

"Good-bye," she said as she reached for her telephone. There was little doubt in my mind I was going to be the subject of her morning bulletin. I only hoped I came out as a sympathetic character and not the villain of the piece.

Either way, I was free from her, at least for now. When I saw the scowl on George's face, though, I almost found myself wishing I were back having tea with Gabby.

The look on his face drained any good cheer I might have felt from my narrow escape. "What is it? Did something happen? Hey, I thought you had to work."

"The case was dismissed," he said as he looked around the sidewalk. "We can't talk here, I don't want anyone overhearing our conversation. Can we go inside?"

I dug through my purse and found my keys. There was no mistaking George's intent gaze of concern.

Once we were in the shop, I flipped the lock shut, then said, "Let's go back to my office. Otherwise people might think I'm still open for business and start banging on the door for donuts."

We walked in back, going past the fryer, the glazing rack, and the dough board, past the proofing station, the dry storage, and the refrigeration units, until we got to my cubby of an office tucked in one corner of the flour-storage area where fifty-pound bags waited their turn for the large flour mixer.

I followed him in, then said, "There's not much room, but at least it's out of sight from prying eyes. Now don't keep me in suspense. What's so important?"

George said, "It turns out Patrick Blaine is more than just a regular, everyday banker. There's a buzz around the squad room that he's into some of the darker areas of finance, and his murder was the result of having a dissatisfied customer."

"Patrick? I can't believe it. He always seemed so sweet to me."

"I trust my sources," he said.

"Even if it's true," I said, "what does that have to do with me?"

George frowned. "Maybe nothing, but I'm wondering how safe you are here right now. If the killer thinks you might be a witness to the body disposal, what's going to keep him from tying up a loose end and getting rid of you?"

I protested a little too loudly for the small space, "But I didn't see anything." Being referred to as an item on a killer's to-do list wasn't something I enjoyed hearing.

"You know that, and I know that, but he might not be willing to take the chance."

I tried to pace, but there was just no room for it. "What am I supposed to do, lock myself up in my house and hope he goes away? I've got a business to run, and if I close Donut Hearts for even a week, I might as well shut down for good. There's a fine line between profit and loss for me here, and I can't afford to let it get any narrower."

He put his hands on my shoulders. "You have to realize that you can't afford to take any chances, either."

Fighting to keep my voice calm, I said, "George, I appreciate your concern, but I can't change my life and go hide in a hole, even if I wanted to."

He shrugged. "Then it's on your head, and not mine. I just thought you had a right to know what you might be facing."

George started for the door when I grabbed his

arm. "Hey, I do appreciate you looking out for me. Don't stop, okay?"

He shrugged. "I'll do what I can, but I'm not making any promises." George knocked on the back door. "Would you mind opening this?"

I did as he asked, and he paused at the door that led into the alley.

"Aren't you coming with me?" he said.

"I've got some paperwork to catch up on since I'm already here," I said. "Don't worry about me. I'll be fine."

"Then I'm staying, too," he said as he moved back inside.

Honestly, I knew he just wanted what was best for me, but I already had one overprotective person in my life in the guise of a mother. "Go. I'm fine. I mean it."

There must have been something in my voice that registered with him, because George studied me a second, then nodded. "I won't be far."

"I know, and it really does make me feel better."

After I bolted the back door behind him, I didn't feel much like doing paperwork after all. There was a constant stream of it in and out of my small business, and I never seemed to catch up on the growing pile, let alone chip away much of its depth.

I started for the front, then paused at the door that separated my kitchen from the public space and peeked outside.

At first, everything looked fine in the world outside my shop, but then I saw a man across the street staring hard at me, using an open newspaper as a shield to deflect my glance after a second. Our eyes met for an instant before he could hide, though, and there was nothing casual about his gaze when he looked at me. He was tall and thin, with a shock of sandy blond hair, and under other circumstances, I would have thought him quite attractive.

But there was nothing appealing about him at the moment.

Ducking back into the kitchen, I reached for the phone and dialed the police. The chief and I might have issues, but I needed someone there, and like an idiot, I'd just sent George away. I was promised an officer immediately, and then I hung up. There was nothing I could do now except wait. I only hoped the police arrived before the man across the street grew bolder and decided to come after me.

No such luck. He folded his newspaper and crossed Springs Drive toward my shop with a firm step and a quick pace. Panicking, I grabbed the first thing I could lay my hands on. I was just glad it was a long, sharp knife instead of something harmless like a roll of paper towels. As he neared the door, I double-checked to see that it was locked, then I made sure he saw the knife in my hand.

"Go away," I shouted, as I looked up and down the street. Where were the police when I needed them?

"You need to let me in right now," he said as he reached into the breast pocket of his jacket.

"If I open this door, I'm going to fillet you. I called the police. They'll be here any second."

I expected to see a gun in his hand when he pulled it out of his jacket, and I knew that neither the thin glass of the shop windows nor the steel of my blade would be able to stop him if he wanted to shoot me through the door.

Instead, he pulled out a wallet, which he opened to show me a badge. "My name's Jake Bishop. I'm with the state police inspector's office, and I'd like to talk to you." He glanced at the knife, then he added with a wry smile, "If you promise not to skewer me when I come in."

"Sorry about that," I said as I started to undo the lock, feeling foolish holding a knife on him in broad daylight on the other side of a locked door. Just then, a squad car pulled up. Officer Moore, the young man who'd taken my statement that morning, jumped out of his patrol car with his gun pointing toward both of us.

After a tense moment or two while the state policeman explained his presence there, Moore reholstered his weapon and drove off without glancing back in my direction.

"Come in," I said as I opened the door. "I don't have any coffee left, but I've got a donut or two you could have." I gestured to one of the boxes of leftovers, but he shook his head.

"I'm fine. I'm here to talk to you about what happened this morning."

"Like I've told everyone else, I didn't see anything. It all happened so quickly."

"Do you happen to have a security camera on the premises?" he asked as he looked around the shop.

"Honestly, I can barely afford napkins. This isn't exactly a gold mine I'm running here. I never considered the possibility that someone might try to rob me, so beefed-up security has never been an issue."

He shook his head. "You're just asking for trouble if you don't take the most basic precautions."

"I do what I can, and I'm being especially careful now, but I just don't have the money for anything else."

"I understand that." He slid a card across the counter to me. "If you think of anything later, call me. If you receive any disturbing messages or threats, call me. If anything out of the ordinary happens—"

I interrupted him and smiled. "Let me guess. I should call you, right?"

He laughed as he left the shop.

I almost threw his card away in the trash can, but something made me tuck it into my purse instead.

I hoped I never needed it, but it would be good to have it with me, just in case.

One thing was clear. This mess wasn't going to just go away, no matter how much I hoped it would. I was going to have to do something myself about my friend's murder, or keep looking over my shoulder for the rest of my life, and that was a sacrifice I wasn't willing to make. I needed to dig into Patrick Blaine's life a little and see how I could take myself out of the equation before someone decided to do it for me.

First, though, I needed something to eat. I locked up, put all of the leftover donuts in the back of my

Jeep, then walked down the tracks across the street to the Boxcar. I needed a hamburger, maybe a milkshake, and a chat with Trish Granger, a friend of mine who owned the diner. As I climbed up the steps into the converted train car, I marveled at how Trish had managed to put a restaurant in it. Booths replaced one section of seats on the left side, and a counter ran the entire length of the restaurant on the right. It wasn't elegant dining by any means, and that suited me just fine. I've always been more of a blue-jeans kind of gal than a dressed-to-kill lady.

Trish Granger and I had gone to school together, and she'd changed very little since we'd graduated fifteen years before. Still fit and trim—with long blond hair she kept in a neat ponytail—Trish always had a smile to serve with her food.

She said, "Grab a menu and I'll be right there."

"No need for that. I'll have a cheeseburger and a Diet Coke." On the walk over, I'd decided against the milkshake, since I'd been sampling so many donuts lately. I took a booth near the back, one of eight that ran down one side of the train car opposite the long counter that offered seating of its own. The kitchen had been added onto the other side of the train car, and the only connection between the two was the pass-through window and a pocket door that was always open. I felt as if I were moving when I ate there, going on some faraway, exotic adventure in the train car, straight out of a black-and-white movie.

After a few minutes, Trish slid my order onto the table and said, "What a mess this morning. You okay?"

"I'm fine."

"Wanna talk about it?" she asked.

"Not really."

Trish smiled. "Good enough. I'm here if you need to chat, you know that, don't you?"

"I'm counting on it."

With that, she went back to the front register. That was one of the things I liked best about her. She always knew just the right questions to ask, and when to press, or fade into the background.

As I ate my burger, I thought about how I was going to approach the bank where Patrick worked, and by the time I was finished with my meal, I had a plan of sorts ready. It would have been bad enough to see a stranger's body dumped from a car in the middle of the night, but I'd known Patrick Blaine, and liked him. That made it personal.

Now it would just take the nerves of a cat burglar to implement my plan to try to find out what had happened to him, and more important, why.

SUZANNE'S PUMPKIN DONUTS

We love these donuts around Thanksgiving, and make them quite often when there's frost or snow on the ground. The flavors are subtle, but the pumpkin taste is there, and makes a nice change of pace from the usual donut.

INGREDIENTS
2 eggs, beaten
1 cup sugar
2 tablespoons canola oil
1 can pumpkin puree (16 oz.)
2/3 cup buttermilk
4–5 cups bread flour
1 teaspoon salt
4 teaspoons baking powder
½ teaspoon baking soda
1 teaspoon nutmeg
1 teaspoon cinnamon
½ teaspoon ground ginger

DIRECTIONS
Beat the eggs well, then add the sugar, mixing until it's all incorporated. Add the oil, pumpkin, and buttermilk, then mix that all in. In a separate bowl, combine all of the dry ingredients, holding back 1 cup of the flour, using 4 cups of flour, the baking powder, baking soda, salt, nutmeg, cinnamon, and ground ginger. Sift the dry ingredients together and add them slowly to the egg mix. Once you've got them well mixed, chill the dough for about an hour.

Once the dough is thoroughly chilled, roll the dough out on a floured surface until it's about ¼ inch thick, then cut out donuts and holes with your donut cutter. While the donuts are resting, heat the oil in your fryer to 375 degrees. Add the donuts to the oil a few at a time, turning them once after a couple of minutes. Take them out, drain them on a rack, then they're ready to eat. These are good with powdered sugar on top, or just plain.

Makes approximately 1 dozen donuts.

CHAPTER 3

I shifted two boxes of glazed donuts in my arms as I walked into the bank where Patrick Blaine had worked until yesterday. Funny, but he'd never talked about his work when he came to the donut shop, and if I hadn't seen him wearing a conservative suit every time he came in, I would have had a hard time believing it.

There were a pair of police officers digging into the files in one of the executive offices, and I realized I was already too late to get any information on my own. The chief's men had beaten me to the punch.

Or had they?

I saw a plump woman sitting at a nearby desk dabbing at her cheeks with a delicately embroidered handkerchief.

As I approached her, I asked, "Are you all right?"

It took her a second to focus on me, and when she did, I could see that her eyes were bloodshot, most likely representing her state of mourning. As she dabbed at her cheeks, she said, "I'll be fine. It was just so sudden, you know?"

"Did you work for Mr. Blaine long?"

"Seven years," she admitted as she dabbed at her cheeks again. She seemed to actually notice me for the first time as she stared quizzically at me. "Why are you carrying two boxes of donuts?"

"They're for you," I said, making it up as I went along. "My name's Suzanne Hart, and I own Donut Hearts over in April Springs."

She looked puzzled. "Are you certain you've got the order right? My name's Vicki Houser, and I can't imagine why *anyone* would send me donuts."

"Mr. Blaine was a good customer of mine," I said. "I thought bringing donuts by where he worked would be better than just sending flowers."

She took the boxes from me as if I were carrying contraband instead of the leftovers from today's donut sales.

"I'm on a diet," she said sternly.

"You don't have to eat them yourself. Feel free to pass them around. It's just my way of saying goodbye."

Vicki nodded. "I don't know what I'm going to do," she said in a sudden moment of emotion. "I'll miss him terribly."

"I'm sure you will. Do you happen to know what he was working on lately?"

"Why do you want to know that?" The suspicion was back in her eyes, and I knew I had to come up with something good, and it had to be done quickly. I thought of another lie, one that was pretty audacious, even for me.

"Actually, he wanted me to deliver a dozen donuts this morning to one of his clients, but I lost the address somewhere in my shop. I know your heart is breaking, but is there any way you could help me? He would have wanted it that way, I'm sure. It would be like you were complying with his final request." It was a little dirty, but I didn't know how else to get her to help me. To my credit, I did feel bad about it.

Vicki nodded as she took one donut from the top box and devoured it in two bites. Through a mouthful, she said, "Sorry, I skipped breakfast."

"Go on. I hope you enjoy them. That's why I make them."

She nodded. "Sometimes the only place I can find comfort is in food, you know?"

"You don't have to tell me. I run a donut shop, remember? Every now and then, it's good to spoil yourself." I wasn't lying now. It was something I firmly believed.

Vicki smiled softly at me, and then said, "Give me a second so I can check his schedule for this week."

She turned on the computer at the desk where she was sitting and started typing. After studying the screen for a few moments, she said, "There are only two pending loan applications on his schedule right now, Allied Construction and BR Investments. He's been meeting with representatives from both companies quite a bit lately. Could it be for one of them?"

"It must be, but I'll tell you what I'll do. I'll take a dozen donuts to each company, and that way I'll be covered. Could you call and tell them I'm on my way, so they'll be expecting me? I'd like to give them directly to the people in charge. After all, I'm sure that was what Mr. Blaine would have wanted."

She fought back a sniffle, then said, "I'll take care of it right now." As she made the calls, she jotted a few things on a sheet of paper, and when she was finished, she handed it to me. "Here are the contacts, as well as the company addresses. Thanks so much for thinking of him. It was sweet of you to come by."

"I'm only doing what I feel I have to do," I said, and that was the complete and utter truth. If it had been a stranger dumped in front of my shop, I wasn't sure I'd go to this much trouble, but I'd known Patrick Blaine and I'd liked him, and that made all the difference in the world to me.

As I walked out of the bank, I felt excited—as well as nervous—about what I'd just done, and what was ahead. Getting that information from her was the most productive use of two dozen donuts I'd ever given away. I had two more boxes in my Jeep, and allotting one dozen for each place, I was hoping I had the right currency to buy the information I was after. So far, it had worked remarkably well; I only wished everyone else involved in this sordid murder had the same love for free donuts as Vicki. I felt a stab of remorse about being the cause of the death of her diet, but I couldn't let that stop me from digging into Patrick Blaine's life. There had to be a clue as to why someone had chosen to kill him and dump his body in front of my shop, and I'd use every last bite of the glazed donuts I had at my disposal to find the truth.

BR Investments wasn't anything like I'd expected. There was a section of professional buildings in April

Springs, but I drove right past them in search of the first address on my list. Instead of at one of the nicer offices where many of the best companies in town operated, I found myself in a strip mall on the outskirts of April Springs. BRI, as the sign over the door proclaimed, was between a manicurist and a Korean grocery whose name I could not read. Who in the world would invest their money in a place like this? As I walked in, I wished I had more than a dozen donuts with me, maybe an armed guard and a weapon of my own.

One man sat alone at a cheap desk in the center of a large room, carpeted entirely in ugly green. There was one other chair, which looked as if it had been stolen from a 1950s coffee shop. A large whiteboard stood on an easel, lettered with acronyms and matching numbers. I noticed that the sevens all had slashes through them, something I'd seen a lot of lately. The desk was a cluttered mess, and a typewriter sat on one edge of it. The man behind the desk was a rumpled mess. His shirt collar was frayed, his tie sported spots of marinara sauce from a long-forgotten meal, and what little hair he had was fighting in vain to cover his sweating head.

I put on my best smile as I asked, "Are you Donald Rand?"

"I must be. That's what it says on my driver's license, anyway." He studied me a second, whistled softly, then said, "Nice."

"Are you talking about me, or my donuts?"

I swear, he had the gall to leer openly at me. "Why can't it be both?"

This guy was too much. But then again, I wasn't

there soliciting new business for my donut shop. I was looking for information. "I believe you were expecting me."

"Just about all my life," he said.

I was painfully aware that we were alone, and I wished I'd had the foresight to bring someone with me. George would have been my first choice, but I would have even preferred my mother's company to being alone.

It was time to guide the conversation in the direction I wanted. "I understand from the bank that you were dealing with Patrick Blaine. It's quite a shock, isn't it? Did you know him well?"

"We did business together a time or two," he said. At least his open leer was gone.

"It's terrible what happened to him, isn't it? Can you believe someone murdered him?" I kept looking for some kind of reaction, but I got nothing from him.

He shrugged. "These things happen. It's a tough world, you know?"

I looked around his office and pointed to his whiteboard display. "Why the slashes through your sevens?"

"I had a teacher in elementary school that started me doing it, and I haven't been able to break the habit since. It's hard to tell how many people around here do the same thing because of one teacher."

At least I had my answer. "What kind of business did you and Patrick Blaine have, if you don't mind my asking."

"You can ask all you want," he said. As he gestured toward the box in my hands, he asked, "So, those are for me, right?"

I handed him the donuts, and he flipped the lid up. "Now that's what I'm talking about."

"I'm glad they meet with your approval. So, about Mr. Blaine."

He looked up at me. "You're the curious type, aren't you?"

How should I answer that? I smiled. "I just like to know why things happen."

He pushed the donuts aside. "Tell you what. Why don't you come back at nine tonight, and we'll talk all you want. I'm kind of busy right now, but I'd be willing to make time for you later."

You wish. "That sounds great. That way you can meet my husband." Okay, it wasn't strictly true, but I knew Max would come with me if I asked him, and maybe this time, an ex would be as good as the real thing.

He frowned. "No, come to think of it, tonight's no good for me."

His phone rang, and I stood there, hoping to hear something that might help.

That wasn't going to happen, though.

Mr. Rand said into the receiver, "Hang on a second." Then he turned to me. "Was there something else?"

"That's okay. Finish your call. I don't mind waiting."

"Sorry, but this might take a while."

When I still didn't move, he refused to say another word. It was clear he wasn't going to let me hear even the smallest bit of his conversation, so I left, although reluctantly.

As I drove to the next place, I wondered what kind of racket BRI was running. Try as I might, I couldn't see Patrick Blaine sitting in that office. Why would a well-respected banker working for a major institution do business with the man I'd just seen? There had to be a reason for it, and if I could find that out, it might help me discover who had murdered him, then dropped off his body in front of my shop.

I wasn't expecting much from the construction company after what I'd seen at the investment firm, but Allied actually surprised me. It was housed in a decent section of town, and the building looked brand-new.

A perky young receptionist met me at the door, and tried to take the donuts from me before I could even introduce myself.

"The bank called ahead. We appreciate the sentiment," she said as she fought to wrestle them away from me.

I held on tight, though. "I'm sorry, but my orders were clear. I'm supposed to give these to Mr. Klein directly," I said.

"Sorry, but he's in a meeting. He wanted me to tell you that he thanks you for the donuts, and hopes you have a nice day."

She had one corner of the box within her grasp, and I had the other. "Are you sure he doesn't have a minute? I'd be more than happy to wait. This will just take a second, and it was Mr. Blaine's wish that he get them."

For a little thing, her strength surprised me. I don't

know how she did it, but she managed to snatch the box from me completely. "As I said, he's in a meeting and he can't be disturbed."

"Do you honestly mean to say he can't give me thirty seconds to deliver them personally?"

"Not even one. He's with the head building inspector for the county. I'll be sure to tell him you dropped by, though."

Then she practically shoved me out the door, and I found myself sitting in my Jeep, without a clue as to what had just happened. I had to hand it to her, she was good.

I thought about what I should do next, but I was tired from my long day, and was already getting hungry again. It was nearing dinnertime for the rest of the world, six o'clock, and two hours past when I normally ate. That was another problem with my schedule. I tended to be out of sync with everyone else. Maybe I could use that to my advantage this time, though I wasn't quite sure how to do it; not yet, anyway.

I drove home, knowing I would get a barrage of questions from Momma, but frankly, not caring. I usually fussed at her for being a mother hen, but just this once, I hoped she had a hot meal waiting for me, and some quiet conversation.

As it turned out, I might as well have wished for the next day's winning lottery numbers, because it was clear the second I walked in the door that I wasn't going to get either dinner or a nice chat.

"There's no food?" I asked as I walked into the kitchen. Momma was sitting at the table doing a crossword puzzle. We lived in a lovely little cottage together, with lots of built-in cabinets and beautiful wood molding and trim everywhere. It wasn't a huge place, but so far, we'd managed to make it work.

"I just didn't feel like cooking tonight," she said.

"When did you ever not feel like cooking," I said as I slumped down on the chair beside her. The day had taken a toll on me, a bigger one than I was used to. My mother was known for her Southern-style food, and I'd been counting on some comfort coming my way with a knife and a fork.

"I didn't feel like it today," she said. "When you didn't come home at your regular time, I assumed you'd get something to eat on your own."

"So you already ate," I said.

She snapped the paper. "No, I waited for you, just in case." She studied me for a second, then asked, "Have you eaten?"

"No," I admitted.

"Suzanne, you have to start taking care of yourself. I'm not going to be around forever, you know."

"Why, where are you going? Is it someplace warm? Can I tag along?"

She was ready to snap at me when she looked up and noticed my grin. "You're incorrigible, you know that, don't you?"

"I learned from the best, Momma."

She accepted it for the apology it was, and smiled. "So, what should we have? How do waffles sound?"

That was our standby meal, something we made when we were both too tired to do much of anything else, and didn't want to go out and face the world.

"That sounds great. Do you mind if I grab a shower first?"

"Take your time. I'll have the first one ready by the time you're back downstairs."

Okay, I admit it, it's not all bad living back home with my mother. I took a long, hot shower—getting the day's cooking smells out of my hair—and came back into the kitchen a new woman, or at least an improved version of the old one.

"That smells divine," I said as the aroma of fresh waffles filled the air. The table was set for two, with a stick of real butter resting between them. Cinnamon apples simmered on the stove, with syrup bubbling gently beside them. One waffle was already out, golden and crisp, sitting on my plate, just waiting for me.

"Do you want to split the first one?" I asked, with less than complete sincerity.

"No, you go ahead."

I didn't even wait for her to change her mind.

It was exactly what I needed, and I was going to enjoy every single bite.

I'll give Momma credit; she waited until I was finished before she started her grand inquisition.

Though just barely.

I was swallowing the last bite when she said, "So, tell me all about it."

"About what?"

She frowned. "Don't be thick, Suzanne. It must have been dreadful finding that body this morning, all alone and in the darkness. I didn't push you this morning so you could have time to deal with what happened, but surely you've come to terms with it by now."

I shrugged. "I've had better days, I'm willing to admit that."

As we started to clean up, she asked, "Do the police have any clues?"

"I don't know, Momma, but you could find out, couldn't you? Why don't you give the chief a call? I'm sure he'd be happier talking to you about it than he would be discussing it with me."

She frowned for a split second, then nodded her acceptance. "If you need me to phone Phillip, I will."

I couldn't believe my mother was willing to make that kind of sacrifice for me, since I knew—more than anyone else—how hard it would be for her to pick up the telephone and call Chief Martin. I couldn't bring myself to do it.

"No, it hasn't come to that yet, but I may take you up on your offer later."

"I'm more than happy to do whatever I can to help. The important thing now is to put it all behind you and forget that this morning ever happened."

"All I can do is try," I said.

I don't know how she does it, but my mother has a built-in lie detector when it comes to me. I hadn't gotten away with stealing Sally Renshaw's crayons in kindergarten, and I wasn't going to slip my detecting activities past her today.

She frowned at me a second, then asked, "Suzanne, what are you up to?"

"Me? Why do I have to be up to something?" I

knew that the more I stalled, the worse it would get, but I couldn't bring myself to chronicle my day's activities just yet, either.

She didn't say a word, but she didn't have to. That look—the one that managed to say she was disappointed in me, that she had hoped for better from me, and that she somehow knew I'd turn out this way, all wrapped into one gaze—always broke me down.

"Fine. If you must know, I'm trying to figure out what happened. Patrick was a customer of mine, and a friend, and I'm not going to let this go."

"There's more to it than that, though, isn't there?"

I couldn't believe how well she could read me, but then again, she'd had lots of practice. "Momma, I turned on my store lights as the body hit the pavement. I didn't mean to, but it lit up the night. Even if I didn't see who did it, how can I be sure that the killer knows that? I've got a bad feeling that whoever dumped Patrick Blaine's body in front of my shop is coming after me next. I'm trying to find out who did it before they decide to wrap me up as a loose end. I knew Patrick, so whoever chose to dispose of him did it in a way that directly involved me."

"That's nonsense," she said sternly.

"I wish I believed that, but if I'm being honest with myself, I have to admit that there's a chance it's true," I said. "Not taking this threat seriously is just foolish."

"What's foolish is that you're attempting to solve the case yourself. Suzanne, you're a donut maker, not a detective."

That was all the scolding I was willing to take. "There's nothing that says I can't do both."

She reached for the telephone, but I managed to catch her hand before she could grab it. "Momma, who are you calling?"

"I'm going to find out what Phillip is doing about this case so you'll stop meddling in police business."

As far as I knew, Momma was the only one in town who didn't call the police chief Martin, and that probably included his own wife.

"Like I told you before, I don't need his help," I said.

"I believe otherwise," she snapped. "Now will you kindly remove your hand so I can use my own telephone?"

"Fine," I said, knowing I'd already lost the battle. "You can call him if you want to, but I'm not going to be here to listen to it."

I grabbed my keys off the counter, and she asked, "Where do you think you are going, young lady?"

"I'm taking a walk in the park," I snapped. That was one of the nicest things about our house. It was close enough to downtown—and my shop—so I could walk to work on pretty mornings if I wanted, and take a stroll across the street in the city park on my way home, though I normally limited those forays to when it was at least a little warmer, and a whole lot lighter out.

Momma said, "Suzanne, it's dark and it's cold outside. Have you lost your mind completely?"

"Apparently. I moved back in with my mother in my thirties. I'm pretty sure that qualifies as going over the bend in most circles."

I stormed out, not even sure why I was so angry

with her. Was it because she was calling her former beau, something I knew she hated doing, or was it because she was right? Sometimes I find myself getting angriest when people call me on my behavior. Did I have any business tracking down a killer on my own?

Honestly, no matter what my mother thought, I didn't have much choice. Sure, I would have preferred that whoever dumped Patrick Blaine's body had done it on the other side of town, but they hadn't. Whether the choice had been planned or random, I was drawn into it, whether I liked it or not. The fact that Patrick had been a customer of mine, and someone I'd liked, just made things worse.

What I wasn't going to do was be a victim and wait for a blow that might or might not ever come. I couldn't spend the rest of the day looking over my shoulder, let alone the rest of my life.

As expected, the park was deserted. I was freezing, and I was getting a massive headache to add to the mix. I needed to go home, patch things up with my mother, and see if I could come up with a plan for tomorrow. If not, it would be time to make the donuts again soon enough, and if I didn't get at least six hours of sleep, I'd be worthless the next day.

My phone was ringing when I got back to my room, a personal line I'd had installed the day I'd moved in. Cell phones were nice, but I needed a landline for my computer, and I wasn't about to tie up Momma's phone while I was online. When I wasn't using the Internet, it served as a way for my friends to get in touch with me, since—likely as not—my cell phone battery would be in dire need of recharging, and they could always leave me a message on my machine.

I should have let the machine pick it up.

At least then I would have had a record of the threat.

After I said hello, a voice said, "Stop digging into the murder, or you are going to be next. This has nothing to do with you. Make sure it stays that way."

The caller, having whispered his warning, hung up.

Evidently, whoever had killed Patrick Blaine was aware of what I'd been up to after work today. The warning was clear enough, and from the hissed words, I didn't doubt they were sincere. Anybody with a lick of common sense would stop now—I fully realized that—but how could I be sure the caller would leave me alone, even if I did as I was told? It might just be a way to get me to back off until he could finish me off without arousing suspicion. Then again, I knew that life would be better if I could just drop it.

But I couldn't bring myself to do it. Having known Patrick, and seeing his body hit the street, was enough to keep me digging, and the telephone threat just meant that I'd touched a nerve somewhere.

If only I knew where.

My alarm clock stays on the other side of my bedroom, a measure I had to take after destroying two others by slamming them on the floor to get them to shut up. One-fifteen in the morning is too early for anyone with any sense to be getting out of bed.

I'd grown somewhat accustomed to the hours, but it was nothing I'd ever relish.

Pulling on jeans and a polo shirt, I grabbed a quick bowl of cereal, then I set off for the shop. It was freezing, but what did I expect? We were in the throes of March, which in our part of North Carolina meant cold weather. We'd even had a snow flurry a few days before, though it hadn't amounted to much. I thought about walking to the shop anyway, as a way to wake up more than anything else, but there were too many shadows out there for my taste. I got into my Jeep and drove to Donut Hearts. I usually parked in back of the old depot building to leave space up front for my customers, but today I was going to break that rule. Leaving my headlights on as the Jeep was pointed toward the front door, I unlocked it, disengaged the alarm, and turned on every light in the place. After that, I cut the lights on the Jeep and raced back into the store, not really breathing again until I was safely inside. There was a lot of glass up front, and I knew it wouldn't slow down anybody determined to get me, but I still felt a level of comfort knowing that at least they couldn't sneak up on me.

I hit the start button as I walked past the coffee-pot, then turned the deep fryer on in the kitchen and set the temperature to 300 degrees. It was Wednesday, and I make old-fashioned donuts on Wednesdays and Fridays. As the oil heated, I checked the answering machine on my desk for any last-minute orders. It's amazing how many people think they can get four or five dozen donuts for parties, fund-raisers, or office breakfasts without warning me ahead of time.

Dunkin' Donuts and Krispy Kreme might be able to do it, but I run a small operation, and I need some kind of warning, or it can throw my whole day off.

Sure enough, a woman's voice was on the machine, and through the constant background noise of kids yelling and screaming, she ordered six dozen glazed donuts with sprinkles and confectionary worms. I had the sprinkles, though I didn't think I'd ever put them on glazed donuts before, but she was on her own for the worms. There are some things even I won't do to a donut.

I was taking down the particulars when I heard someone banging on the front door. My hand automatically reached for my largest rolling pin—a ten-pound maple monster—as I peeked around the corner. It was time to stop running.

If whoever was after me was looking for a fight, they'd just found one.

"Emma, why didn't you use your keys?" I asked my assistant as I let her in through the front door. She was petite, with fine red hair, freckles that sparkled when she blushed, and pale blue eyes. Emma was saving money for college by working at my donut shop, and I didn't know what I was going to do without her when she finally made enough to head off to school. I'd have to hire someone else. One day a week making donuts by myself was plenty of experience to tell me that I couldn't sustain it on a regular basis or I'd kill myself from overwork.

"I left my key ring on my dresser at home," Emma said sheepishly.

"Then how did you get here?" I looked outside, but couldn't see her car anywhere.

"Don't bother looking; it's in the shop again. Dad dropped me off."

"I bet he just loved getting up in the middle of the night to do that," I said. Emma's father, Ray, was the editor of the *April Springs Sentinel,* a small paper known more for its advertisements than its in-depth reporting.

"Let's just say that he was less than pleased, and leave it at that. He's working on some ultra hush-hush story about local police corruption, and he's driving us all crazy with it."

"Is that true?" The thought of corruption in our tiny little North Carolina town made me nervous.

"I'd be totally shocked if it was. Dad's always going off on one wild-goose chase or another looking for a Pulitzer Prize-winning story that he's never going to find."

Emma hung her coat on the rack, then said, "I'm so sorry I didn't call you yesterday, but I was out of town, and my dear old dad didn't think it was newsworthy enough to tell me what happened until he dropped me off just now."

"How did he find out about the telephone threat? I haven't even told anyone about that yet." Was there some kind of tap on my telephone, or did he know who had made the call?

Emma looked shocked by the news. "You were threatened, too? I was talking about finding Patrick Blaine's body in front of the shop. I think Dad intentionally didn't tell me because he thought it would worry me. You know what? He was right. So, tell me about this call." Emma's voice went into a whole other octave when she was excited, and she was clearly agitated now.

Reluctantly, I admitted, "Someone called my house and tried to intimidate me last night."

Emma frowned. "What's happening to this town? First you see one of our customers dumped in front of the shop, and then some random idiot calls you and threatens you. Dad makes me carry pepper spray, and I've been giving him a hard time about being over-protective, but now I'm starting to think that he was right."

"It wasn't random at all," I said softly. "He told me that if I didn't butt out, I'd be sorry."

"Butt out of what?" she asked me.

I didn't want go into what had been happening, but we'd be working together all morning, and I couldn't see keeping any of it from her. Besides, by being near me, she was in danger herself, and Emma had a right to know what she was going up against.

"I'm trying to find out who killed Patrick Blaine myself," I said.

Emma smiled.

"What's so funny about that?" I asked.

"Dad said that's exactly what you would do, but I told him you were too levelheaded for that. So, what have you done so far?"

I looked outside, feeling exposed in the darkness. "Come on. We've got donuts to make," I said.

Emma wasn't about to give up that easily, though. "We can talk while we work. We do it every morning, don't we?"

I reluctantly agreed. "You clean the glaze left in the reservoir, and I'll make more to top it off." We don't make new glaze every morning, since it would be too wasteful to throw the old out and start fresh. Instead, we skim the top layer of collected grease—along with some of the water that has separated from the glaze overnight—dispose of that, then add new glaze to the mix when the reservoir gets too low. I added thirty-four pounds of powdered sugar to the big floor mixer, put in a gallon of water and some flavoring, tossed in some thickening agent, and then started the mixer. It wasn't a delicate operation, so I didn't have to set one of the four timers we had in the kitchen. I could turn it on and forget about it until I was ready to add it to the old glaze.

Emma had just finished stirring the remaining glaze together using a large loaf pan, which is how we apply the glaze to the donuts once they are fried. There's nothing sophisticated or even automated about our operation, but it is quick, and very effective. The poured glaze runs over the donuts, drops through the rack, and slides down a stainless steel incline back into the waiting pool.

"So, talk to me," Emma said.

"Let me measure out some ingredients first," I said.

I set up individual stations for our cake donut mixes and measured out the dry ingredients, water, and flavorings into neat little grids.

"Come on, give," Emma asked.

I was at a point where my total concentration wasn't required anymore. "After I found Patrick's body, I realized that the police weren't taking my protection too seriously, so I decided to dig into this myself."

"You should ask George for help," Emma said.

"I don't want to put him at risk any more than I have to," I said, "but he's checking on things at police headquarters, so he can keep me informed if Chief Martin actually stumbles over a clue, even if it's just by accident."

"What does he think about all of this?"

"He's worried about me, but should that really surprise anybody? You know how overprotective he is," I said as I combined the ingredients in each individual mixing bowl by hand.

"But you're going to do it anyway, aren't you," Emma said.

"I am," I admitted. "Let me make these old-fashioned donuts first, and then we'll talk more about it."

I checked the grease temperature, and it was right at 300 degrees, which was exactly what I needed it to be. It was time to load up the dropper, a device that looked like a cross between a large steel teacup and a funnel. There was a spring-operated disk inside that dropped a perfect ring of batter into the oil every time, and cake donuts would be impossible for me to make without the nifty little device. I added the batter, then swung the dropper from side to side like a pendulum to force the batter to one end. I'd never dropped the tool yet, but if I did, it could do some serious damage to anyone unlucky enough to be standing nearby. There might be other ways to get the air bubbles out of the batter and force it to the bottom, but I hadn't found anything else that worked for me.

I dropped ten or twelve rounds into the oil, where they quickly settled on the bottom rack. After a few seconds they floated up to the top, and I took my flipping sticks and nudged them over once I thought they were ready. There's more of an art than a science to doing it, and I didn't use timers for this stage. Once the donuts were the perfect color on both sides, I used the handles and lifted the donuts from the hot oil and emptied the rack onto the glazing station. Scooping up glaze in the loaf pan, I poured a cascade of white sweetness over them, put a new rack in the bottom of the fryer, then started over.

"Swinging," I said, and Emma ducked out of the line of fire.

"Clear," I added as I finished, then dropped new rings into the oil while Emma transferred the donuts from the rack to one of our trays. It was a many-tiered stainless steel rack on wheels, and it would hold twenty trays on each side, allowing us to store forty dozen donuts until we added them to the case out front. After the old-fashioned donuts were finished, I made each batch of cake donut we were offering today, then I turned up the fryer in preparation for the yeast donuts. Those we cooked at 365 degrees, and I'd learned early on that it was much easier to start at the lower temperatures and work my way up, instead of the other way.

As Emma washed the things we'd used so far in the industrial sink, I mixed the yeast dough. After I was finished, I pulled a wad of dough out of the mixer and covered it so it could rise. We had forty minutes now, but there was still a lot to do before we were ready to make more donuts.

First, though, it was time for our break. Emma and I normally sit outside for twenty minutes every morning—rain or shine, snow or sleet—just to get some fresh air and escape from the kitchen for a little while.

She started toward the front door when I said, "Maybe we should have our coffee inside tonight."

"Are you sure? We never have before." She looked into my eyes, then added, "Hey, you really are spooked."

"Let's just say I don't want to take any chances that I don't have to," I said.

"Inside is fine with me, then."

I got us each a mug of coffee, and we moved to one of the best couches in the place, one that also offered a great view of the front parking lot. At least no one would be able to sneak up on us.

Emma tucked her legs under her, something I hadn't been able or even willing to try in years, and said, "Now that we have a few minutes, tell me what you've been up to."

I reluctantly brought her up to speed on my visit to the bank, the so-called investment house, and the construction company. She listened with rapt interest, interrupting now and then with a question or two.

After I was finished, she said, "You should really talk to Dad."

"I'm not ready to talk to the press about this yet," I said.

"He won't print what you talk about if you ask him to keep it off the record," Emma said, "but he may know some things you don't. I know the paper's a joke around town, but Dad's got sources everywhere, and he'll help you. I know he will."

"How can you be so sure it won't end up in his paper?"

"Believe me, if I get him to promise, you'll be all right, and I won't let you talk to him until he gives us both his word. For Dad, that's more binding than any contract that's ever been written."

I thought about it, then I said, "I need to have something more concrete before I even think about talking to someone else about it."

"I understand that. Don't dismiss him out of hand, though. He just might have something that helps you. Have you thought about what your next step is going to be?"

"I'm not sure," I admitted. "I guess I'll keep digging and see what I can turn up."

"Don't worry, we'll find out who killed Patrick."

I put my coffee cup down on the table. "Hang on one second. I'm not going to let you get involved in this."

"Why not?"

"It's too dangerous. Besides, this isn't your fight, it's mine." The last thing I wanted was Emma's life in jeopardy because of me.

She frowned as she asked me, "Did you say the same thing to George?"

"No," I admitted.

"Why not?"

"This is different," I said.

"Why, just because he's older than I am? I don't just work here, Suzanne. I thought we were friends."

"We are," I said. "That's why I don't want to put you at risk."

"That's the wrong way to think of it. I'm involved because I want to be. I knew Patrick Blaine, too, and I liked him. Besides, I'm over eighteen, and I've been making my own decisions for a lot longer than that." She grinned at me and added, "If you don't believe that, just ask my dad."

"Fine, you can help, but I'm not going to let you take any chances, do you understand?"

"I won't take any you wouldn't yourself," she said.

I was about to reply when the timer went off.

Emma bounced off the couch. "I'd love to sit and chat all morning, but those donuts aren't going to make themselves."

She was entirely too happy to be involved in my unofficial investigation. The real reason I was reluctant to use her was because I was afraid Emma thought of this as a game instead of real life, with its matching levels of danger. If anything happened to her because of me, I'd never be able to forgive myself. It meant that I'd have to keep a closer eye on her, and that was a distraction I really couldn't afford at the moment.

MOMMA'S HOMEMADE WAFFLES

We love these waffles, especially on the weekends when everyone has more time to relax and enjoy a meal instead of rushing off into the world. These are especially good with a side of baked apples and some steaming hot syrup, along with real butter. It's a great time to indulge a little, and enjoy some wonderful taste sensations.

INGREDIENTS
1¼ cups flour
2 teaspoons baking powder
Dash of salt
1 tablespoon sugar
2 eggs, separated
1¼ cups buttermilk
2 tablespoons vegetable oil

DIRECTIONS
Combine the flour, baking powder, salt, and sugar in a medium-sized bowl and set it aside. In another medium-sized bowl, beat the egg whites until stiff, moist peaks form. In a third bowl, beat the yolks lightly, stir in the buttermilk and oil, and blend it all together well. Pour the liquid at one time into the dry ingredients, then beat this mixture until it's smooth. Next fold the beaten egg whites into the mix, and you're ready to bake the waffles in your waffle iron.

MODIFICATIONS

You can add blueberries, mashed bananas, bacon, or chopped nuts to the batter to create different types of waffles with the same basic recipe.

It's fun to experiment, and you can test several different combinations with the basic mix once you've folded the beaten egg whites into the batter.

Makes 8–10 square waffles.

CHAPTER 4

By the time we were ready to open our doors for business at 5:30 A.M., Emma was prepared to charge out into the darkness and find Patrick Blaine's killer before noon.

"Remember," I said before I undid the dead bolt, "you're not going to do anything until you talk to me first."

"Fine," she said, though I could hear the reluctance in her tone. "But I want to be a part of this. Remember, I have a stake in it. He was my friend, too."

"I said I would, now let's sell some donuts."

I opened the door, and George was waiting patiently for us.

"You're early two days in a row," I said.

"What can I say? I had an early-morning craving for donuts," he said as he brushed in past me. "Hi, Emma."

"'Morning, George. I've got your coffee ready."

She handed him a mug, and he took a sip, then he smiled. "You're an angel, young lady. Marry me."

Emma laughed. "I'm not sure you could handle me."

He grinned in return. "You want to know the truth? I think you might be right. Just be glad I'm not a hundred years younger, or you'd be in trouble."

As he took his seat at the counter, he said, "Emma, could I trouble you for a lemon-filled donut with chocolate icing and some of those sprinkles you're always carrying on about?"

She didn't even have to check our inventory. "We don't have any in the case, but I can make one just for you."

"I'd be much obliged," he said.

She was almost through the door that led to the kitchen when she stopped dead. Emma pivoted, then stared hard at George for a split second. "You're trying to get rid of me, aren't you?"

"What are you talking about? I just want a donut."

Emma put her hands on her hips. "I doubt you've had a sprinkle in your life, and you don't seem like the type to start now. If you're going to talk about Patrick Blaine's murder, you can speak freely in front of me. Suzanne's agreed to let me help."

He gave me a troubling glare. "Did she, now?"

I wasn't about to accept a scolding from him. "George, she's as much at risk as I am working here. It's only fair she gets to help figure out what really happened."

I tried to warn him off that particular line of

questioning with my eyes, and he caught it without faltering. George's years as a cop had made him pretty observant, something I was counting on.

He nodded. "That's all well and good, but I really do want that donut."

"I'll make it for you right now," Emma said, "but don't say a word until I get back. Do you two understand me?"

George just nodded.

"Suzanne?"

I shook my head. "I'm sorry, were you under the impression that you were in charge here? Would you like to fill our customer's order, or would you rather join him on the other side of the counter as an unemployed donut maker?" I'd said it in my sweetest Southern accent, but she heard the steel beneath the surface.

"Yes, ma'am. I'll get right on making that donut."

When she disappeared in back to create the requested treat, George said, "We need to talk, but not in front of her. I don't like this."

"I didn't have much choice, but we can protect her."

"We're not even sure we can protect you," he said. "Tell her what you want, but I'm just going to talk to you about what I found out."

"Can it wait until closing?" I whispered.

"I think so. I'll meet you by the back door at noon. Send her on some fool's errand before then, but don't put her in the line of fire."

"I'm sorry, George. Agreeing with her seemed to be the only way I could keep her out of trouble."

"That's fine, as long as that's the way it stays." If it were possible, George was being even more over-protective of Emma than he was of me. He might be a gruff old bear to the rest of the world, but I knew just how big the soft spot in his heart really was.

Emma came back with the requested donut on a plate, and it was pretty clear to me that George wished he'd been more careful placing his order. I could have saved him with an excuse, but what fun would that have been? I watched him struggle to eat it, then he smiled brightly when he finished.

I asked, "Would you like another one just like it?"

George pushed his plate away. "No, thanks, I'm good."

"So, why are you here?" Emma asked.

"Like I said, I came by for a donut," he said.

My assistant frowned. "I don't believe you."

He just shrugged. "That's entirely up to you, now isn't it?"

George slid a five under his plate. "See you later."

"That's way too much, and you know it."

He looked at the bill, then George swapped it out with another one from his wallet. "Sorry. I thought it was a single."

"You could at least tip me something," I said, shaking my head. His one barely covered my morning special of coffee and a donut for a dollar before six A.M.. It was a way to encourage early-morning business, since very few people who came in could stop at just one donut.

He dug a quarter out of his pants pocket, then laid it beside his plate. "I'll talk to you later."

As soon as he was gone, Emma asked, "What

was that all about? I thought you were going to include me in what's going on."

"Emma, if you have a problem with the way George acted, I suggest you talk to him about it. Now, we've got work to do. You need to ice the plain cake donuts, and make a few peanut ones while you're at it."

"Yes, ma'am."

At a quarter after six, George came back into the donut shop.

"Did you change your mind?" I asked him. "I knew one donut wouldn't be enough for you."

"Suzanne Hart, have you lost your mind?"

"Probably. What are you talking about?"

"You're making yourself a target by being so obvious in your digging; you realize that, don't you?"

I had no idea where this conversation was going, but I'd never been a big fan of being scolded, even if it was coming from a good friend. Especially since it was. "What do you mean?"

George shook his head. "You're an amateur, and don't take that as an insult, because it happens to be true. If you stumble along blindly looking into this case, you're going to attract the wrong kind of attention. Did you think what you're doing would go unnoticed? One of the cops at the bank noticed you talking to Blaine's assistant. He told me about ten minutes ago, so don't try to deny it."

I took a deep breath, and then admitted, "I'm guilty as charged. I also talked to two of Blaine's clients. I can't solve this with a Ouija board; I need to talk to people."

"Were you really under the impression no one

would notice? You're going to get exactly the wrong kind of attention acting that way."

I thought about keeping what had happened the night before to myself, but it wasn't fair to ask George for help, then not tell him everything.

Reluctantly, I admitted, "I got a phone call last night warning me to drop it, or I was going to be in trouble." Maybe I edited it a little, but if I'd repeated the conversation to George verbatim, he'd never let me out of his sight again.

"Did you tell Bishop about the call?"

"No," I said.

He frowned for a moment, then said, "How about the chief?"

"George, I appreciate your concern, but there's no way to tell who called me. For all I know, it could have just been a prank."

He looked into my eyes, then said softly, "But you don't think so, do you?"

"No," I admitted. "It was real enough. But I still can't let that stop me."

"Just be a little more discreet then, okay?"

I shrugged. "I can try, but I won't make any promises."

After George left, I started wondering if he was right. Should I sit back and wait to see what might happen? If I did that, I might end up as a target, with no chance to stop an attack before it could happen. No, I had to keep doing what I was doing, and if it ruffled some feathers, so be it.

Twenty minutes later, I was still fretting over my conversation with George when a friendly face walked in through the door. "'Morning, Suzanne,"

Bob Lee said as he came into the shop. "Are my pies ready yet?"

"I finished them ten minutes ago, but you were late, so I sold them," I said.

Bob looked as though he wanted to cry, so I said quickly, "I'm kidding. I would never sell your pies to anybody but you." The retired gentleman came by three days a week for fried apple pies, turnovers I made with apple filling. They weren't that popular with most of the crowd that came into Donut Hearts, but Bob loved them, and I was happy to oblige.

He greedily took the box of palm-sized pies and breathed in their aroma of apples, cinnamon, and fried dough. "If I have anything to say about it, that's what heaven's going to smell like."

"You won't get any disagreements from me," I said as I rang up his sale. I loved making the pies. For one thing, they were the perfect use for the third rising of the yeast dough, one that was too stiff for donuts, but perfect for fried pies and fritters. Not much went to waste at the donut shop, and that helped the bottom line. Honestly, though, I hated throwing anything out, and using the scraps of dough left over from everything else really appealed to me.

After he was gone, Emma said, "You shouldn't tease him like that. One day he's going to have a heart attack, eating like he does."

I said softly, "Would you mind lowering your voice? Do we really want folks to think about what they're eating when they come here?"

She blushed, something that was remarkable to see in a redhead. "I'm sorry. I didn't mean anything by it."

"Emma, don't get me wrong," I said, "donuts are a wonderful treat, but even I don't recommend them as a steady diet. But think about how dull the world would be if it was only filled with whole wheat and granola."

"You're preaching to the choir," Emma said. "Nobody around here is about to argue with you."

"If we're lucky, maybe we'll have a quiet morning," I said.

Emma pointed toward the door. "I wouldn't be too sure about that."

I turned around and saw my ex-husband, Max, coming into the donut shop. It was too late to duck into the kitchen, so I put on my best smile as he neared the counter.

"What can I get you this morning?" I said.

There was a gleam in his eye, which I needed to quell immediately. I added quickly, "I'm talking about donuts, Max."

He nodded. "That's why I'm here. I'll take two dozen. You pick them out for me, okay?"

"Are you going to eat all of these by yourself?" I said idly as I collected the donuts in two of our boxes.

Max smiled, and I felt my heart flutter a little. "Why, are you jealous I might have company helping me?"

"Hardly," I said, putting two blueberry donuts inside, a treat I knew from experience that Max hated. It served him right for goading me.

"If you must know, they're for my theater group. We're putting on *West Side Story* in May."

I taped the boxes shut and told him how much he owed me. As I made change from the twenty he handed over, I said, "Out of curiosity, who's the youngest member of your troupe?"

He scratched his chin, then said, "I guess that would be Hattie Moon. She's not sixty yet."

"At least not according to her," I said. "I'd love a peek at the driver's license, though. That lady has had at least six birthdays for fifty-nine."

Max winked at me. "A woman never tells the truth about her age anyway, does she?"

"Mabel Young does."

He shook his head. "Mabel doesn't count. She's the only woman I've ever known who adds ten years to her real age."

"Think about it," I said. "When Mabel tells folks she's eighty instead of seventy, they always make a fuss about how young she looks. She does it for the attention."

Max said, "If I live to be a thousand, I'll never understand women."

"That's okay, we don't get you, either. Bye, Max."

"Good-bye, Suzanne."

I couldn't believe it. He hadn't asked me about my investigation, or scolded me once for anything. That was a record for Max. Was he really changing? Was it even possible? Should I give him another chance? There had been a lot that was right about my marriage to Max. I'd tended to ignore all of that with the image of him and that trollop together, but it was there, nonetheless. Even if I could forgive him for cheating on me, though, could I ever forget? I sincerely doubted it. No, if I was being honest with myself, it was probably time to move on.

Three older women, two brunettes and a redhead, walked into the shop half an hour after Max left, and approached the counter like a force of nature. They were all obviously well off by the way they dressed and carried themselves, but there was nothing haughty about them.

The redhead spoke after looking happily around at the donut shop's décor.

"This shop is absolutely perfect," she said.

"I'm glad you like it," I replied. "If it's donuts you're after, you came to the right place. I've got coffee, too."

"No, that's not it at all. Well, of course we'll enjoy those, as well, but what we really need is a quiet place for our book club to meet, and we are hoping you'll let us hold the first meeting here."

I had visions of hordes of women gathered in my shop, buying up all of my stock as they discussed the latest literary novel. "We might be able to arrange something. What day did you have in mind?"

She looked at me oddly for a second, then laughed. "Why, right now, of course."

I looked behind her and saw her two friends waiting patiently for us to finish our conversation. "Are you all out in search of a location?"

She frowned. "No, so far there's just the three of us. Hazel's apartment is being painted, so we can't meet there. Elizabeth's cousin is staying with her, and she hasn't read a book since the eighties. Since my husband retired, I can't get him to leave the house, so we decided we had to find a place that would work for all of us. I'm Jennifer, by the way. Please, won't you help us?"

How could I say no to that? "As long as you don't disturb my other customers, you're welcome to have your meeting here." It might be nice to give the place a literary edge.

She said, "Thank you," and the three women took a couch in the corner. After they settled in, Jennifer came back to the counter and stared at my display racks.

After a few moments, she said, "We'll take three of those pinecones—they look delightful—and three of your most exotic coffees."

"Coming right up," I said. I poured three cups of a new blend I'd let Emma talk me into buying, then added three donut-pinecones. I loved making them, snipping the dough with scissors until I had them looking perfect.

She paid me with a fifty, and as I started to make change, she said, "I'm sure we'll want something else. Just keep that and let me know when we run out."

I nodded, and made a note on the pad by the register where we kept track of things. After the host distributed the coffees and treats, the three women pulled out copies of the same book, a current mystery I'd just finished reading myself.

Keeping her voice low, I heard Jennifer say, "First, let's discuss the significance of the ornamental dagger and the weathered shotgun in chapter one. I thought for sure one of them would turn out to be the murder weapon. Did anyone else?"

"I admit, I never can figure these things out," Hazel said.

"I don't know why everyone always tries to guess who did it before the end," Elizabeth replied. "I read mysteries for the characters and the setting. The mystery's just an added bonus for me."

"I still never saw the bust of Poe as a murder weapon," Jennifer said.

I grabbed a pot and filled it with the blend they were drinking. As I refilled their cups, I said, "I thought the foreshadowing was well done. The way the light from the hallway reflected in Poe's eyes when the detective came into the room gave me the shivers."

"You've read it?" Jennifer asked, the delight clear in her voice. "Won't you join us?"

"I'd love to, but I've got my hands full at the moment."

Jennifer nodded. "I understand completely, but if you have anything else to add, feel free." She looked at her friends, then asked, "Isn't that right, ladies?"

After two nods of eager agreement, I smiled and said, "If you're sure."

I came back to the counter and Emma asked, "What was that all about?"

"They wanted me to join them," I said.

"You really should. I can handle things here, and if I need you, I'll just shout."

I was tempted. It had been a long time since I'd discussed something I'd read with anyone but Momma and Grace. "Are you sure?"

"Absolutely."

"Then I will." I filled a cup of coffee, then took a

pinecone for myself. If I was going to join them, I might as well indulge all the way.

As I joined them, I said, "I thought the missing book was an especially nice touch, don't you?"

"We were just talking about that," Jennifer said, clearly pleased that I'd changed my mind.

After half an hour, Elizabeth looked at her watch, and then frowned. "I hate to break this up, but I have to get back. This is so wonderful. Thank you for joining us, Suzanne."

"Thanks for having me," I said.

As they got up to leave, I said, "Hang on a second, Jennifer. I'll get your change."

"Put it on my tab for next month," she said.

"I'll never remember," I protested.

"Then consider it a tip, and our way of saying thank-you. We're reading *A Deadly Wicked Murder* next month, and we'd love to have you join us."

"I can't promise anything," I said. "I never know how busy things are going to be around here ahead of time."

"At least promise us you'll try," Hazel said.

Jennifer added, "Come on, Suzanne. We loved having you join us."

"If you're sure," I said.

"See you next month," Jennifer said.

After they were gone, I couldn't keep from smiling. It was another benefit of owning Donut Hearts. I made new friends nearly every day I was open for business, and that was something that would never show up in the bottom line, but made the place worth all of the trouble nonetheless.

*   *   *

"I'm telling you, the Panthers are the best team in the NFC South," Officer Moore said as he and Officer Grant walked into the donut shop.

"You know I don't care about football," Officer Grant said.

Moore smiled. "You don't know what you're missing. I live for football season. You should come with me to a game sometime."

"No, thanks," he said.

"Good morning," I said to them, trying my best to be cordial as they both smiled at me. Officer Grant moved to a chair by the window as he nodded to me, and I caught a slight smile as he turned his head away and pretended to watch the traffic go by on Springs Drive.

"'Morning, Suzanne," Officer Moore said as he approached the counter.

What on earth was he up to?

"Can I get you two something?"

He looked over at Officer Grant, who just shook his head. Moore studied the donut sign behind me, then said, "I'd love a cup of coffee, and maybe a blueberry donut."

I was surprised by the change in his demeanor. The day before, he'd been abrupt to the point of rudeness, and now he was being downright civil. His long-sleeved shirt was neatly pressed, and his shoes sported a high-gloss shine.

I grabbed a blueberry donut and a coffee for him, and then said, "I was under the impression that you didn't like donuts."

He frowned. "That's kind of why I'm here. This isn't official or anything. Grant and I are on a break, and I wanted to come by and apologize to you. I was a little shook up yesterday morning, and that's the way I deal with it. To be honest with you, I haven't seen that many bodies, either, at least not up close like that. I'm sorry if I was rude to you. You had enough to worry about without dealing with my attitude."

"I understand completely," I said. "I appreciate you coming by to apologize."

He smiled slightly. "What can I say, I'm trying to be a better person, but I'm not all the way there yet."

"I don't think any of us are," I said. "Sometimes it's the fact that we're trying that counts."

He took a sip of coffee, then said, "Since I'm already here, I'd like to ask you something. Have you remembered anything else about yesterday? You said you turned on the outside lights just as it happened, right? Have you recalled seeing anything else since we spoke the last time?"

I wasn't about to tell him about the threatening telephone call I'd received the night before, and it really wasn't an answer to the question he'd just asked me. "No, there's nothing else. I didn't see anything."

He took a bite of donut, smiled, then said softly, "You had a tough day yesterday, didn't you?"

"I have to admit, I've had better," I said as I topped off his mug, as well as those of some of the other customers around him. This was certainly a different man from the one I'd spoken with last night. He was going out of his way to make up for his behavior, and I appreciated it.

"I can't even imagine how you must feel," he said.

After finishing his donut, he asked, "You're sure there's nothing else you need to tell me about?"

"I'm positive," I said. "Do you want that in a to-go cup?"

He pushed it away. "No, I'd better not. It was delicious, though." He slid two singles under his plate, and the officers left.

"What was that all about?" Emma asked as soon as he was gone. "Was he here to interrogate you again?"

"The man wanted a cup of coffee and a donut. There's no crime in that, is there? Even cops are allowed to get hungry now and then, aren't they?"

What an odd day it was getting to be. Folks were surprising me with their behavior by the bucketful, from my ex-husband to a once-belligerent cop who'd suddenly turned nice. Was there something in the coffee that I didn't know about?

If there was, I was going to have another cup myself.

My best friend, Grace, came in twenty minutes before my closing time of noon.

I said, "Hey there. I thought you were going to be in Charlotte all week."

"I am," she said as she smiled at me. "At least my boss thinks so. I finished up early for the day, so I came back home. As far as she knows, I'm doing paperwork. Why don't you close up early and we can play hooky? How does that sound?"

"Like heaven," I said, "but this isn't exactly a good time for me. I've got a lot to do after I close up the shop." George had promised to come by, and I'd been dying to hear what he wanted to talk about.

Grace lowered her voice, though there was just one customer in the shop, an older woman who could make a donut last longer than anybody I'd ever seen in my life. One day a week she came in at ten, bought a donut and a cup of coffee, then she sat at a table reading until I locked up at noon. I'd tried to start a dozen conversations with her, but her answers were always terse, and I'd finally given up. Emma was in back working on the never-ending supply of dirty dishes we seemed to accumulate in the course of a day.

Grace asked, "Are you going to investigate the murder? I could help, you know. It sounds like fun."

"So far, it hasn't been all that exciting," I said, recounting all I'd been through lately.

"You know what I mean. Come on, I could be a big asset to you. I've read every Nancy Drew ever written, and even a few of the Hardy Boys books."

"We're not trying to solve the case of the strange light in the bell-tower," I said. "This is real life."

"I know that. I'm just saying, I've got skills you should be using."

I thought about telling her no, but then realized that it would be good having someone watching my back.

Before I could answer, my assistant came out front wearing her jacket. "I'm going now."

I looked at the clock. "It's a little early, isn't it?"

"Suzanne, I told you three days ago about my dentist's appointment. I just need to get the donuts for

Dr. Frye." Emma always took a dozen glazed donuts with her to Dr. Frye's office when she had an appointment. Some folks would think we'd be natural enemies, but he was a good guy who liked a little sweet treat every now and then himself, and as long as his patients brushed their teeth after they ate at my place, he was fine with it.

"I'm sorry. You're right, I forgot all about it. See you tomorrow."

"'Bye," she told both of us as she tucked the box under her arm and left.

Once she was gone, I turned back to Grace. "It's not fair that I ask you to put your life in danger for me," I said.

She took my hands in hers. "In all seriousness, who's in a better position to do it than your very best friend? I want to help."

"If you're sure," I said. "Then I accept. There's only one problem."

Grace nodded. "What is it? Between the two of us, we'll figure something out, or a way to get around it."

"George was supposed to come by to talk about the case, but he's late."

Grace nodded. "Then until he gets here, why don't you tell me what you've done so far, and we'll see where things stand?"

That made sense. Maybe talking about it would help me figure things out. I kept glancing at my sole customer, and realized that I couldn't do this in front of her.

I approached her, after putting a single donut in a

bag. "Ma'am, we're closing early today. I'm sorry for the inconvenience."

She was about to cloud up when I thrust the bag toward her. "Please accept this donut on the house as my apology."

That flustered her, and the clouds vanished as quickly as they had appeared. "Why, thank you. That's most generous of you," she said as she scooted out of the shop.

After I locked up behind her, Grace said, "What an odd old bird. She was awfully grateful for a free donut, wasn't she?"

"Maybe it's a windfall for her," I said. "She buys just one donut a week, along with a small coffee. Sometimes I feel guilty charging folks who don't look like they can pay."

"Suzanne, I'm not about to get into the economics of giving away food with you. Let's make a list and see where things stand right now. That's the only way we'll know where to go next."

"Fine," I said. "Here's where things stand. After what happened yesterday morning, I decided to dig a little myself. I spoke with Patrick Blaine's secretary at the bank, and she told me that he was working on two pending loans, one for a brokerage and the other for a construction company. I went to talk to both, but neither one gave me much to go on. I didn't even get in to see the construction company owner. After that, I got a threatening telephone call, and that's all I've managed to do so far."

Grace whistled. "That sounds like a lot to me. How did you get those folks to talk to you at all?"

"It's amazing what people will tell you in exchange for free donuts," I admitted. "But they'll only go so far."

"True," she said. "This time, let's take fritters."

I glanced in the case. "There aren't any left. In fact, I doubt there are enough donuts here to get anyone to tell us anything."

"Then you can make more," she said. "Come on, I'll do Emma's part. How hard can it be?"

"Harder than you think," I said. "If you don't believe me, you're welcome to come by some morning at 2 A.M. and help us make some. I'm even willing to let you sleep in, since I get here around one-thirty myself."

"No, thanks, I don't get this gorgeous by waking up in the middle of the night," she said with a laugh. She put a hand on my arm. "We all can't be natural beauties like you."

"Please, spare me. I'm not making any more donuts today, and that's final. We're going to have to find another approach, but that's the problem, isn't it? I don't know who to talk to next, and Chief Martin isn't exactly being forthcoming about the investigation."

"So George is helping you, too."

"He is," I said as I took the opportunity to start cleaning up. "But he's retired, and that limits his access."

"Then we need to find out more ourselves."

"How do you propose we do that?" I asked as I finished sweeping the floor. Grace had sat at the counter the entire time I'd been working, but I hadn't minded. I had a routine I went through every day at noon to close up the shop, and the work left my mind free to think while I performed the tasks on autopilot.

"I think I've got an idea, but you're going to have to go along with me," she said.

"I'm not making a blanket promise like that," I said. "It's gotten me into trouble in the past, and you know it."

She shook her head. "You're losing your nerve in your old age, girl."

"I'm seven months younger than you," I said.

"It doesn't matter. Age is nothing more than a state of mind, anyway. So, how's your nerve?"

"I guess there's only one way to find out." I wasn't sure what Grace had in mind, but whatever it was, I was sure it would be risky, but something with a chance at a big payoff. That's how she ran her life, but this time, I was the one who had everything to lose.

My cell phone rang as we walked outside and locked up.

It was George.

"I've been waiting for you," I said.

"Sorry, I got hung up. We'll talk later."

"What's it about?" I asked.

"Can't talk now. I've gotta go."

Then he hung up on me.

Grace looked at me and asked, "What was that about?"

"I don't have the slightest idea."

As we started walking together, I put a hand on Grace's arm. "Wait a second," I said. "My car's over there."

Grace said, "I know, but we're not driving, at least not yet."

I wasn't about to let go of her. "We're not going to Gabby's, are we? She's the biggest gossip in April Springs."

"Don't you think I know that? Who better to ask about Patrick Blaine?"

This was a bad idea; I could feel it in my bones. "We shouldn't do this. She's going to suspect something."

"If you ask the questions, she probably will. You, my friend, have a character flaw that's going to be fatal someday."

I stopped dead. "Do you mind telling me what it is?"

Grace laughed. "Don't be so serious about it. I'm just saying that you're not that great a liar. In fact, you're pretty lousy at it."

"That's what you call a character flaw? I wonder what that says about you."

She shook her head as she said, "I'm in sales, so of course I know how to lie. It's not always a bad thing, you know? I shouldn't call it lying, even. It's more like embellishing the truth, and massaging it until it says what you want."

I couldn't believe we were having this conversation, especially in front of Gabby Williams's shop.

The door to Gabby's business opened, and the proprietress herself stepped out and said, "Are you ladies coming in, or are you just loitering in front of my shop?"

Before I could say a word, Grace spoke up. "We

came to see you. Is there any chance we could get some of your marvelous tea?"

Gabby was taken aback by the request, and obviously delighted. "Why, that would be lovely. Let me put a kettle on. Don't tarry now, come in."

"We'll join you in one second," Grace said, and Gabby disappeared back into her shop.

The moment she was gone, Grace turned to me and said, "Suzanne, do me a favor and don't say anything."

"I'm not going to sit there like some kind of lump," I protested.

I could tell Grace was exasperated as she said, "Then at least follow my lead. Wait until you see where the conversation is going before you chime in."

"Grace, do you honestly even know where the conversation is headed?"

Her smile was bright as she said, "I don't have a clue. That's part of the fun of it, don't you think?"

Gabby poked her head back out the door. "Are you coming, ladies?"

"We are," Grace said as she threaded her arm through mine.

We walked in, but before we could make it to the back, Grace stopped at an ivory jacket. "This is absolutely lovely."

"It is, isn't it? I only wish I could keep them all."

I touched the sleeve. The fabric was silk, which was nice to the touch, but wouldn't wear well at all. "That kind of defeats the purpose, doesn't it?"

"Whatever do you mean?"

I shrugged. "I wouldn't have much of a business if I ate all the donuts myself, would I?"

Grace said, "You must forgive her, Gabby. Suzanne's been awake a long time, and I think the poor girl is sleep deprived."

"I understand. These past few days must have been hard on her."

"Hey, I'm standing right here," I said.

Gabby looked at me for a moment. "Of course you are. Now, let's have some tea. I have some wonderful new cookies I just found the recipe for, and you have got to try them."

"They sound delicious," Grace said. Once Gabby's back was turned to us, Grace put a finger to her lips, making a shushing sign.

Fine. If she wanted a mute witness, then that was what I was going to be, if I could just manage it.

We took our seats in back, and as Gabby poured tea for us, Grace said, "The shop is wonderfully organized. How do you manage it? I imagine your inventory turnover is tremendous, and yet you always seem to keep a perfect balance of offerings."

"It can be difficult at times," Gabby said. It was pretty obvious she was pleased by the compliment. I had to hand it to Grace. She'd managed, in just a few words, to put Gabby at ease, something that would have taken me hours to do, if I could succeed at all. She truly had the touch when dealing with people.

After more inane conversation, much of which I didn't participate in, Grace said, "I keep thinking about poor Patrick Blaine."

"From what I've heard, 'poor' is exactly the right

word I'd use to describe him," Gabby said. "I understand he was overextended on several fronts, if you follow me."

Grace nodded sagely, and I had to bite my tongue to not ask her how she'd heard anything about him, since twenty-four hours ago she hadn't even known his name. It had to be the power of the grapevine at work. I was starting to see that Grace's choice of first stops had been a wise one. Evidently Gabby had done a great deal of our legwork for us.

Grace took a sip of tea, then she said, "Still, whenever a life leaves us, someone feels the sorrow. I wonder who his significant other might have been."

Gabby put her teacup down, and leaned forward, though there was no one in the shop but the three of us. She must have loved the conspiratorial edge to our conversation, because her eyes were absolutely gleaming. "His divorce was completed just last week, according to a friend of mine. I have it on very good authority that his ex-wife, Rita Blaine, wasn't aware that it had already become final, and the woman tried to collect his life insurance before the body was even cold. Can you imagine how shocked she must have been? She'd been expecting a windfall, and instead, she gets nothing, the poor woman." It was pretty clear that Gabby didn't think Rita was a poor woman at all.

"It's tragic, isn't it?" Grace added. "I wonder who does inherit the money?"

"I haven't heard that myself, but I'm willing to wager anything that Rita knows. Would you like more tea?"

Grace put a hand over her cup. "I'd love to, but I'm afraid Suzanne has had a difficult day. I think I should get her home."

"I'm fine," I insisted.

"Nonsense," Gabby replied. "With the discovery of the body yesterday, and the trauma you must be feeling from it, it's amazing you even made it in today."

Grace was standing, and I felt her arm tugging at mine. "Let's get you home, Suzanne." The pressure of her grip on my arm was getting stronger, so I just nodded. Before we left, though, I turned to Gabby and asked, "How have you managed to learn so much about Patrick Blaine so quickly?"

"Suzanne, in a county as small as ours, do you honestly think anything stays a secret for long? I understand he was a loyal customer of yours, which must make the shock to your system even worse. You need to go home and get some rest. You look like you could use it." She hesitated, then added, "If you don't mind my saying so, you might want to try a little concealer under your eyes. You mustn't go around town looking like a raccoon, no matter how you feel."

"Thanks, I'll get right on that," I said as Grace dragged me outside.

Back on the sidewalk, Grace said, "You just couldn't keep quiet, could you?"

I asked, "Aren't you the least bit curious how she goes about collecting her information? How can any of it be accurate?"

"I would imagine she has a pretty good set of sources, but even if she's dead wrong about everything, she's given us a good place to start. He never mentioned Rita to you, did he?"

I shook my head. "No, our conversations were always light. That doesn't mean he didn't matter to me, though."

"I never thought so."

I headed for my Jeep, but Grace said, "Suzanne, I think it would be better if we took my car. Too many folks around here know what you drive, and if they see your car parked in front of your shop, they'll think you're still here."

"I'm not going home," I said. "I don't need to rest."

"That was just to get us out of there, you nit. If I hadn't made up some kind of excuse, we'd be sitting there sipping tea till midnight. Come on, let's go."

"I'm guessing we're going to pay a visit to Rita Blaine so we can find out if what Gabby heard about the life insurance was true," I said.

She nodded her head in satisfaction. "That was my thought, unless you can think of something else we should be doing."

"Not off the top of my head."

Grace frowned as we approached her car. "I'm just not sure I know how to get her to talk."

"You mean you're not going to just charm the information out of her?"

As Grace called information for Rita's phone number and address, she said, "There's just so much I can finesse my way through. You don't have any ideas, do you?"

My mind raced for some excuse we could use to get Rita to talk. I'd almost given up when I saw a newspaper vending machine on the corner.

"I've got it," I told Grace as she hung up her phone.

"Okay, I'm listening. What's your idea?"

"We're going to pretend to be freelancers writing an article for the *Charlotte Observer*. If Rita thinks she's going to be in the newspaper, I'm willing to bet that she'll tell us things she wouldn't ordinarily admit to a pair of strangers."

Grace smiled softly. "That's a Nancy Drew idea if I've ever heard one."

I looked at her. "Are you making fun of me?"

"Are you kidding? I'm applauding. That's brilliant. Now here's what we'll do."

By the time we got to Rita's house, we were ready with our act. Grace dug a couple of notebooks out of her trunk, a space that was always a cornucopia of office supplies, since she traveled so much.

But when we got to Rita Blaine's address, the front door was standing wide open, and I had a feeling in the pit of my stomach that we were too late.

EASY FRIED APPLE PIES

These are some of the easiest things in the world to make, and they are absolutely delicious. Even if you're a seasoned cook, sometimes a shortcut is still a good thing. Try them, they're worth it!

INGREDIENTS

Precooked apples, 8 oz., from the can
1 tablespoon sugar
1 teaspoon cinnamon
1 ready-made pie crust

DIRECTIONS

Warm the apples on the stovetop over low heat, adding the sugar and cinnamon and mixing it well, then take the pan off the heat to cool a little. Unroll the pie crust onto the countertop. Flour the rim of a bowl or glass and cut circles out of the dough by pressing down and twisting. I usually make four fried pies out of one crust. Place a small amount of apple in the center of each circle, then wet the edges of the dough all the way around. Fold the dough over in half, and pinch the edges together, sealing in the apple. The shape will look something like a curved half-moon.

Drop the pies into 375 degree oil, and give them three to four minutes on each side before turning them with skewers. The crusts will puff out a little along the edges, and they will get golden, with maybe a little brown as well. These usually take about eight minutes to cook, but the time can vary. Don't be afraid to leave them in a little longer than you would normally fry something. Pull them from the oil, dust them with powdered sugar, and they're ready to eat.

Makes 4 pies.

CHAPTER 5

"Should we just go on in?" I asked. "Or should we call the police?"

"Why on earth would we do that?" Grace asked.

"I've got a feeling that something's wrong."

"Nonsense," Grace said as she brushed past me and went inside. "Hello? Is anyone here? Hello?"

I followed her, albeit reluctantly. What would Chief Martin say if I found another body, so soon after the last one? Was that a conversation I really wanted to have, or an experience I needed to endure? The image of Patrick Blaine's body on the asphalt in front of my shop was still so vivid in my mind that if I closed my eyes, I knew I would see it.

"Who's there?" a woman's voice asked, coming from the bedroom.

"We're with the *Observer*," Grace said.

An older woman wearing a stained blue blouse and Capri pants came out. Her hair, its original color long forgotten, was frosted platinum blonde, and from the state of her makeup and the unsteady way she walked, it was clear she'd been drinking heavily. Okay, two empty bottles of vodka on the coffee table helped me reach that conclusion, as well.

"Don't need a paper," she said. "I've already got one. What I need is a drink."

She stared at the empties with an accusatory glare. "Did you kill that bottle while I was in the bedroom?"

"We just got here," Grace said.

I pointed to a tumbler half full on the fireplace mantel. "Is that what you're looking for?"

She spotted the glass, held it to her lips, and drank the entire contents in three straight swallows. "That's what I needed, something to take the edge off."

Rita noticed us again after she removed her rapt attention from the alcohol. "Like I said, I already subscribe."

"We're not here to drum up business," I said. "We're writers working for the paper, and our editor thinks your story is one worth telling."

She frowned, as if the focus cost her something. "What story?"

Grace jumped in. "How you lost your husband so soon after the divorce was finalized."

"He rammed it through, the horse's hind end," she said. "It wasn't supposed to be done until next week. That money's rightfully mine."

"What money is that?" I asked softly.

"The insuranche, insurance," she said, the vodka starting to take hold.

"Was it a lot?"

"That depends. Do you call a million bucks a lot?" She looked around her shabby living room. "I do. And now that cupcake gets it. She gets all the icing. It's just not fair. He cheated me on my alimony, and then he did it again with his insurance. All because of that woman." I wasn't sure if she was laughing or crying, but Rita had an emotional jag that lasted nearly a minute before she collected herself.

"She should be exposed," Grace said. "What's her name?"

Rita pointed her empty glass at us. "Deb. Deb Jenkins. The tramp. She lives in Union Square."

I asked, "How long had your ex-husband been seeing her?"

Rita snapped, "Let me put it this way. He wasn't my ex when she took up with him. Now she's got my money, and all I've got is this." She looked around the room, then the glass tumbled from her grip onto the carpet.

"I need a drink," she said.

Rita started digging through the cabinets, and I put a hand on Grace's arm. "Let's go," I said softly.

After hearing a string of curse words, directed at bottles that somehow had managed to empty themselves, Grace nodded her agreement.

I closed the door behind us, setting the lock as we went. At least Rita would be left alone with her bender, unless she chose to open the door again herself.

Once we were in Grace's car, I said, "I feel sorry for her."

"She brought it on herself," Grace said. Her father had been an alcoholic, and I knew there were still wounded spots in Grace's heart from it.

It was no time to get into a philosophical debate about the perils and causes of alcohol abuse. "At least we've got a new lead. Let's go find Deb Jenkins and find out her side of the story."

Grace got a new address, and as we drove there, I said, "You know, we've got to add Rita Blaine to our list of suspects."

"Why's that?"

"By her own admission, she didn't know the divorce was final when he died. She might have been trying to get her hands on that insurance while she still thought she was entitled to it. I wonder if Chief Martin has spoken to her yet."

"Let's call in an anonymous tip," Grace said. "I'd love to hear him interview her."

"Not even I'm that cruel," I said. "Why don't we leave her alone, at least for now? I have to admit, I'm dying to hear Deb Jenkins's take on things."

Grace parked in front of a condo, then asked me, "Are we still newspaper reporters?"

"I don't see why not. It's worked okay so far."

Grace frowned. "We didn't even need a cover for Rita Blaine."

"No, but I've got a feeling we're not going to be so lucky with Deb Jenkins."

"There's only one way to find out, isn't there?"

Grace got out of the car, and I followed her lead. Hopefully, Patrick Blaine's girlfriend might be able to shed light, where the ex wife had failed.

*   *   *

Before we had the chance to walk up the steps to Deb Jenkins's house, my cell phone rang.

"Don't answer that," Grace said. "We're doing something important here."

"How do you know this isn't?" I flipped the phone up and saw that the caller was restricted. Who on earth could be calling me from a blocked phone?

"Hello," I said.

"Why aren't you home?"

"Hi, Momma. I'm sorry, I didn't realize I had to check in with you after work. When did you start blocking your caller ID?"

I shrugged as I looked at Grace, who tapped her watch.

"Don't get an attitude with me, young lady. You know I'm concerned about your welfare."

"My welfare's just fine," I said. "Is that all you wanted? I'm kind of in the middle of something right now."

"What are you doing, Suzanne? Are you taking unnecessary chances with your life?"

"How would I know if it is necessary or not? I'm with Grace. Would you like to speak with her to be sure I'm all right?"

"That's exactly what I'd like to do."

I handed the phone to my friend. After she put her hand over the receiver's mouthpiece, she asked, "What? Why are you giving it to me?"

"She wants to talk to you," I said.

As Grace said hello, walking a few paces away, I saw a curtain flutter at the house. Someone was watching our comedy routine from the second floor. What must Deb Jenkins be thinking? Maybe it was a good thing Momma had called. It might give our next interviewee a chance to think about why we were there, and if that kept her off balance, it might be just as effective as alcohol had been for Rita Blaine.

After a full minute, Grace handed the phone back to me. I was surprised to find that my mother was no longer on the line.

"What did she want with you?" I asked.

"I had to promise to keep you out of trouble," Grace admitted reluctantly.

I laughed, in spite of the humiliation of what she'd promised. "Good luck with that. Let me know how you do."

"I didn't know what else to say. Your mother is a force of nature sometimes, isn't she?"

"You don't have to tell me," I said as I put my phone back in my purse.

I looked back at the house, but the curtain had returned to its closed position. "Someone's been watching us from inside."

Of course Grace looked at the house. "I don't see anyone there."

"That's because you spooked her. Let's go have a chat with Ms. Jenkins and see what she has to say."

Deb Jenkins opened the door before I even had a chance to knock. She wasn't anything like I'd expected the "other woman" to look like. Deb had mousy brown hair and wore no makeup that I could detect. I couldn't really see her body, since it was hidden by a bulky sweater, but I had to admit, I was beginning to wonder what Patrick Blaine had seen in her that he liked enough to leave his wife. Maybe she was a sweetheart, or had a bubbly personality that belied her appearance.

"What do you two want?" she snapped.

So much for that theory.

"We're from the *Observer*," I said, "and we'd like to include you in an upcoming article we're working on."

"Is it about my moth collection? I wrote your editors several times, but I've been amazed by their lack of interest."

"Absolutely," Grace said. "That's why we're here. Could we possibly see it?"

"Come in," she said, the change in her personality striking. "Where's the photographer? I told them in my letters that the article won't be anything without photographic evidence. My collection would be rather difficult to describe in print."

"He's coming," I said, "but he was held up at a wreck."

"So that's who you were talking to out on the walk."

I said, "We're sorry for the delay, but perhaps you could show us your work while we wait. That way we can finish the interview before he arrives."

"That would be fine," she said. We followed her through an ordinary enough home, filled with frilly pillows and framed needlepoint works hanging from the walls.

"It's in here," she said, as she led us into what had to be a spare bedroom at the top of the stairs.

Grace and I followed her in, and I immediately started wishing we had an exit strategy, despite why we'd come. In place of needlepoint, the walls were covered with framed display boxes featuring the wildest array of dead moths I'd ever seen in my life. Each specimen was carefully labeled, and there were tables filled with displays, as well. I've never been that big a fan of moths in the past, but my heart went out to them when I saw this torture chamber dedicated to their demise.

"It's really something," I said, searching for anything that would hide my disgust.

Grace seemed fascinated by the displays. "What drew you to moths? There has to be a flame somewhere in your life."

The reference zipped right over her head. "I began my collection when I was nine, and it just seemed to grow and grow. Moths are lovely, and they need to be protected from man's devastation and development. Their lives are too fragile."

Especially with her on the loose. The main thing they needed to be protected from appeared to be Deb Jenkins.

"I'm curious," Grace said. "Does your husband share your love of moths with you?"

"I'm not married," she said curtly.

"Your boyfriend, then," Grace pushed.

"What does my love life have to do with your article? It should be about my moths, not my life."

"It's part of the human-interest angle," I said.

Grace nodded. "Our editor won't even look at the story if we don't have human interest."

Deb seemed to mull that over, then said, "Fine. If you must know, my boyfriend wasn't a big fan of my hobby. He didn't get it."

"Is that why he's not your boyfriend anymore?" I asked.

"He died," she said curtly. "I really don't want to discuss it any further, if you don't mind."

Grace closed the notebook she'd been scribbling in. "I'm sorry you feel that way. We're sorry to have bothered you." She turned to me and said, "Call Max and tell him we don't need him for the photo shoot after all."

"Wait, you can't leave," Deb said as she grabbed my arm. She had a grip like a longshoreman.

"Sorry. It's out of our hands," I said as I tried to pry her loose.

"I'll talk about him," she said. "He was murdered, and the police don't know who did it. They haven't even talked to me, and I could help them."

"What would you tell them if you could?" I asked.

"They should focus on his ex-wife. She wanted his life insurance money, only Patrick fooled her."

"And left it to you instead?" I asked gently.

"That's what he promised me. What's wrong with that? We were in love."

Grace said, "Some folks might think that gave you a motive for murder. Was it a lot of money?"

"Not really. I wanted him alive and with me. What good would the money be to me without Patrick? I haven't even contacted the insurance company yet."

"So you and his ex-wife both had motives," I said. "She thought she was going to benefit from his death, but it sounds as if you're the one who really did."

Deb wasn't about to take that. She snapped, "You know what? There are more people than me who had a reason to kill him. You should talk to his secretary at the bank. Her name's Vicki Houser, and she had every reason in the world to want to see him dead herself."

I thought of that sweet and caring woman I'd spoken to the day before, and I couldn't imagine her as a killer. "Why do you say that?"

"She's been in love with him for years, and Patrick finally had enough of her pining and sickening adoration. He told her he wasn't the least bit interested in her romantically a month ago. She wouldn't accept his rejection, though, and when she found out he was seeing me all along, she said she'd see him dead before she'd let him throw his life away on me. There's the one you should talk to."

Could she be telling the truth, or was Deb Jenkins just trying to muddy the waters? I'd been focusing on the business end of motives, but this afternoon's interviews had revealed an entirely separate line of investigation. I wondered if Chief Martin had even thought about the possibility that Patrick Blaine had been killed for love, instead of money. Then again, if Deb Jenkins had done it, it might be because of a little bit of both.

Grace's cell phone rang, and she excused herself.

Deb looked at me, then said, "Can we please talk about my collection now? It's fit for the finest museum."

"You've certainly been thorough in your dedication," I said.

Grace hung up, then said, "We've got to go."

"What about the photographer?" Deb asked.

"I'm sorry, they bumped the story. Thanks for your time, though."

Deb snapped, "So that's it? You're just going to walk away?" Her voice had gotten louder with each word she spoke.

"Easy," I said. "There's no reason to lose your temper."

She nearly shouted, "I don't have a temper!"

Grace's eyes grew large while I envisioned both of us pinned and labeled on a board under glass, and added to her collection.

I said, "We'll do our best to convince our editor that this is a worthy story. We'll be in touch."

That seemed to mollify her somewhat. "Do you have a card?"

"Sorry, I'm all out," I said. "Maybe there's one in the car."

We got into Grace's car and drove off as fast as we could.

Once we were out of sight, I turned to Grace and asked, "What was so urgent about that telephone call?"

"My dentist's office called to remind me of my next appointment. I had to get out of there. She was creepy, wasn't she?"

I fought back a chill. "What did he ever see in her? She isn't pretty, by any stretch of the imagination, and she has the personality of a psycho. I just don't see the appeal."

"Are you asking me to explain a man's behavior? You're talking to the wrong gal. I haven't been able to figure them out yet."

I noticed that we were driving away from April Springs, instead of toward it. "Where are we headed now?"

"I thought we'd have a chat with Vicki Houser."

"The reporter angle isn't going to work," I said. "She already knows I'm a donut maker."

"Then we'll just have to ask her point-blank if she had anything to do with her boss's death."

"This could get ugly," I said.

"Uglier than Moth Girl? I don't see how."

We didn't even get to find out. At the bank, we learned that Vicki Houser had turned in her notice, and was taking accumulated vacation time, as of that morning.

It appeared that one of our suspects had gotten away.

At least for now.

As we were driving back to the donut shop, I had an idea. "Let's find out where Vicki Houser lives."

"You heard her replacement at the bank. She's gone."

"Do we know that, really? Just because she quit her job and took her vacation time doesn't mean she's left town. It takes time to pack up everything you own. I'm willing to bet she hasn't left town yet."

"I knew there was a reason I kept you around. That's not a bad idea."

As Grace called Information yet again, I wondered what I'd say to get Vicki to talk. I could appeal to her sense of loyalty to her former boss, or Grace and I could let her know right away that we knew she had more of an interest in him than just as her boss.

It was an ugly business, and I hated airing people's dirty laundry if I didn't need to, but I didn't have much choice. How long would it take until the killer came after me? I wondered if I might not be speeding up the process by ignoring the warning, but I couldn't see any other way around it.

The hard questions had to be asked.

There was a moving van parked in front of the apartment where Vicki Houser lived.

Grace smiled. "You were right. She's not gone yet."

We knocked on the door three times, tried the handle, even walked around to the back.

No Vicki Houser anywhere in sight.

"We could leave her a note to call us," I said.

"What possible reason could we give her to do that?"

I thought about it a minute, then said, "Why don't we tell her we found some money that we think might belong to her?"

Grace asked, "Why would she ever believe that?"

"How many people do you know who would be willing to turn their back on found money, whether it belonged to them originally or not?"

"I guess it's worth a shot," Grace said. "We certainly can't stay camped out on her front lawn waiting for her to come back home."

"I've got a feeling that would get Chief Martin's attention pretty fast," I agreed. "And I don't want to confirm what he already suspects. Let me borrow that notebook of yours so I can leave her a note."

"Put my number on it, not yours," Grace said.

"No way. I'm not dragging you that far into this."

"Think about it, Suzanne. You'll be asleep in a few hours. It's hard to tell when Vicki's going to get back here to finish packing."

I shook my head. "I'm not going to do it. Even if she calls at midnight, I'll take it."

"I don't mind."

I touched her shoulder lightly. "Thanks, I appreciate that, I really do, but I'm still not letting you put your neck on the line like that."

"Fine, then we'll do it your way."

I wrote the note, with a promise of cash, and tucked it into the door frame where she'd be sure to see it.

As we drove back to Donut Hearts, I wondered if the lure of money would be strong enough to reel her in, or if Vicki's desire to get out of town would supersede everything else.

I collected my Jeep back at the shop, thought about going in and having one last look around the place, but I was dead tired, hungry, and ready for some sleep. It was time to go home.

To my delight, dinner was on the table, and it was my favorite. My mother was known over seven counties for her pot roast, and there were grown men who cried at the thought of getting a single taste of it.

"What's the occasion?" I asked Momma as I walked into the kitchen.

"What are you talking about? I cook dinner almost every evening."

"Not pot roast," I said. "I feel special."

"You should," she said. "Are you ready to eat?"

I took my seat. "You'd better believe it."

A large helping of roast, carrots, potatoes, and onions made it quickly to my plate. The smells of the cooked meat and vegetables, along with a handful of Momma's secret spices topped off with two Bay leaves, made my mouth water.

There were definite advantages to living back at home with her, and the wonderful meals she cooked was near the top of the list.

Momma said a quick grace, and then we ate.

I took a piece of her sourdough and slathered it with butter before taking a big bite of the warm bread.

As we ate, I tried to steer the conversation away from what I'd been up to.

I cleaned my plate, thought about getting seconds, then realized that I'd better stop.

"I don't suppose there's dessert," I said.

"Can you honestly eat anything after all that?"

I grinned. "Try me."

She bit her lip, then finally admitted, "There's peach cobbler, but we can have it tomorrow, if you'd like. It saves beautifully."

"If there's any left by then, that's fine with me. Do we have any vanilla ice cream to go with it?"

"It's in the freezer."

She gave me a penurious slice of cobbler along with a dollop of ice cream, but I knew I could raid the fridge in the morning before work, so I didn't protest.

It was probably a good thing. By the time I had the last bite, I wasn't sure I'd be able to hold a thimbleful more of food.

The phone rang just as I was pushing my plate away. "Could you get that, Momma?"

She picked up the phone, and after a few seconds, gave it to me.

"Hello?" I asked.

"Is this Suzanne Hart? Your name sounds familiar, but I can't place it."

Was I about to get another threat? "It is."

"This is Vicki Houser. I'm not exactly sure what money your note was talking about, but I thought I'd give you a call."

"Hi, Vicki. We met at the bank yesterday. I'm the woman who brought you donuts."

She paused, then said, "I'm sorry, but how does that involve my money?"

That was a good question. Unfortunately, I wasn't all that sure I had a good answer. I said, "I was talking to Rita Blaine, and your name came up."

Vicki's voice went deadly cold. "What did she have to say?"

"She was going through her ex-husband's things, and she found some money in an envelope with your name on it. She thought you should have it, so I volunteered to deliver it to you, since we'd already met."

The woman's tone shifted yet again, this time with a new level of warmth in it. "How thoughtful of her. Do you happen to know how much it is?"

"The envelope's sealed, but you can see a twenty through a tear." I was going to have to fork over some of my own money, something I hadn't planned on, but I really didn't have much choice.

"Is there a letter with it that you can see?"

I suddenly realized how I could have gotten Vicki Houser's attention without spending my money to do it. A promised letter from her ex-boss, fantasy love, and who knew whatever else, would have been more enticing to her than cash.

"I'm not sure," I said. "Can you meet with me now?" I'd call Grace and pick her up on the way. There really was safety in numbers.

"No, I'm afraid I'm tied up until midnight. Then I'm leaving town. I'll swing by the donut shop on my way out of town. What time do you get there?"

"Not until two," I said.

"Meet me there at one-thirty, and you can give it to me then. Thanks for calling."

"Good-bye," I said. I wasn't sure Grace would be able to meet me so late, or early, depending on the point of view. She wasn't picking up her cell phone, so I left her a voice message. The meeting wasn't ideal, but I didn't have much choice. I needed to talk to the woman before she left town.

I just wasn't sure I wanted to do it alone. Maybe Emma would come in early.

I dialed her number, and got her answering machine. After the command to leave a message, I said, "Emma, this is Suzanne. Could you come in a little early tomorrow?"

Momma came back in from the kitchen. "What was that all about?"

"Nothing," I said, trying to avoid a direct conversation about what I'd been up to.

"It didn't sound like nothing to me."

I suddenly remembered I'd forgotten to go by the bank before it closed, and the only ATM I could use was out of order. Some idiot had tried to steal it a few nights before, going so far as pulling it out of the bank wall, but there he'd been thwarted in his grand larceny attempt. What the fool hadn't counted on was that the machine was wired into the bank's alarm system, and the sirens had driven him away.

In the meantime, law-abiding citizens were being inconvenienced until they could get a new machine. I looked in my wallet and found a twenty, four ones, and a coupon for Hobby Hood. It made for an anemic envelope.

"Momma, do you have any singles?"

"Has it gotten that bad at the shop?" she asked.

"No, this isn't for me. It's for a friend."

Her hand stopped in midair as it had been going toward her purse. "Suzanne, which of your friends is in need of money?"

"It's too long a story to tell you. I'll pay you back tomorrow."

She raised an eyebrow as she retrieved six one-dollar bills and handed them to me. "I'm sorry it's not more."

"This is perfect," I said as I stuffed them into the envelope. It didn't look like a fortune, which it surely wasn't, but it might be enough to keep Vicki Houser occupied while I talked to her about what had happened between her and her boss, and why she was leaving town so abruptly.

I scrawled Vicki's name on the front of the envelope, then jammed it into my purse.

It was just in time, too. I heard the front doorbell

ring, and when I looked up, I found State Police Inspector Jake Bishop watching me from my front porch. How long had he been standing there, and how much had he heard?

I had a feeling I was about to find out.

BAKED CINNAMON APPLE DONUTS

Baked donuts are more of a breadlike consistency, and if you're hesitant to begin your donut journey with frying, this is a good place to start. In fact, my daughter prefers these over most of the fried varieties. Be warned, though; baking means these donuts take quite a bit longer from when you start to when you can start enjoying them.

INGREDIENTS
2 packets dry yeast
½ cup warm water
½ cup granulated sugar
1½ cups applesauce
3 tablespoons butter or margarine, melted
2 teaspoons cinnamon
1 teaspoon nutmeg
½ teaspoon salt
2 eggs, lightly beaten
5½ to 6½ cups all-purpose flour

Topping
½ cup butter, melted
½ cup sugar
1 tablespoon cinnamon

DIRECTIONS
Dissolve the yeast in the warm water in a large bowl, allowing it to sit 5 to 10 minutes.

Then add the sugar, applesauce, melted butter, cinnamon, nutmeg, salt, beaten eggs, and 3 cups of the flour. Beat it at low speed with an electric mixer or by hand until the mixture is moistened throughout, then beat at medium speed for another minute.

Stir in 2½ cups of flour, ½ cup at a time, adding it until you've formed a soft dough. The consistency of the dough is more important than the exact amount of flour you use. Turn it out onto a lightly floured surface, and knead it about 5 minutes, until it's smooth and elastic.

Place the dough in a bowl coated with cooking spray, then lightly spray the top. Cover it with a clean cloth and let it rise in a warm place, free from drafts, for about 1 hour. It will have almost doubled in size by then. Punch the dough down, and then turn it out onto a lightly floured surface.

Roll the dough to ½-inch thickness, and then cut it with your donut cutter.

Place the donuts and holes on greased baking sheets, then brush the tops of donuts with some of the melted butter. Let the donuts rise, uncovered, in a warm, draft-free place for 30 minutes.

Bake the donuts at 425 degrees for 11 minutes or until they are golden. Immediately brush melted butter over baked donuts as soon as you take them out, and then dip the donuts into the sugar-cinnamon mix.

Makes 12 to 16 donuts.

CHAPTER 6

"I need a minute of your time," Jake said as I walked to the door.

"I thought we already covered everything we needed to discuss before, Inspector." I wasn't ready to admit to my own mother what I'd been up to, and I certainly wasn't going to admit it to somebody who could put me in jail for my meddling. Actually, I wasn't sure he could do that, but I wasn't ready to take the chance.

"Like I said, call me Jake, and our last conversation happened before you started snooping around on your own."

This wasn't going to be good; I could tell that from the tone of his voice. It was time to see if my innocent act might work.

"I'm sure I don't know what you're talking about," I said as I kept the screen door between us.

"You know what? I'm pretty sure you do," he said.

I was ready to wait him out all night with the door between us, when Momma popped up behind me.

"Won't you come in, young man? I swear, Suzanne, sometimes you act as though you were raised by wolves."

"He doesn't need to come in, Momma," I said.

"Actually, I'd be delighted," he said as he stepped inside. "I'm Jake Bishop."

"He's with the state police," I said.

Momma looked positively delighted. "Oh, an officer of the law. We're pleased to have you in our home. Would you care for some peach cobbler?"

"He doesn't have time for a treat, Momma."

Jake laughed. "The day I turn down homemade cobbler is the day they can have my badge. I'd be delighted, ma'am, thanks for the offer."

As Momma disappeared into the kitchen to get his cobbler, I said, "I don't have anything else to tell you."

"Why don't you start by filling me in on what you've been up to the past two days?"

"Have you been following me around April Springs, Inspector?"

"How many times am I going to have to tell you? It's Jake," he said as he smiled. "And you and your friend haven't been all that hard to keep up with. You have the subtlety of a wet fish slapping someone in the face."

"That's not the point," I said. "I don't like being watched by the police."

"Then maybe you shouldn't interfere with our business," he replied, so sweetly that sugar wouldn't melt in his mouth.

My mother came back in, holding a piece of cobbler at least twice the size of the one she'd given me.

After Jake took it, she said, "We have coffee, or cold milk if you'd prefer."

"Milk would be fine," he said.

As Momma disappeared yet again, I said quietly, "There's something I need to tell you. I don't approve of you."

"Your mother doesn't seem to mind." He took a bite of cobbler and whistled. "Did you make this?"

My baking pride was at stake, and while I probably couldn't replicate my mother's cobbler perfectly, I knew that I could come close. "No, but I could have, if I'd wanted to."

He looked at me with more than a hint of skepticism.

"I can," I insisted.

"Can what, dear?" Momma asked as she rejoined us with Jake's milk.

"I can make a cobbler every bit as good as yours," I said.

"Of course you can," my mother said, with just enough hesitation to condemn the statement as a lie.

I was about to protest when she added, "Now I'll leave you two young people alone so you can get better acquainted."

"Momma, I don't care if you stay or go. This isn't a date."

"Of course it isn't," she said with that same hitch in her words.

She was gone before I could stop her, and I found myself alone with Inspector Bishop.

What on earth had I gotten myself into? "No matter what my mother may think, I'm fine just the way I am."

Jake took a bite of cobbler, then said, "Were you under the impression I thought otherwise?"

"I'm happier divorced than I was when I was married," I said, not sure if that was true or not. "I don't need a man to complete me, and I don't have to have one in my life to have fun. I'm doing fine."

"I'm not here to discuss your love life," he said. "If I were, this conversation would have started out on a completely different foot. Who knows what might happen after we solve this homicide, though. But at least for now, we need to keep things strictly professional."

"That's what I've been trying to tell you," I said. Somehow he'd turned my words around into something else entirely.

"Good, I'm glad we cleared that up. Suzanne, as a police officer, I can't stress how important it is that you stay out of this investigation. You are making things harder by butting in where you have no business being."

"Are you scolding me, Inspector?"

"What happened to calling me Jake?"

I was going to let that go. "I'm beginning to feel like I've got a target on my back, and I'm not sure you or Chief Martin are doing anything to alleviate that fear. I have a right to find out what's going on."

He put the plate down. Despite our bantering, it appeared that I'd tweaked something in him with that one. "You want to talk about rights? You're running around town doing more harm than good to an official inquiry, and then have the nerve to sit there and crow about it? I was right the first time."

"About what?"

"I should have locked you up on the spot the second I found out what you were doing," he said.

"That's the only way I'm going to stop, so you might as well," I said.

"Suzanne, have you ever listened to anyone in your entire life?"

"I do when they make sense. You people didn't even talk to Patrick Blaine's ex-wife, or his new girlfriend. That doesn't exactly give me much confidence in your abilities."

"You're not in a position to judge our competence, are you?" I had definitely crossed the line with that last crack. A vein I'd never noticed before started pulsing on his forehead, and his face was beginning to darken.

I was about to try to ease my hard stand when there was a knock at the front door.

It was the last person I wanted to see there, but then again, I hadn't gotten to choose.

"Max, I'm busy," I said as I saw my ex-husband at the door.

"So am I," he said. "I need to see you, anyway."

"I've got company," I said, hoping he'd get the hint and go away.

"Then I'll wait until you're through," he said as he took up a seat on the front steps of the house.

Jake shook his head, then he said to me, "You might as well let him in. We're not getting anywhere, are we?"

"I'm sorry," I said. "I don't mean to be a thorn in your side, I really don't. I just think there's more going on here than you realize."

"Funny, that's the same thing I was getting ready to say to you."

"So, can we agree to disagree on this?"

He looked at me intently, and I felt myself getting swept up in his eyes, no matter how much I'd protested that he didn't have any effect on me. "Suzanne, if you keep digging into this, I can't guarantee your safety."

"Nobody's ever been able to do that," I said, "but I promise I'll be careful."

"I hope so."

As he left, I saw Max glare at him, but if Jake noticed, he didn't respond.

"What do you want?" I asked my ex-husband as Jake Bishop drove away.

"I didn't know you were dating again," Max said sullenly.

"That wasn't a date."

Passing me, he stepped inside and spotted Jake's empty plate. "If he got your mother's cobbler, she must think so."

"What she thinks doesn't really matter at this point."

Max frowned at me. "You shouldn't be seeing him. He's trouble."

I laughed out loud, but there wasn't an ounce of joy in it. "That's rich, coming from you. Max, you should wear a warning label so women will know to be careful around you. I'm thinking something like a radiation sign, or even worse."

"I made one mistake, and that's in the past," he said. "You've got to let it go, Suzanne. How else are we going to move on?"

"In case you haven't noticed, I already have."

"Have you forgotten this?" he asked as he took a step toward me. I swear, I could feel the heat coming off him, and for an instant, I wanted to kiss him more than anything else in the world.

But that would be exactly the wrong thing to do, and I knew it.

I took a step back, tripped on the coffee table, and nearly fell before I righted myself. So much for dignity and grace, but at least it broke the tension in the air.

"Good night, Max. It's late, and I've got to get up early tomorrow."

"Time to make the donuts, right?"

"It's a steady income; I'm my own boss; and I meet a lot of interesting people. What more can you ask?"

"You used to want to be an artist, remember?" he said softly. "Whatever happened to those dreams?"

"I still paint now and then," I said. "Besides, there's art in everything done well, and I'm great at what I do, despite what you might think."

He held his palms up toward me. "Don't get me wrong, I know feeding people is noble and all that, but how creative do you have to be to make donuts every morning?"

"Max, you're showing your ignorance. Have you ever made a pinecone out of dough, or a fritter? Have you twisted a cinnamon stick, or built a honey bun by hand? I use my artistic skills every day, and if you don't see it, that's your problem, not mine. Now go. I'm too tired to keep arguing with you."

I could see in his eyes that his visit had taken a

wrong turn somewhere, interfering with what he'd been hoping to accomplish, but we weren't married anymore, and the time when I was supposed to make everything right was long past. Max was just going to have to deal with it.

"Good night," he said gently, and I felt my pique with him suddenly fade away.

"'Night," I said, as I closed the door and deadbolted it behind him.

Momma came out of the other room, and said, "That was the oddest thing."

"What's that?"

"I know you were talking to the police inspector, but then I could swear I heard Max's voice." She looked outside just as Max drove away. "What did he want, and where did Mr. Bishop go?"

"The inspector and I had a disagreement, so he left just as Max arrived."

Momma gave me that curt, disappointed look that I'd earned so often as a child. Well, I wasn't a child anymore. She asked pointedly, "What did you say to him, Suzanne?"

It was time to tell her what I was up to. "I told him I wasn't going to stop digging into Patrick Blaine's murder. I'm not going to sit around and wait for something to happen. I have to tackle this myself."

"Suzanne, it sounds so dangerous."

"I'm being careful, Momma."

She decided to let that go, at least for now. "That explains his absence, but why on earth did Max come by?"

I bit my lower lip, then said, "Do you want to know the truth? I think he was jealous." It was a revelation to me, but I don't think I surprised my mother at all.

"Why shouldn't he be? Max had his chance with you, and he threw it away on a cheap imitation. Now that there's a new man in your life, he clearly sees the error of his ways."

"Momma, there are so many things wrong with that statement that I don't even know where to start. Jake isn't in my life, at least not the way you mean, and if Max is having regrets, that's nobody's business but his own. As I told both of them, I'm happy with my single status. Having a man in my life just complicates things too much."

Momma smiled. "But think of how much fun they add to the party."

"If you feel that way, why don't you find someone new yourself? Dad's been gone for quite a while."

She looked sad for a moment, then Momma said, "There hasn't been a man born who could compete with your late father."

"Momma, I was almost as big a fan of Dad's as you were, but that doesn't mean you had to die when he did."

She wanted to speak, I could see it in her eyes, but instead, she said, "It's late, and you have to get up early tomorrow."

I could tell there was no way she wanted to talk tonight, and honestly, I was out of things to say myself.

Instead, I kissed her forehead, then said, "Good night, Momma. I love you."

"I love you, too," she said.

I lay in bed half an hour wondering exactly what

had happened that evening. There was a definite vibe between Jake and me, a tingling I hadn't felt in a very long time. Then again, Max wasn't just going away, no matter how much I wanted it. Or did I? It was all too confusing.

I needed to quit thinking about my love life—or complete lack of it—and focus on the task at hand; figure out who had killed Patrick Blaine and dumped his body in front of my shop, and more importantly, do it before the killer decided to come after me.

My alarm clock went off half an hour earlier than normal, and for an instant, I wanted to hit the snooze button and capture a few more minutes before I had to get up. Then I remembered my early-morning meeting with Vicki Houser on her way out of town, and I managed to drag myself out of bed. I'd debated telling Jake about it the night before, but his scolding had killed that idea. I couldn't very well ask him to watch my back while I was going against his express wishes. Hopefully, either Grace or Emma would show up and I'd be fine.

If not, I'd confront her by myself. Just because I'd met Vicki Houser didn't mean I was going to be reckless while I was around her. If she'd killed Patrick Blaine and thought I had any idea of it, I had no doubt she'd get rid of me, as well.

And I was going to make sure she never got the chance.

There was a moving van parked in front of Donut Hearts when I got there, and I felt my hands shaking as I started to get out of the Jeep. At the last second, on nothing more than impulse, I took the envelope I'd prepared the night before and shoved it under my car seat.

The van was dark, but I could see a figure inside behind the steering wheel.

I tapped on the window, trying to get Vicki's attention.

For a second, I thought she was dead. I was troubled to realize that the first thing that went through my mind was that someone had killed her in front of my shop to make the police suspicious of me, instead of worrying about her well-being.

She awoke with a start, then rubbed her eyes as she opened the door and got out. "Sorry, I hadn't planned on falling asleep. It was a long day yesterday, and I nearly killed myself taking care of everything."

"Don't apologize. I know how tough early mornings can be. Come on in. I'll start a pot of coffee, and it will be ready in a jiff."

She looked at her watch. "I don't know. I'm getting a late start as it is."

"One cup, that's all I'm offering," I said. Where on earth were Emma and Grace? I'd been counting on at least one of them backing me up, but it looked like I was on my own. So be it. I'd stall Vicki with the coffee, and while it was brewing, I'd ask her about her relationship with her boss, and what was driving her out of April Springs in the middle of the night.

"I suppose it's all right," she said.

She followed me inside, and I flipped on the lights for Donut Hearts. I wanted the world to know that someone was there with me, and if something happened to me, a car driving past might remember the parked moving van.

"I'm surprised you're leaving town so suddenly," I said as I turned the coffeepot on.

"It was a long time coming," she said, as she stifled a yawn. "Losing Mr. Blaine was just the final push."

"I understand you two were close," I said, trying to keep my tone light.

Vicki shook her head sadly. "It didn't take long for the gossips to dig their claws into me, did it? What did you hear, that Mr. Blaine and I were having some kind of torrid affair? Am I a spurned lover in the rumor mill?"

"I admit that I heard something like that. Is it true? Don't get me wrong, I'm not judging you. You certainly wouldn't be the first woman who was taken advantage of by her boss, and then thrown away. The same thing happened to my cousin Kim, and it nearly ruined her." Okay, I've never had a cousin named Kim, but I could have, and I was doing everything I could to get Vicki to open up.

"I feel bad for her, but it never happened to me. We worked together, and that was all it was. I was loyal to him, but when he died, my loyalty to the bank did, as well. I need a fresh start in a new town, and I'm determined to get it."

"Can you afford to just pick up and leave?" I asked delicately.

"I can't afford not to. That's the point, isn't it?"

I shook my head. "How can you leave town with

folks talking about you like they are? Don't you want to set the record straight before you go?" I needed more from her, especially before she left town forever.

"You're more involved in this than you claim, aren't you?" Her gaze had gone cold all of a sudden, and for some reason, I felt I was treading on dangerous ground.

"Don't forget, I saw him out there on the street," I said. "In my opinion, that gives me a stake in all of this."

"I'd be careful, if I were you," she said as I poured her a cup of coffee.

"Vicki, is that a threat?"

She hesitated, then said, "Not from me, but there are dangerous people involved in this, folks who don't care who gets hurt."

"Is that experience talking? Has someone threatened you?"

She took a sip of coffee, then said, "Nothing that blatant, but things were hinted at, and I didn't need any extra incentive to leave."

"Who's been pushing you? Someone from the banking business, or is it something more personal?"

She sighed. "Despite how Mr. Blaine's ex-wife and his mistress might feel, I'm not the least bit afraid of either one of them."

"So it's business," I said.

Vicki pushed the coffee mug away. "I really do need to get on the road. I've got a long drive ahead of me."

"Where are you going?"

She started to answer, then said, "You know what? If you don't mind, I think I'll keep that knowledge to myself. I'd hate for anybody in April Springs to find out where I am. About that envelope, may I have it before I go?"

I couldn't stall her any longer, and there was no earthly reason I could keep the money I'd promised her, even if it did really belong to me.

"It's out in the car," I said.

She followed me out, and I felt a tingling on the back of my neck as I opened the car door and bent down to get it from under the seat. It would have been simplicity itself for her to hit me over the head or stab me in the back, but fortunately, neither one of those things happened, and I straightened back up with the envelope clutched in my hands.

"It's not his handwriting," she said as she took it from me.

"No, it's not." I wasn't about to admit that it was mine.

Vicki tore the envelope open, did a quick count, then said, "I don't even know why he bothered."

It was all I'd had, and I guess I wanted her to be a little more grateful for it, since the money had come straight from my own pocket and not her boss's. "I'm sorry. Were you expecting more?"

"I guess that's been my problem from the start. I've always expected more than I've gotten."

On what was clearly an impulse, she leaned forward and hugged me.

"Thank you," she said as we broke apart.

"What for?"

"You're the only one in this town who was ever

straight with me, and I want you to know how much I appreciate it."

I'd lied to her from the first moment we'd met, and if I had to find a kernel of truth in anything I'd said to her since, it would be a tough battle. I wasn't about to tell her that, though. All I could manage was to say, "You're welcome."

I hoped my face didn't burn with my shame from one more lie.

I'd just finished locking the front door when Emma pulled up.

I unlocked the door again and let her in.

"What's so important?" she said as she shed her jacket. "I got here as soon as I could."

"You just missed it," I said.

"Sorry, I must have hit the snooze button without realizing it. What happened?"

I thought about it a second. "I'm not sure yet."

"What does that mean?"

"I'll tell you as soon as I know. Are you ready to make some donuts?"

"Lead the way," she said.

As we worked on preparing the day's donut offerings, different scenarios kept playing through my mind. The first thing I had to consider was that someone was lying to me. They all couldn't have been telling the truth, but who should I believe? Blaine's secretary, Vicki, had a motive if the mistress, Deb Jenkins, was telling the truth, while Deb had plenty of reasons to want Patrick Blaine dead if his ex-wife, Rita, was right. Then again, if Vicki was telling the truth, her insinuation was that none of the women had killed her boss. Instead, she'd pointed the finger in a direction I'd already started exploring, the construction company and the financial advisor. Maybe it was time to look a little more closely at them.

"Are we seriously making three batches of pumpkin donuts today? I know some of our customers like them, but isn't that overkill?"

I hadn't realized I'd made the same cake donut mix three times while I'd been lost in my thoughts, but I wasn't about to admit that to Emma. "I wanted some extras for this afternoon."

"What's going on, are you having a Halloween party in March?"

"No, but I thought I might use them around town. You know me, I'm always trying to drum up new business."

"Is that really all it is?" she asked.

"That's all I'm willing to admit," I said. I'd have to pay more attention to what I was doing.

By the time we were ready to open our doors at five-thirty, Emma and I had somehow managed to make the donuts yet again.

But I wasn't any closer to figuring out who had killed Patrick Blaine.

I needed help—even I could see that—and I knew just who to ask.

As George came in a little before 6 A.M., I said, "Today's donuts are on the house, but there's a catch."

He pushed the plate of donuts away. "No, thanks, Suzanne. I'd rather pay my way as I go."

"Is that any way to be? I know there's no chance

you're not going to help me, so why not take an offering that's meant to be a thank-you for caring?"

George said, "Sorry, you're right. I guess I'm a
little too stiff-necked these days for my own good. It
comes from getting older."

"Now about that catch."

George said, "Whatever you need. I'm sorry I
said anything."

I took a deep breath, then said, "I'm afraid things
have gotten a little too out of hand for me. It's tough
running this donut shop ten hours a day, and then
spending the rest of my time snooping into Patrick
Blaine's life. Plus, Chief Martin's watching me pretty
closely, not to mention the inspector from the state
police who's been called in to work on the case.
George, I need you to see if there are any new devel-
opments at the police station. Don't get yourself in
trouble with the chief, but it would be helpful for me
to know what they're up to."

"I'm a trained investigator, Suzanne, you know
that, don't you? I can do a lot more than sit around the
station listening to idle gossip. Why don't you let me
help you on the case itself?"

"I may take you up on that a little later, George,
but for now, I need you to do this for me."

"Fine. I'll do it, but you're not taking full advantage of your resources here, that's all I'm saying.
You shouldn't hold it against me that I turned down
your donut offer at first."

I patted his hand. "You know I'm not doing that.
As to your offer, I thank you kindly, and I promise
that I'll keep it in mind." Another thought crossed my

mind. "I suppose there is something else you could do, but I need you to be discreet."

"Whatever it is, I can handle it," George said.

"I need to find out anything you can learn about Allied Construction and BR Investments, but I don't want them to know that I'm looking into their businesses."

"Consider it done," George said, looking happy with the expanded assignment.

I frowned, then said, "I'd like to dig into Patrick's home life, but I'm not exactly sure how I should go about it."

George thought about it a few moments, then said, "I've got an idea, but I need to make a phone call first."

He stepped outside the shop, whether for privacy or better reception, I didn't know. After a few minutes, George came back in, smiling.

"Good news?" I asked him.

"I have a way of getting you inside Patrick Blaine's house, and once you're in there, you'll be able to snoop around to your heart's content."

"You've got my attention. How am I going to manage all of that?"

"It's easy. We have the same cleaning lady, and I've managed to get you hired on for a few hours as an apprentice to Mary Paris for the day. She was planning to clean the place anyway, and she said she'd love an extra set of hands."

"That's brilliant," I said. "When is she going to clean his place?"

"It's today, or it's no deal," he said. "Can Emma manage the shop while you're gone?"

"She can handle things," I said. "Most of the work is done. Now all she has to do is wait on customers. I hate to do it to her, but I really don't have much choice, do I?"

"Not if you want to see inside his house before Mary cleans it out." He glanced at his watch, then said, "Meet her at Blaine's place in an hour. She starts at seven sharp, and you don't want to be late. I can't promise you'll be there all day, but it's a way to get your foot in the door. Now if you'll excuse me, I've got to be on my way."

"Thanks for doing this, George."

He grinned at me. "You know me. I'm always happy to help. Enjoy your new cleaning job."

"It's what I live for," I said as he walked out.

I called Emma to the front and said, "How do you feel about running the place by yourself this morning?"

She didn't look exactly thrilled by the prospect. "Why? What's going on?"

"George has managed to get me inside Patrick Blaine's house, but it has to be today. If you aren't comfortable doing this, I'll get him back in here and tell him no."

"I can't do that to you. I know how important this is." She bit her lip, then Emma added, "If things get too crazy, I could always call my mother."

"Call her anyway. I'll pay her for her time, and she can keep you company while I'm gone."

"If you're sure you don't mind," Emma said.

"She's doing me a favor, of course I don't mind. I just don't see how I can say no after George went to so much trouble to do me this favor."

Emma said, "You have some great friends here, don't you?"

"That's one of the best parts of owning this business," I said. "And it doesn't hurt that I've been living in April Springs my entire life."

"Don't you ever get the yearning to live someplace else, though?" she said as she wiped down the counter. "It's a big world out there, and we're in a little tiny piece of it. I feel like I'm missing something every day I stay."

"I love it here," I admitted. "I can walk outside and see the mountains in the background, and we're less than an hour away from the Blue Ridge Parkway if I want to see some beautiful scenery. Then again, if I get the yen to go to the beach and see the ocean, that's less than five hours away."

"But there's more out there, don't you think?" She brushed an errant strand of red hair from her face.

I thought about it. "I guess so, but this is home for me. I don't know anybody out there," I said as I gestured to the outside world. "Here, I know who I can count on, and who I can't. There are people I can call at midnight, and they won't even ask why, and there others I wouldn't turn my back on under any circumstances. There might be dangers here, as well as pleasures, but they're things I know, and can count on. I guess what it comes down to is that I've got everything I need right here in April Springs."

"Not me," she said. "I can't wait to get out of this town for good."

I smiled at her. "And you just might find that you miss this place more than you ever could imagine once you're gone."

"I doubt that," she said.

I laughed. "Let's talk again in ten years and see." I looked at a few empty tables with remnants from earlier customers. "I don't have to leave for another half hour, so why don't you call your mother while I start getting this place cleaned up?"

"You've got yourself a deal."

After Emma's mother showed up, it was time for me to leave. Sadly, I didn't even have to go home and change clothes for the cleaning job. My jeans and T-shirt would be just fine for the work I was about to do.

I arrived at Patrick Blaine's house three minutes before seven. A car was in the driveway with a metallic sign on its side that said MERRY CLEANERS. That had to be Mary's Subaru.

"You're late," she said as she opened the house door. As she sized me up, I did the same to her. Mary was a tall, thin woman with graying hair pulled back in a no-nonsense bun. She wore a maid's uniform straight from the movies, and I wondered if that was her preferred attire, or if she did it as good public relations with her clients.

I definitely looked shabby standing in front of her.

I looked at my watch as I protested, "I've got two minutes."

"Anything short of five minutes early is too late in my book. Come on in, I don't have time to do a thorough job here and stand around talking all morning." She glanced at her watch, and added, "I've got to be across town at 10 A.M., so we need to get moving. You take the master bedroom, and I'll start on the kitchen and bath. Dust, vacuum, and straighten the place up. George implied that you're interested in more than just cleaning, but I'm warning you now, you mustn't take anything. Do you understand?"

"I'm not a thief," I said.

"I'm not saying you are, but my name is on the line, and so is George's reputation."

"You can trust me," she said.

"Good. Let's get to work then."

I made my way down the hallway of the small brick ranch and found what had to be the master bedroom. I wasn't even sure why we were there. It was the neatest place I'd ever been in, including the house Momma and I shared.

Then I realized that this was his transition place. He'd had to have somewhere to go after leaving Rita and before taking up with Deb, though it might just be a refuge from his mistress's moth room.

As I dusted the dresser top, I peeked behind me and started pulling out drawers. Socks were neatly paired, and underwear carefully folded. I tried my best not to disturb anything as I searched, but it was frustrating not finding anything of value or interest to me. It might as well have been a hotel room.

I'd just closed one of the bottom drawers when I heard soft footsteps on the hardwood floor behind me. Without a moment's hesitation, I dropped to one knee and started running my cloth over the dresser's molding.

"Very good," Mary said. I was just glad there wasn't carpet in the house. There was no way I'd have been able to hear her checking up on me then. "Do you need anything?"

"No, ma'am, I'm fine," I said.

She nodded curtly, and then went back to her own work.

I kept cleaning the room as I searched it, though there wasn't that much dust there to begin with. I'd about given up when something fluttered out of the nightstand as I closed the drawer.

It was a receipt for a bank account withdrawal, showing Patrick had taken ten thousand dollars out of his account on the day he'd been murdered. What on earth could that mean? No one had mentioned finding that much cash, not that Chief Martin would run to me and tell me that he had. But I had to guess that George would have heard something about it at the police station, so I was going to assume that the money hadn't shown up. Was it possible it was here, in his house? I'd have to look harder for it, just in case. What other secrets had Patrick been hiding?

Looking in the drawer for something else that might tell me where the money had gone, I stumbled across a parking ticket from the April Springs Police Department, but then I noticed something odd about it.

Nothing had been filled out on the front. The spaces for the name, the driver's license number, the address, and other information were all blank. I flipped the ticket over and found a time and date printed on the back: "7:00, 3/03." The seven had a slash through it, something I'd been seeing more and more lately around town. It was for a week before the murder occurred, but I had to wonder if there wasn't some significance to it. Its presence made me dig deeper around the room, but if he'd hidden the money in his bedroom, I wasn't able to find it.

I was still searching the place when Mary came in. She looked around the bedroom, then said, "It looks good enough. We need to go."

There were still nooks and crannies I hadn't searched yet. How much room would it take to hide ten thousand dollars? "I'm not finished, though."

"Sorry, but I need to get going. One of my clients had a grapefruit-spill emergency, and I've got to get over there pronto."

"I don't mind staying behind," I said. There were other parts of the house I wanted to explore.

"Sorry, I can't do that, even if you are a friend of George's. Let's go."

I reluctantly let her lead me out of the house, then said, "You can call me when you come back here, and I'll be glad to help."

"That won't be necessary, but thanks for the offer."

I was standing near the front door as she drove off. I wasn't finished with Patrick Blaine's house, but still, I'd found a few things that might be significant. For now, that would have to do.

I headed back to the donut shop where I belonged, and hopefully I'd have more time to think about what I'd uncovered.

When I got back to the shop, it was empty, except for Emma and her mother. "Hi, Eileen. Thanks for filling in on such short notice. I've got it covered now."

"It was my pleasure. Are you sure you don't need me for the rest of the day? Emma and I have been having the nicest chat."

"Between customers," Emma said quickly. "We've been busy most of the morning."

"Of course we have," Eileen said. "Suzanne knows that."

One glance at the display cases showed me that they'd done well enough in my absence. "I do." I reached into the cash drawer and pulled out a twenty. "Is this enough?" I asked as I handed it to her.

"Honestly, I can't take that," she said. "It was too much fun to charge you for it."

I shrugged. "Then how about two dozen donuts? Your choice."

"That I'll do," she said. As I started boxing them for her, Eileen said, "Won't your father be surprised when I bring these by the paper?"

"He'll be surprised, all right," Emma said. According to my assistant, Eileen's visits to her husband's newspaper office had elicited a long list of negative comments in the past from him, but it appeared that she considered the donut delivery acceptable.

As soon as she left, Emma dove for the phone. "Dad, Mom's on her way over with two dozen donuts. Act surprised, she earned them helping me out today. Love you, too."

"Did I do something wrong?" I asked.

"No, he just hates to be caught off guard. It'll be fine," Emma said. "Did you find anything at Patrick's house? You weren't gone long."

"I was dismissed," I said, not wanting to share the information I'd found with her. I was still trying to keep Emma out of my impromptu investigation as much as I could.

"You got fired?"

"No, she had another emergency job across

town," I explained. "Now, let's get busy on the dishes while we're slow."

"I'm on it," she said, and disappeared back into the kitchen.

The lull didn't last for long, and a steady trickle of professional folks, mothers with kids in school, and retirees started trickling in soon after I got back.

When the front door opened a little after ten, I was surprised to see Gail and Tina come in, two regulars who were widows and now roommates. Their children had left long ago, and the two women had grown tired of living alone, though I wasn't sure their current arrangement was much better.

"Ladies, I thought you were on a cruise."

Gail, a rail-thin woman with straight black hair, said, "We were, but the captain threw us off the boat."

Tina, short and round and all kinds of soft, said, "It was a ship, and we didn't get thrown off. You'd rather lie than tell the truth, wouldn't you?"

"Don't listen to her, Suzanne. What I said was all true," Gail said as she ordered a cup of coffee and an apple fritter.

"The ship ran aground," Tina said. "Everyone had to leave, not just us. You keep making it sound like we were singled out for bad behavior or something."

"Oh, my, that sounds dreadful," I said as I got Tina three donuts and a cup of whole milk.

Gail said, "Actually, it was quite fun. I've never been on a life raft before. It felt like we were in a Hitchcock movie."

"It was nothing like that," Tina said. "We were twenty feet from shore, and everything was rather mundane."

"Mundane?" Gail asked. "How about the man who had a heart attack?"

"It wasn't a heart attack, it was a panic attack, and as soon as he breathed into a paper bag, he was fine. I do wish you wouldn't embellish the truth so much."

Gail frowned. "It's not lying. I'm just telling the story from my own perspective."

"From wherever that is," Tina said.

After they were settled onto one of the couches, I was restocking some of the trays in the display when Grace walked in.

"I just got your message," she said, looking more frazzled than I'd ever seen her. "My voice mail's messed up. Why didn't you keep calling me until I answered?"

"I'm fine," I said, "and would you mind lowering your voice?" We were attracting quite a bit of attention, and not the good kind.

"Sorry," she said. "I'd kill for a cup of coffee. I'm sorry about that, as well. Not the best choice of words, was it?"

I put a full mug in front of her, and after she greedily drank some down, she said, "Tell me what happened."

"Vicki came by on her way out of town this morning, but she didn't think Rita or Deb had anything to do with the murder. She was pretty suspicious of the two businesses Blaine was dealing with, though."

"Good. So after work today, we go see them."

"Are you sure you want to keep digging into this with me?"

Grace looked surprised by my question. "I told

you that as long as you're doing this, I'm right beside you. You're not having a change of heart, are you?"

"It's not that," I said. "I just seem to be attracting a lot of attention from the police lately."

"Who said something, the chief? Come on, he's had you in his sights for years."

"Actually, Jake Bishop came by the house last night."

That got her attention. "Was it for business, or pleasure?"

"What are you talking about?"

Grace shook her head. "Come on, don't be coy with me. You like him, don't you? I can hear that hitch in your throat when you talk about him."

I threw my dishtowel down on the counter. "He's done nothing but aggravate me since he came onto the scene."

Grace waved a hand in the air. "You can protest all you want, but I know I'm not imagining it."

"That's nonsense," I said, but was it? Did Grace see something in me I wasn't ready to acknowledge to myself, or admit to the world? He was a handsome man, there was no denying that.

She asked, "So, how did you leave things with him? I'm not foolish enough to think you kissed him good night, but was there at least a lingering good-bye at the door?"

"No, Max picked the worst time in the world to show up on my doorstep, and Jake rushed off as soon as my ex showed up."

"What did he want?" Grace asked. She wasn't a big fan of my ex-husband, and clearly wasn't afraid who knew it.

"Believe it or not, I think he wants to get back together with me."

Grace frowned. "You aren't going to, are you? Please tell me you didn't promise him anything."

"If you want to know the truth, I threw him out," I said.

"Good for you."

"Grace, he made a mistake, and he's asked me for my forgiveness."

She shook her head.

I asked, "What?"

"Just because he asks for your forgiveness doesn't mean you have to give it."

I sighed. "I know you're right, but I can't keep holding this grudge forever. It's not healthy."

"Forgive him if you want to, but I was the one who was there helping you pick up the pieces of your life, remember? Don't try to tell me he's suddenly repentant about the affair, because I don't believe it." Grace threw a ten onto the counter, and I noticed that we'd amassed quite an audience.

I didn't care. "Hey," I called out, "are we okay?"

She waved. "We're fine. I just need some air."

"Call me later," I said.

She nodded absently, and then walked away without a single look back.

SOUTHERN PEACH COBBLER

My family clamors for peach cobbler all year long, and when peaches are in season, I like them the best. But canned peaches make a great cobbler, too, so over the years, I've developed this recipe using what I can find on the grocer's shelf. This one's a real hit at home, and it has the added benefit of being really easy to make!

INGREDIENTS

1 stick butter (½ cup)
1½ cups granulated sugar
1 cup flour
1 tablespoon plus 1 teaspoon cinnamon
1½ teaspoons baking powder
½ cup milk (2% or whole)
1 can (29 oz.) sliced peaches in heavy syrup, drained, keeping ¾ cup of the syrup

DIRECTIONS

Preheat the oven to 350 degrees. Melt the butter, then pour it into the bottom of a 9 by 13 casserole dish. Set aside ½ cup sugar and all of the cinnamon, then separate the peaches from the syrup, keeping the syrup in another container for use later.

Mix the remaining 1 cup sugar and the other dry ingredients together in a bowl, then stir in the milk and the heavy syrup from the peaches. Next, put the peaches in bottom of the dish on top of the melted butter. Pour the batter over the top of the peaches.

Mix the cinnamon and the remaining ½ cup of sugar and sprinkle that over the top of the mixture.

Bake this at 350 degrees for about 1 hour, or until the top crust is golden brown and has pulled away slightly from the sides of the dish.

Serves 6–8

CHAPTER 7

"Don't worry, she'll be back," Tina said from her vantage point as Grace disappeared.

"You don't know that," Gail said. "She may never set foot in here again."

"Are you helping or hurting, Gail, helping or hurting?"

"I do wish you'd stop saying that, Tina," her friend said. "It really aggravates me, and it annoys everyone else, too."

"All I'm saying is that you should ask yourself that question before you say something that might hurt someone else's feelings."

Gail stood abruptly. "I don't have to take this, you know."

She stormed out of the donut shop herself, but Tina never moved a muscle to try to stop her.

I walked over and topped off her coffee. "Sorry, I didn't mean to pull you two into my argument."

Tina offered me a slight smile. "Are you kidding? I welcome the peace and quiet."

"But what about Gail?"

Tina laughed. "It will do her some good, storming around town until her temper settles down. This has been brewing since we had to get off the ship, and I for one am relieved it finally blew. Once she's over her fit of pique, things will be fine again." She nodded to me, then added, "Your friend will feel the same way, I'm sure."

"I hope you're right."

Tina said, "Well, Gail's probably had time to cool off by now. I'd better go track her down." She touched my shoulder lightly as she added, "Keep your chin high, and don't let the monkeys of the world get you down."

"I'll do my best."

"Must have coffee," Terri Milner said an hour later as she presented herself at the counter. She was, at that moment, the epitome of a frazzled mom.

As I poured her a cup, I said, "What happened, did you have a rough night?"

She waited for the mug, then she took it from my hands the second I offered it to her. After taking a bigger gulp than I ever would have recommended, she smiled blissfully. "That almost made what I just went through worth it."

"I'm still waiting on the update," I said.

"The girls have discovered boys," she said. "Eight is a little young for that, don't you think?"

"How have they discovered them, exactly?"

Terri took another deep drink, then held the mug out for a refill. As I topped her off, she said, "There's a boy in second grade named Ethan Marks, and he's all my girls can talk about it. I'm so tired of Ethan this and Ethan that, I could scream."

"It sounds rough," I said, as I looked out the window. "Where's Sandy?"

"She's on her way. Her son forgot his homework— yet again—and she had to take it by the school first." Terri pointed out the window. "Here she comes now."

As the second mother came in, I had another mug of coffee poured and waiting for her.

The second she saw it, she smiled and said, "Thanks for thinking of me, but I'd rather have apple juice."

I started to dump it down the sink when Terri made a grab for it. "Don't just waste it. I'll take it."

I laughed as I handed it to her. After the women placed their donut orders, I heard Terri say, "Has your son ever talked about Ethan Marks?"

"Sneezin' Ethan? Sure, why?"

"Why do they call him that?" Terri asked.

"The poor boy's allergic to just about everything," Sandy said.

"Well, apparently he's not allergic to my girls. They both appear to have raging crushes on him. Tell me something, and be honest with me. Doesn't the second grade seem too young to start noticing boys?"

Sandy patted her friend's hand. "I had my first true love in first grade, so by my clock, they're a little late."

Terri looked a little mollified. "What about you, Suzanne?"

I gave them their donuts, then I said, "I can beat that. Kyle Peters shared his mat with me in kindergarten after Jenny Grace stole mine, and he had my heart forever, at least until the next day, when Steve Brewer gave me his juice box. What can I say, my head's easily turned."

Terri stared at us both intently. "So, you two don't think it's anything to be worried about?"

"Not until they start bringing him home with them," Sandy said.

Terri's face fell.

Sandy said softly, "What did I say?"

"He's coming home with them after school today."

Sandy and I grinned at each other, and Terri finally said, "Go ahead and get it out of your systems. I don't want you two exploding on my account."

We laughed, and she finally joined in. "I feel better just talking about it."

"I'm always here for you," Sandy said as they found a couch to share.

That was one of things I loved about Donut Hearts. There was more to the place than donuts and coffee. It was, in its own way, a safe harbor in the storm of life.

Twenty minutes later, two grown men came into the shop wearing Carolina Panthers football jerseys and matching hats. They barely glanced at me as they ordered a dozen donuts to go. Instead, they were debating the team's off-season acquisitions as though the coach were standing by waiting for their advice.

After they were gone, I realized that Emma was standing right beside me.

"I don't get it," she said. "Why do grown men get so attached to their sports teams?"

"It's usually innocent enough," I said.

She shook her head. "I don't know. You'd think that bankers, cops, and even judges had better things to do with their time."

"Hey, as long as they come in here for their donuts, they can talk about whatever they want to."

I got a call from George a little later. He said, "I've got some news about Blaine. I've been doing some digging, and to be honest with you, I don't like what I've been hearing."

"Go on, tell me," I said. "I know he wasn't perfect, but he was still my friend."

George said, "From what I've heard around the courthouse, he was in some pretty severe financial trouble when he died. His credit cards were maxed out, the house Rita lives in is mortgaged to the rafters, and his car was about to be repossessed. Does that sound like a successful banker to you?"

"What on earth did he do with his money?" I asked, remembering the ten-thousand-dollar withdrawal. I suddenly realized that I'd forgotten to tell George about finding the receipt. After I told him about it, I said, "I don't know how anybody manages to get into that kind of debt."

He nodded. "That makes sense, based on some of the rumors I've heard swirling around. I suspect he was a gambler, and not a very good one at that. I should have more answers for you later, but I thought it might help you to know what I've been hearing."

"It definitely gives me something to think about," I said. "It sounds like he was in some real trouble."

George said softly, "Well, we know that he didn't shoot himself and then throw himself out of that car. So at least we can rule out suicide. Sorry, that wasn't very tactful, was it?"

"I'm sure you're as frustrated as I am trying to figure out who did this."

After George hung up, I started thinking about what he'd told me. If Blaine was really that over-extended, was there anything he wouldn't do to get his hands on some cash? Was that why he'd been dealing with the investment broker and the construction company? Was he looking for a way to dig himself out, or had he gone for broke pushing through a dirty deal, and ended up losing everything?

I didn't know, but I had high hopes that before I was through digging into the man's life, it would lead to more answers than questions.

"I need ten dozen glazed donuts," a heavyset man with gray hair said when he walked into the shop a little after eleven.

That's what I liked, big orders. "Sure," I said as I got out my pad. "I'll be glad to help. When would you like them?"

"Right now," he said, looking at me as if I were some kind of moron.

I put my pen down. "I'm sorry, but I can't help you."

He looked up at the Donut Hearts sign over the register. "This is a donut shop, isn't it?"

"I hope so, or I'll need to change all of my business cards."

"So what's the problem?" he asked. "You make

donuts, and I need some. I would think it would be a simple business transaction."

I wasn't a big fan of being treated in such a condescending way, but then again, if I explained the situation to him, maybe he'd come back another day. "It takes twenty or thirty minutes to mix the dough for yeast donuts. Then it has to rise for forty minutes. After that, I punch the dough down, roll it out, and cut out the donuts. They proof for around thirty minutes then. After that, I can fry them and glaze them in fifteen minutes."

"So it takes two hours," he said. "Is that just for the glazed jobs?"

"It is," I admitted. "The cake donuts don't take nearly that long. Maybe we can work something out after all."

He shook his head. "No, they have to be glazed." The man checked his watch, then said, "Fine. I suppose I can wait that long if I have to. I'll be back in two hours."

I stopped him before he got out the door. "I don't think so."

"Now what's the problem?" he asked.

"We've already made the donuts for today. The kitchen is closed. If you'd like to order them for tomorrow, we'll have them ready by 6 A.M."

I swear the man looked like he wanted to wring my neck. "That won't do. You see, I need them today," he said. "I don't know what the problem is. I'm willing to pay you your going rate."

"That's not the issue. I've been here since one-thirty this morning."

He nodded. "Now I understand. So, I'll pay for

the privilege. How much do you usually charge for ten dozen donuts?"

If he'd been nicer to me, I would have quoted him a bulk rate with a nice discount, but instead, I gave him the same price he'd pay if he bought each donut individually.

It didn't even faze him. "I'll double the price, then. What do you say to that?"

"You'll have to pay for them up front," I said, still not all that enthused about going back into production, but slowly warming to the idea with the profits we'd make.

"Put it on my credit card," he said as he handed me his corporate account charge card.

I rang up the order, watched as he signed the receipt, and then said, "See you in two hours."

I was starting to wish I'd padded the time it took. It was going to be tight having them ready by then.

At least we'd make good money for the extra work.

Emma had been sweeping the back room, so I called her out front.

As she stowed her broom, she said, "It's kind of quiet. Do you mind if I take off early today?"

"Sorry, I was just about to ask you if you could work a little overtime. We just got an order for ten dozen glazed donuts."

"And you took it?" she asked.

"Let's just say the customer sweetened the pot a little."

Emma smiled. "Just like you're going to sweeten my paycheck, right?"

I nodded. "You're absolutely right. I don't see why we both shouldn't profit from it."

"Sounds great. I'll start measuring the yeast, the water, and the flour."

I thought about closing the shop while we filled the special order, but I didn't want to turn away legitimate customers who were used to having Donut Hearts stay open until noon. We'd be able to wait on them most of the time, and during the critical times when I was kneading dough and cutting out rounds, Emma could handle the front on her own.

Our impatient customer was back just as the last dozen donuts took their glaze bath. "Are they ready?"

I'd unlocked the door to let him in, since we'd shut down at noon, just like always.

"Nine dozen are boxed up, and while you load those, I'll get the last one ready. I'm throwing in some donut holes as an extra," I said.

"No, thanks, you can keep them. The donuts are all I want."

What were we going to do with ten dozen donut holes? I'd fried them after the rounds, since I hated to see anything go to waste. Maybe I'd take them by the grade school and give the kids an afternoon snack. No, I'd had a few complaints the last time I'd done that, not from the students, but from parents who objected to their children eating my treats at school. I noticed that didn't keep them from supplying their little darlings with gummy concoctions and beverages loaded with sugar whenever they asked for them.

Then again, maybe there was some way I could use the donut holes to further my investigation. I'd learned early on that not many folks could say no to donut holes, especially when they were free.

"Come again," I said as I locked the door behind him once the last dozen was handed over.

Emma let out a woosh of air and said, "I'm beat. I can't believe we just did that."

My back was stiff from the extra work. "It's because I keep forgetting how much trouble it is to make a special order." I reached into the cash register and pulled out a twenty-dollar bill. "That's for your overtime. Maybe that'll help a little."

"Thanks," she said as she slipped it into her jeans. "I was going to go see a movie, but I'm beat. I think I'll grab a nap before class tonight."

"I don't know how you do it," I said. "Tell you what. Why don't you go on home? I'll take care of the cleanup myself."

"Are you sure?" she asked as she grabbed her jacket. "I'd hate to put you out," she said, two steps from the front door.

"Just go," I said, laughing.

As I cleaned up after our unscheduled donut production, I wondered how I could best use the holes.

I was still pondering over it when there was a tapping on the front door that wouldn't go away.

"We're closed," I said as I walked out of the kitchen.

"It's me," George said. "You need to hear this."

"Come on in," I said as I opened the door. "I didn't know it was you. How'd you know I was here?"

"I saw your Jeep out front. Do I smell fresh donuts?"

"Yes, I just finished making a special order. Ten dozen glazed walked out the door five minutes ago."

He looked so disappointed, I asked, "Would you like a dozen donut holes on the house?"

"I hate to rob you like that."

"Please, I'd love it if you'd eat them."

He grabbed a few napkins. "Well, then, if it would help you out . . ."

"Come on, you can eat them in back while I finish cleaning up."

George nodded. "Let me grab some coffee first."

I looked at the pot, now empty. "Hang on. I'll make a fresh batch. It'll just take a second."

"Don't do it for me. I'll have some chocolate milk instead. That I'll pay for myself, though."

I nodded. "I guess I can live with that."

After I had him set up in back, I asked, "So, what do I need to hear? Or was that just an excuse to get your hands on some of my donuts?"

He finished a hole with one bite. "No, it's just a bonus. I've been digging into Allied Construction and BR Investments."

"You've got my undivided attention," I said as I finished rinsing the equipment I'd used to make the rush batch of donuts. "The investment broker is the dirty one, isn't it?"

"No, it's just the opposite," George said. "That guy checks out. But Allied has been doing something with construction loans that isn't kosher. Their contact with the bank was Blaine, and it looks like he didn't come through on some promises to get them more cash. It turns out that they're in a real bind, and with the banker dead, everything's getting a closer look from the authorities."

I frowned. "Wouldn't they have known that was going to happen? If their business was in trouble, and Patrick was helping prop them up, he'd be the last person they could afford to murder."

George scratched his head. "I guess that makes sense, but there's one thing you're forgetting."

"What's that?"

"Most criminals don't think things through that thoroughly. I'm guessing he made somebody mad and they got rid of him, no matter what the consequences."

"I guess it's possible," I said. "What do we do now?"

"I'm going to keep digging," he said as he polished off the last donut hole. "I figure as long as I'm on the payroll, I might as well earn my keep."

"Would you like more donut holes to go? I've got a ton of them on hand."

"No," he said as he patted his belly. "I better not. I'm getting a little heavier than I like."

"Join the club," I said. "Thanks for coming by."

"Thanks for the treat," he said. After he looked around the shop, he asked, "How long do you plan to hang out here all by yourself?"

"I'm nearly done cleaning up," I said.

"Good. Then I'll walk you out."

"George," I said. "I thought we already had this conversation. I appreciate your concern, but I'm a grown woman. I can look out for myself."

He held his palms up. "Take it easy, then. I'll touch base with you later."

We were nearly to the door when he stopped.

"There's something else you should know. If you find yourself in trouble, call me or Jake Bishop."

"Not Chief Martin?" I asked, curious because I knew that he and George had mutual respect for each other from his time on the force.

"There are some bad stories going around about cops taking payoffs to look the other way, and I'm not sure who you should trust."

"You think the chief is dirty?" I asked, not able to believe it.

"No, I'd vouch for him with my life." George frowned, then he said, "You can call him, too. I'd stake my life on the fact that he's clean."

"Sure, but are you willing to risk mine?"

"Suzanne, this isn't a joke. It's happened in towns smaller than ours, and from what I hear, once a cop starts going around with his hand out, the slide the rest of the way down isn't that hard to make."

"I'll be careful," I said.

I let him out, then I finished the few chores I had left to get the place cleaned up and ready for the next day. I was worn out. That double batch of donuts had been enough to push me over the edge, and I thought about going home to catch a quick nap before I went out hunting for a killer again.

Then I remembered the donut holes. What on earth was I going to do with them? I was too tired to go on a fishing expedition with them, so it would be a good idea to donate them to the church.

I saw Gabby standing out in front of her shop, no doubt waiting for me to appear, and I decided to kill two birds with one batch of donut holes.

As I locked the shop up, I looked over at Gabby. "I'm so glad you're here. I need a huge favor."

Gabby looked startled by my preemptive question, no doubt killing the dozen queries she was readying for me.

"Of course, all you have to do is ask."

I put the boxes of donut holes into her arms. "I need to get these to the church, but I'm so beat, I might not make it. Would you take them for me?"

I knew Gabby would jump at the chance, no doubt taking the credit when she delivered them, but I didn't care. While I kept regular hours no matter what, she was known to shut down on the slightest whim.

"Yes, I'd be delighted. You do look weary. You're not getting any younger, you know," she said smugly.

"None of us are," I replied, trying not to put any sting into my words. I knew I wasn't getting enough sleep, and that I probably looked like something the cat dragged in, but I didn't need to be reminded of it.

"You're a dear," I said.

"It's my fatal flaw," Gabby said. "I give too much."

Too much unwanted advice, I said to myself.

I got into the Jeep, and drove back to the house.

As I went past our local newsstand, Two Cows and a Moose, the pretty young brunette proprietress, Emily Hargraves, waved at me. When she'd first opened up shop, I'd asked her about the unusual name. She'd told me that growing up, she'd had three stuffed animals that she loved more than anything else in the world, named—appropriately enough— Cow, Spots, and Moose. When I told her that she might want to choose a name that said something more about the kind of business she ran, she laughed the suggestion off, but I had to wonder if the moniker had caused a lot of unnecessary confusion in her clientele. Word had gotten out, though, and even I had to admit that the stuffed cows and the moose perched on a shelf of honor above the cash register was an amusing touch. Oddly enough, in our town full of eccentrics, she fit right in.

Back home, Momma was out, thank goodness, doing who knows what, but it saved me from explaining my need for a nap, so that was good enough for me.

As I walked up onto the porch, I found myself wishing for springtime. I had a hammock I mounted on brackets between two posts during nicer weather, something that let me sway in the breeze from the park. If it hadn't been in the low fifties, I might have put it up anyway, but the folks around April Springs thought I was crazy enough without adding to the legend of the donut lady.

I couldn't bring myself to go into my bedroom, so I grabbed my favorite blanket and curled up on the couch. I must have fallen asleep before my head hit the cushion, because I didn't remember a thing until the telephone rang a few minutes later.

I steadfastly ignored it, promising myself that I'd earned my nap, and I wasn't going to let someone else ruin it.

The phone rang three more times, and then it kicked over to the answering machine.

It was Momma.

"Suzanne, are you there? Pick up. I'm worried about you."

I grabbed the phone. "Hey, I'm here."

"Why didn't you pick up, then?"

I sighed. "I was napping."

"In the middle of the day?"

"Momma, I'm worn out. I'll talk to you later."

I hung up the phone, and settled back down onto the couch.

Just then, the phone rang again.

I grabbed it. "What."

"You never gave me a chance to tell you why I was calling," my mother said. "I won't be home for dinner tonight, so you should make your own plans."

I couldn't resist. "What's going on? Do you have a hot date?"

She sighed heavily. "Suzanne, I've had the love of my life. Why on earth would I care to look for a pale imitation? I'm having dinner with Jenny White."

She and Jenny had been friends since elementary school, and they had had dinner together once a month for as long as I could remember. I felt duly chastened, which I was certain was my mother's intent. "Have fun."

"Oh, I plan to."

I hung up a second time, and had settled back on the couch when the phone rang again. It appeared that a nap was out of the question.

I picked it up, then without waiting, I said, "I'm getting tired of this. If you have that much to say to me, you should just come home and tell me face-to-face."

"Okay, if that's the way you want it, it suits me fine," Jake Bishop said. "I'll be there in ten minutes."

He hung up before I had the chance to respond.

"Blast it, when am I going to learn?" I said out loud.

I decided to meet Jake outside. The day had warmed up after a chilly morning, and the temperature had to be near sixty. With our southern-facing porch, I could feel the afternoon rays on my cheeks, and it felt good. Sitting on the steps, I could watch the birds and squirrels in the park. It had been a great place to grow up, with a woodland wonderland just outside my bedroom door, and I felt sorry for any child who didn't have their own personal park nearby.

As good as his word, Jake Bishop drove up before ten minutes had passed.

As he approached, he said, "That looks like a little slice of paradise."

"It is," I said. "Can I get you a cup of coffee?"

"That would be nice," he said, his tone gentler than it had been before. "Do you mind if I drink it out here?"

"I think that's a perfect idea."

I ducked inside, grabbed two mugs, filled them from the pot on the counter, and rejoined him.

His eyes were closed when I got back, and there was a cute little crooked smile on his lips. For a second, I could see what he must have been like as a boy.

He must have sensed me staring at him. His eyes opened, and he admitted sheepishly, "That sun feels so good. What a great place this must have been to grow up."

"I was just thinking the same thing," I said as I handed him the mug. "What brings you out this way?" Before he could answer, I added quickly, "I'm sorry I was so abrupt on the telephone. I thought you were someone else."

"Do I even want to know who?"

I shook my head. "My mother seems to be inordinately worried about me lately."

"She's a good woman," Jake said.

"I know, but sometimes she pushes just a little too hard."

He took a sip of the coffee. "I thought that was what mothers were for."

I put my mug down, then I said, "So, now that we've got that settled, what brings you out my way, besides my forceful invitation?"

"I was wondering if you were free tonight."

My neck tensed. "Why? Do you have more questions for me?"

He grinned. "No, I'm all out at the moment, but I thought it might be fun taking you out to dinner. I'm tired of eating dinner every night by myself, if you want to know the truth of the matter."

"What a romantic proposition," I said. "I'm guessing you're not married, but what's your girlfriend going to think?"

"What makes you think I have one?"

I shrugged. "I don't know. I just took a stab in the dark."

Jake ran a hand through his hair. "I know it's hard to believe, but I don't have a girlfriend at the moment."

"Trust me; it's not that hard to believe."

He smiled at me, and I felt that same rush I'd felt before. It was the budding of something new, full of possibilities and promise.

Jake said, "Now it's your turn. Why aren't you with someone? Do you still have feelings for Max?"

"How do you know about my ex-husband?" I asked. "Have you been digging into my life?"

"Relax, Suzanne. This is a small town, and folks talk. I don't want to step in where I'm not welcome. If you and your ex-husband are trying to work things out, I don't want to get in the way of that."

"My ex-husband, no matter what impression he may be under, is part of my past, and I intend to keep him there." A thought suddenly occurred to me. "What about your stand on not going out until the case is solved?"

"Ordinarily, I'm a real believer in rules, but this is one I'm willing to bend, just for you."

I thought about that, then I nodded. I'd been thinking entirely too much of Max lately, and Jake just might be a way for me to break out of that bad habit. "In that case, I'd love to have dinner with you."

"It's a date, then," he said. "Should I pick you up around seven?"

"You could, if you want me to yawn until eight, which is my bedtime. Sorry, but I keep some odd hours."

"Of course you do," he said, laughing. He glanced at his watch. "It's a little after four. Would you like to go get something to eat right now?"

"Aren't you still on duty?"

"I won't tell anybody I'm playing hooky if you won't," he said. "What do you say?"

"Give me half an hour, then come back to get me," I said. "I need to get ready."

"You look fine to me just like you are."

I took the mug from him and smiled. "Thirty minutes, Jake, and not a minute sooner."

He stood, and I caught myself looking into his eyes. This could be trouble, and I knew it. But that still didn't keep me from feeling that flutter again.

"Thirty minutes it is."

I waited on the porch until he was gone, then raced upstairs to shower and change. I wasn't sure what the evening would bring, but I was excited about the prospects, and that was something that hadn't happened in a very long time.

GINGERBREAD "STICKS AND STONES" DONUTS

These donuts are wonderful, a real gingerbread treat that fries up beautifully. I have to admit, I used to make these as regular donuts, but one day I decided to make logs and balls from the dough, and thus "sticks and stones" were born. They taste even better than the rounds, in my opinion.

INGREDIENTS

½ cup brown sugar, firmly packed
1 egg, beaten
½ cup molasses
½ teaspoon baking soda
2 teaspoons baking powder
3 teaspoons ginger
½ teaspoon salt
2½ to 3 cups flour
½ cup sour cream

DIRECTIONS

Beat the egg, then add the brown sugar and mix well. Stir in the remaining ingredients, except the flour, mixing well again. Then add enough flour to make it into a soft dough. Pull off 4 pieces of dough, each the size of your thumb. Roll half of them into short sticks, and the other half into balls. Drop them immediately into 375-degree oil, and keep turning them until they're brown on both sides. Drain. You can dip the tops into sugar or a glaze, but I like them best plain.

Makes 12 "stones" and 4 "sticks"

CHAPTER 8

"You look nice," Jake said as he rang the front doorbell thirty-one minutes later.

"I'm sure it would surprise most folks in town,
but I do own a dress or two," I said, "though I rarely
seem to wear them these days."

"Then you should try to make the effort more often. I like your hair, too."

I'd curled and styled it after a quick shampoo,
something I rarely had time for on a typical day
making donuts. Besides, the hairnet would just ruin
it anyway, so I'd grown accustomed to putting my
hair back into a ponytail and forgetting about it. It
felt good dressing up for someone, and I suddenly
realized how much I'd missed it.

"Shall we go?" Jake said, all but offering me his
arm.

"I'm ready if you are."

"Since I'm new around here," Jake said as he es-
corted me to his car, "I was hoping you could recommend a nice restaurant."

I thought about it a second, then asked, "Do you like Italian?"

He nodded. "That sounds great."

"Then you'll love this place. The owners make all of their pasta by hand, but I should warn you, the ambiance is not what you'd expect."

"I think I can handle it," he said.

He actually held my car door for me, something that Max had refused to do, even when we'd first started dating. I slid in, and then Jake walked around the car and joined me.

We sat there a few seconds, then he said, "I need some directions, unless you want me to drive around blindly hoping to find this place by luck. It's fine by me, but you're the one with the early bedtime."

"It's in Union Square," I said.

"Oh ho, so we're going out of town to eat. You're not afraid of being seen with me around town, are you, Suzanne?"

"Of course not. We can eat around here if you'd like, but I don't get out much, and this sounds like fun to me."

"Then it does to me, too," he said as he pulled out.

"So, you don't need directions now?"

As he drove, he said, "I think I can find Union Square on my own."

We had to drive down Springs Drive to get out of town, and as we passed my store, I saw Max standing in front of Donut Hearts, peering in through the window. What on earth could he want? I kept repeating a silent prayer that he wouldn't turn around, but as we approached, he pivoted and we made eye contact. It was just for a split second, but I could see his emotions shifting from surprise to disappointment, and before we passed him, I could have sworn I caught a hint of anger.

Wonderful. My ex had managed to spoil the evening before it had a chance to start.

"You're awfully quiet," Jake said as we drove on the highway toward the restaurant. "Not having second thoughts, are you?"

"No, I love Napoli's," I said.

"I'm not talking about the restaurant, and you know it," he said. "I mean second thoughts about going out with me."

"We aren't eloping," I said. "It's just dinner."

"Well, when you put it that way . . ." he said.

"That didn't come out right. I guess I just have a lot on my mind."

Jake nodded. "Your plate's pretty full at the moment, isn't it? Between making donuts and conducting your own investigation, it's amazing you even have time to eat."

"I feel like the chief isn't doing much to help me," I said.

"Or me either, right?" There was an edge to his voice, and I could feel that he wanted to clear the air.

"Just for tonight, can we forget about all of that? I'd love to ignore what's been happening and have a nice dinner out. Is that possible?"

The clouds over his expression quickly broke up. "That's fine with me." He drove for a few more minutes, then said, "So, tell me about yourself."

"You already know all there is to know," I said. "I'm divorced, I live with my mother, and I own a donut shop."

"Come on, Suzanne, there's more to you than that. What do you like to do in your spare time? What's your favorite book? Do you have a favorite movie? Do you like going to the theater, or would you rather stay home and watch something on DVD?"

"My, my, my. Once a cop, always a cop."

"What do you mean?"

As I looked at him, I said, "That sounds more like an interrogation than dating conversation."

I wasn't sure if he'd get mad—I hadn't meant to be so curt—but he laughed instead. "You got me. What can I say? I'm interested in you."

"That's the nicest thing anyone's said to me in a long time."

He started smiling, and I asked, "What? What's so funny?"

"That's what I like, a bar set low to impress you." He drove a little longer, then said, "To be honest with you, I'm a little out of practice."

"Come on, it's hard to believe you don't date much," I said.

He shrugged without really answering.

I said, "I'll make you a deal. I'll talk about myself, but that means you have to, as well. What do you say?"

"Okay, we'll take turns. You first. Theater or DVD?"

I thought about it a second. "If it's something epic and grand, a theater's worth the trouble, but for romantic comedies, which are my favorite, I'll take my couch at home and a bowl of popcorn."

"I can see how that makes sense. Okay, go ahead. It's your turn."

I asked, "When was the last date you went on?"

He frowned, and I thought for a second I'd overstepped my bounds.

Quickly, I added, "You don't have to answer that. I'm just being nosy."

"No, I'll tell you. I just wasn't planning to bring it up, at least not tonight."

"Then don't. It's okay, I promise."

He took a deep breath, then said, "I gave you my word. The last date I was on was three years ago, come June tenth."

"That must have been some date," I said.

"It was. My wife and I were celebrating our tenth-year wedding anniversary, and as we were driving home from the restaurant, a drunk driver blindsided us. She died on the spot." Tears were carelessly tracking down his cheeks.

I felt suddenly very small. "Jake, I'm so sorry. I didn't mean to . . . I've got such a big mouth."

He wiped at his eyes with his free hand, then he said, "Sorry. I didn't mean to spoil the evening."

"You haven't," I said.

We drove on in silence, and I broke it only to give him directions until we arrived at Napoli's.

When he stopped the car, I put a hand on his arm and said, "We don't have to do this tonight. It's all right. I understand if you'd like to cancel and take me back home."

"If it's okay with you, I'd like to have dinner. It's time I put all of that behind me and got on with my life. That's why I asked you out in the first place." He suddenly smiled, giving me the soft whisper of a grin. "Besides, I'm starving."

"So am I," I admitted.

"Then let's eat."

As we walked across the parking lot to the front door, I marveled that Jake had layers and levels I hadn't even guessed at. He was taking a big step going out with me tonight, and I was going to make sure it was memorable. I promised myself that I'd be the most charming dinner companion in the history of modern dating. After what he'd been through, the least I could do was try to make this the most positive experience possible.

"Hey, this is nice," Jake said as we walked into the restaurant.

I'd been watching his face to see his reaction, and was pleased with his smile. Napoli's looked like any other building in a strip mall anywhere in America, at least from the outside. But once we walked through the front door, that all changed. Murals of Italy greeted us as we walked in, and a fountain gurgled pleasantly in one corner of the vestibule. The deep red carpet was lush, and the fixtures were all faded brass. I tried to eat there at least once every few months since my divorce. It was nice to get out of April Springs now and then, just to confirm that there was a world beyond my small town, though some folks would say that Union Square barely qualified as someplace different.

Maria DeAngelis, one of the owner's daughters, was working the front tonight, and she offered me a tender smile and a quick hug the second she saw me. Barely into her twenties, she was a real Italian beauty, with jet-black hair, large brown eyes, skin the color of olive oil, and a figure I could only dream about owning myself.

"Suzanne, it's so good to see you."

"Hi, Maria. I'd like you to meet a friend of mine. This is Jake Bishop."

She offered Jake her hand, and I could tell he was disappointed he wouldn't be getting a hug himself. I didn't blame him one bit.

"It's nice to meet you, Jake."

"Thanks, it's a pleasure meeting you, too."

Maria grabbed a couple of menus, then she led us through the entry into the dining room. It was twice as large as anyone would expect, and the first time I'd been there, I'd asked idly how they had room for a kitchen. That had led to a grand tour, given by the matriarch herself, Angelica DeAngelis, the Angel's Angel. With four daughters all working shifts at the restaurant at various times, Angelica always managed to smile, even though life had dealt her more than her share of hardships. We'd become friends on that first visit, and it had felt as though we'd known each other for years from the very start, and were just renewing a relationship instead of starting a brand-new one.

Maria gave us her best table, which wasn't difficult, since Jake and I were the first ones there. It was something I was used to, but it was pretty clear Jake wasn't.

As he held my chair for me, I said, "I know it feels odd at first, but it's really kind of nice when you eat early. There's no feeling of being rushed, or crowded by too many other diners."

"I can see it has its advantages."

After Maria left us with our menus, we were alone all of two minutes before Tianna came by. She was two years older than her sister, and the girls had grown close enough in appearance to look like twins.

"Suzanne, how nice to see you again," she said.

"Tianna, this is Jake."

He actually stood this time, and I wondered if he was hoping to capture an elusive hug, but if that was his goal, he was thwarted when she offered a hand, as well.

After he was reseated, Tianna asked, "Would you like more time to look over the menu? I can start you with something from the bar."

"I'll have water, no lemon," I said.

Jake said, "That sounds good."

"You don't drink?" I asked Jake.

"A little red wine with dinner is all I want, but don't hold back on my account."

I shook my head and laughed gently. "Some wine sounds good."

Tianna said, "I'll be right back."

Jake looked at the menu, a heavy affair with thick pages filled with dozens of Italian delights. As he studied the offerings, he asked, "What's good here?"

"Everything," I said.

"That doesn't help." He gestured to my menu, still closed and sitting on the edge of the table. "What are you going to have?"

"A house salad, and an order of ravioli," I said.

He frowned. "I never liked that stuff."

"Let me guess. Your only experience with it so far is what you get out of a can, right?"

He nodded. "Once was enough. I took some camping, and it was a toss-up which was tastier, the ravioli, or the label on the can. No, thanks."

"Fine, but when you taste one of mine, don't you dare ask for more, because I won't be in the mood to share."

He put his hands up. "Trust me, that's not going to be a problem."

Tianna was back with a bottle of red house wine, and after she poured us both glasses, she brought a pair of ice waters, as well. "Are you ready to order, or would you like more time?"

Jake looked at me, and I said, "I'll have a house salad and the cheese ravioli."

Tianna grinned at me. "I don't even need to ask anymore, do I?"

"Hey, why mess with perfection?"

She looked at Jake, who said, "I believe I'll have the spaghetti and meatballs, with a house salad, too."

Tianna nodded. "I'll bring some bread and olive oil in a minute," she said as she departed.

Jake looked around, soaking up the ambiance of the place, and I spent the time studying him. He hadn't changed after work, but then again, since he wore a suit instead of a uniform, there had been no need. I'd seen him several times over the past few days, but somehow, this was a different man with me tonight. He was attentive, polite, and appeared to be interested in whatever I had to say. In other words, a perfect date, at least so far. I still couldn't believe I was going out with a state policeman who was investigating a murder I was involved with, even if it was just around the edges.

"What are you thinking about?" he asked, and I realized that he'd been watching me for more than a few moments himself.

I couldn't very well tell him. "It's nice here, isn't it?"

"Yes, but that's not what you were thinking about."

I smiled at him softly. "So, you're a human polygraph all of a sudden?"

He blushed slightly, something that I found charming. "There's nothing all of a sudden about it."

"Let me guess, you have the power to read people's thoughts."

I'd said it jokingly, but he simply nodded. "It comes from years of training, and experience working in the field. Some people call it good instincts, but I think it's trainable, and I've been honing my skills ever since I first became a cop."

I took a sip of wine, then I said, "What made you join the police force?"

He shrugged. "My dad was a cop, and his dad, too. It seemed like a natural thing to do."

I'd been watching his face, and it was obvious there was more to the story than he was willing to share. "But that's not the only reason, is it?"

Jake paused a moment or two, then he said, "I'm not the only one who can read people, am I?"

I laughed out loud at that. "And to think that I haven't had any training at all."

"What can I say? For some people, it's a natural gift."

"You didn't answer my question," I pressed him.

"No, I didn't, did I?" There was a twinkle in his eyes as he replied, but no further information was forthcoming, so I let it drop and focused on enjoying this rare treat, a night out with a man who wasn't just a friend marking time.

The salads were good, but nothing spectacular, but then our main courses came. My ravioli, white and pristine under a layer of lush red marinara sauce, looked just as good as it always did, but I had to admit, Jake's dinner looked good, too.

"Enjoy," Tianna said.

"We will," I replied.

Jake put some freshly grated parmesan cheese on his spaghetti, and I added a bit to my ravioli, as well. I didn't take a bite, though. I wanted to see what Jake thought of his meal. I knew Angelica and two of her other daughters were working the kitchen, creating their magic out of the most basic ingredients, and I wondered why the place wasn't even more popular than it was. I supposed too many people let the exterior fool them, and didn't dig deep enough to find the gem within.

Jake's face transformed as he took his first bite. His look of sheer pleasure had been worth delaying my own meal.

"This is incredible," he said. "I've been to Little Italy in New York, and I've never had anything this good."

"Angelica is a wizard with pasta," I said. It was time to take my first bite, as well. I cut one of the hand-formed raviolis, dipped its exposed edge in sauce, then I took a bite. The cheeses inside, melted perfectly, exploded in my mouth, and the pasta shell, lightly enhanced by the marinara, danced across my tongue.

"That looks good," Jake admitted reluctantly.

"It's cruel, but I'm going to give you one bite, and one bite only," I said.

I grabbed a clean fork, speared one of the ravioli squares, and handed it to him.

As he ate it, I watched him savor the bite before he said, "Okay, I was wrong. Yours is even better than mine."

"Too bad, because that's all you're getting."

"I could always add some to my order," he said, smiling.

"If you do, you'll have to share it with me."

Jake said, "I admire that."

"What, my ability to eat?"

"No," he said, "your willingness to stuff yourself in front of me."

That generated a laugh he deserved. "In case you hadn't noticed, there's nothing coy about me. Mind if I snag a bite of yours?"

"I guess it's only fair," he said. I didn't know if he was feigning his reluctance, or if it was real, but I didn't care. He had to make up for my lost pasta he'd sampled. The spaghetti and meatball combination was good, but not as good as mine, I was happy to see.

"You really enjoy your food, don't you?" he asked.

"I do when I'm eating here. It makes a great change from donuts, not that I don't love them, too.

It's a constant battle between my waistline and my appetite."

"How'd you happen to get into the donut business?" he asked. "Is it a family tradition like mine?"

"No," I said with a smile. "I bought the place as a part of an overhaul of my life. I never had a bit of interest in donuts until the day I bought the shop."

"So, what was so bad about the way things were before?" he asked, his big brown eyes showing a real interest in what I had to say.

"I'd just gotten a divorce from my husband, and I'd moved back in with my mother. I had a job I didn't really like, and a bad taste in my mouth about the world. So I took my settlement—which I earned every penny of, believe me—and bought the shop."

"Do you mean that it was a donut shop before? Surely it wasn't called Donut Hearts then."

"No, it was Murphy's. I liked the idea of having my name in the title, though, so I added an 'e' and changed it to 'Hearts.' You wouldn't believe how many people come in expecting to find heart-shaped donuts."

"Could you do that? It might be a nice addition to what you're offering now."

"I've thought about it, but I've never looked into how much trouble it would be to make a donut cutter in the shape of a heart."

He took a sip of wine, then said, "I've got a brother in Hickory who's good with his hands. Should I ask him to take a stab at making you one?"

"No, thanks, but I appreciate the offer."

After a while, I noticed his pasta was gone. "How was your dinner?"

He smiled. "I have a new favorite restaurant. I just wish it wasn't so far from home."

"That's right," I said. "I keep forgetting that you live in Raleigh."

"That's where I get my mail," he said, "but I travel all over the state, so I'm not there as much as you might think."

"I guess we're getting too close to our forbidden topic," I said.

"I don't mind if you don't."

"Let's not, though. We've done so well all evening." The place was starting to fill up as Tianna presented the bill. Out of habit more than anything else, I reached for the check, but I was a second too late.

Jake took it and said, "You're not going to insist on paying, are you?"

"No, sir, you asked me out. I'd never dream of stealing that privilege from you."

He nodded. "Good. I guess if you go deep enough, I'm just an old-fashioned kind of guy."

I put my hand on his, and said, "Then you might not like this. I'd like to see you again, and since I'm asking, I should be the one who gets to pay the next time. Do you have a problem with that?"

He studied me a moment, then asked, "Which part? You asking me out, or the fact that you're insisting you'll pay?"

"Either one, I guess," I said with a smile.

As he took out his wallet, he said, "I'd love to go out with you again, and I've got no problem with you paying."

"That's two right answers in a row," I said.

Before we could leave, Angelica came out of the kitchen, and I marveled that the woman had four daughters in their late teens and early twenties. She was more my size than her daughters', but somehow, on her the pounds just added to her attractiveness, whereas I didn't think mine did anything for me at all.

After I made the introductions, Jake finally got his wish and received a warm hug from one of the DeAngelis women.

She broke free, then Angelica looked him straight in the eye. "You'll do."

Jake grinned. "I'm glad I passed the test."

Angelica said, "You passed it long ago. I've been watching you from the kitchen. I like a man who enjoys his food."

She dropped his hands and hugged me. "Suzanne, it's always so nice to see you. We must get together sometime."

"I just wish our schedules allowed it," I said. With my killer mornings, and Angelica's afternoons and evenings at her restaurant, it didn't allow us much free time that overlapped.

"One of these days, we'll make the time."

"Excuse me," I said as I nearly bumped into another couple on the way out of the restaurant.

"Pardon me," the woman said. The man with her was tall and swarthy, but I was willing to bet that when they were together, no one spent much time looking at him. She was drop-dead gorgeous, but there was something familiar about her. I knew we'd met before, especially when her pupils dilated upon recognizing me. I couldn't for the life of me figure out who she was, but then it hit me once they were gone.

I grabbed Jake's arm and said, "That was Deb Jenkins. She's beautiful!"

"She's a little too flashy for my taste," Jake said.

"Come on, you've got to be kidding me. There's no way."

"No way what? I like my women more subdued in their appearance. Now, my brother always liked that type, but I think they're trying just a little too hard, don't you?"

"That's not what I meant, and besides, I saw your eyes light up, so save the snow job for somebody else. I can't believe that she could look as bad as she did when Grace and I spoke to her, at least not without a conscious effort."

"Maybe she just likes to get dressed up sometimes," Jake said. "She looked fine when I spoke to her."

"So, you admit that she's a suspect in the case?"

Jake stopped in the middle of the sidewalk outside the restaurant. "Suzanne, I'm doing my best to ignore the fact that you and your friends are interfering with my ongoing investigation. Don't make it any harder on me, okay?"

"Fine, we won't talk about it," I said.

But that didn't mean I couldn't think about it. Reconciling the Deb that Grace and I had met with this glammed-up version was too much to take. I knew some women who let themselves go when they were by themselves, but never to that extent.

She'd been purposely trying to throw us off her trail, which meant she had something to hide.

And who was that man she'd been with? For someone supposedly still in grief over the death of her paramour, she'd rebounded awfully fast.

There was a distinct chill in the early evening air as we walked back to Jake's car. I tried to put all thoughts of Deb out of my mind and enjoy the evening. It had been just about perfect. I'd nearly forgotten how good it felt to be out on a date again, and I realized that I was hoping we could have the second one soon.

I couldn't believe it, but I actually felt butterflies starting to flit around in my stomach as I contemplated the first good-night kiss I'd gotten in a long time.

Then I sensed Jake tense beside me.

"What is it?" I asked.

He didn't speak, just pointed to the tires of his car. All four were flat against the ground.

"Could all of them have gone flat all at once?" I asked.

Jake said, "I can't imagine it happening," as he leaned down to check.

When he stood back up, he said, "This was no coincidence, someone did it deliberately."

"Do you mean that somebody slashed your tires?"

He shook his head. "No, the rubber looks fine." Jake held a small black cap up to me. "They let the air out of all four tires, though. I'll call a garage to come take care of this."

As he made his calls, first to Information, and then to the garage, I kept wondering who might have done it.

Once he hung up, he said, "It's going to be a few

minutes. Would you like to go back inside the restaurant while we wait?"

"And explain what happened to Angelica? She'll feel responsible, I know her. No, if you don't mind, I'd rather just wait out here with you."

I didn't want to say what I was thinking, but I couldn't help myself. "I think I know who did this."

"It was probably just kids out making mischief," he said.

I looked at some other cars parked near us. "And they just happened to target you? I don't think so."

"Then who did you have in mind?"

I admitted, "As we were driving through April Springs, I saw my ex-husband, and more importantly, he saw me."

Jake shook his head. "I can't see a grown man doing this."

"Then you don't know Max. Jake, I'm sorry this has spoiled our evening."

He surprised me by taking my hand. "Suzanne, it doesn't have to. Let's not worry about why it happened. I don't want the evening ruined, either. It's been quite a while since I've felt like this."

He was going to kiss me, and I was more than happy about the prospect, when a pair of bright headlights pinned us in the darkness.

An overweight driver in greasy overalls got out of the tow truck's cab.

"I was just around the corner," he said.

Lucky me, I thought.

He studied the deflated tires, then said, "I've got a tank of compressed air here. I'll have you on the road in no time."

As the tow truck operator filled the tires, I kept looking at Jake, hoping that what I'd seen in him hadn't been a mistake. He'd been leaning in toward me to kiss me, I knew it.

But that's where it had ended. I couldn't help wondering if he'd try again once we got back to my place, and I'm afraid my conversation skills suffered a little because of the suspense.

But I never found out.

As Jake walked me up the sidewalk to my house, I saw a figure looming on the porch.

If the killer had decided to come after me, he'd picked the wrong time to do it.

I had a state police escort with me, and I was suddenly very glad that I'd agreed to have dinner with Jake after all.

"Hang back a second," Jake said, as he pulled a gun from under his jacket. I hadn't even realized he'd been armed during our entire date.

"Come out of the shadows," he barked.

The figure hesitated, then Jake's demand grew louder. "I'm going to count to three, and then I'm coming up there after you. One. Two."

Max stepped out of the shadows, a defiant look on his face.

I felt relief wash through me, but Jake's gun never wavered.

"It's okay," I said. "He's my ex-husband."

Jake ignored me.

He asked Max, "What are you doing here?"

My ex-husband was defiant as he said, "I came to check on Suzanne. Is that illegal?"

"It is if you had something to do with my car," he said.

In the dim glow of a streetlight, I saw a look flicker across Max's face, and hoped that Jake had missed it. It was surprise, anger, and there was a hint of triumph there, as well.

"I don't know what you're talking about. Now how about getting that gun out of my face?"

Jake barked, "Turn around."

"He's okay, honestly." This was getting worse by the moment.

Jake glanced at me for a split second. "You don't know that, though, do you? Leave this to me."

He looked at Max and said, "If you don't do as I ask, I'm taking you in."

"On what charge? A man can visit his wife, can't he?"

I meant to stay out of it, but my mind had another plan. "Ex-wife," I said.

Nobody even looked at me.

"What's the charge going to be?" Max asked again.

"I'll think of something, don't worry about that."

Max apparently decided he'd had enough. He turned around, and Jake patted him down with a surprising coolness and efficiency.

"There, are you satisfied?" Max said.

"Not by a long shot." He turned to me. "Can we have some light here?"

The porch light instantly came on, and I realized that Momma had witnessed the entire thing. I walked to the door, and saw her peeking out.

To my surprise, she didn't say a thing; she just stayed inside watching the two men.

I saw her lips mouth the question to me, "Are you okay?"

I nodded, and I could see some of the stress melt from her.

Jake said to Max, "Let me see your hands."

"What? Why?"

"Don't push me, Max."

My ex-husband shoved his hands toward Jake. "Fine. There they are."

Jake checked them over, then he said, "You could have been smart enough to wear gloves."

"What are you looking for? What happened?"

Jake said, "Somebody let the air out of all four tires on my car, and Suzanne said she spotted you as we were leaving town."

Max laughed. "And you think I did it? Come on, you can't be serious."

"That's where you're wrong. You don't want to mess with me, Max."

"That goes double for you," my ex-husband said.

"Is that a threat?"

Max didn't back down. "I don't know. Is it?"

Jake stared at him a few more seconds, then turned to me and said, "What do you want me to do about him?"

"He's harmless," I said. "Don't worry, I can handle him."

"Are you sure?" Jake looked into my eyes, and I could tell he was searching for permission to run Max off.

"I can handle him from here. Thanks for a lovely evening."

Max snorted, and I turned to him and said, "Just do yourself a favor and shut up this instant, do you understand me?"

He looked more nervous about my threat than he had when Jake had been holding a gun on him. Instead of risking a word, Max nodded once, so I knew we were good, at least for the moment.

Jake stared at me wistfully for another few seconds, then said, "Good night, then."

"Good night. And thanks again."

He didn't respond, just gave Max one last glare, then he left us there.

Jake was barely out of hearing when Max said, "I can't believe you're actually dating him."

That was it; the last bit of my patience was gone.

I got right in his face and said, "Who I see is none of your business anymore. You lost that privilege the day you slept with Darlene."

"How many times do I have to apologize for that? I made a mistake."

"And yet you keep on making more, don't you?" I stared hard at him so there would be no doubt in his mind that I was serious. "Max, go home and leave me alone. You don't have a stake in what happens to me anymore. Do you understand that?"

"I'm not willing to accept that."

I shook my head. "You don't have any choice. Now leave, and do yourself a favor. Butt out of my life."

He knew he was beaten; I had to give him that. Without another word, Max walked off the porch, and I saw a shadow in the trees just beyond the house shift with him. I nearly called a warning out to Max when I realized it had to be Jake, hanging around in case I needed him. What was wrong with these men? I wasn't some delicate flower that needed to be protected. Then again, it was nice to have someone who cared.

I just hoped Max hadn't ruined things for me.

I walked inside, and Momma asked, "Would you mind telling me what just happened out there?"

"I was on a date with Jake, and someone let the air out of all four of his tires. He thinks Max did it, and so do I."

She looked like she was going to burst, her smile was so broad.

I asked, "What's that for?"

"You were on a date," she said, as if repeating it made it real to her.

"Yes, I've been known to do that in the past a time or two."

Momma laughed. "The operative word in that sentence is 'past,' isn't it?"

"Don't sound so giddy," I said. "It makes you look like a fifteen-year-old girl."

"And we both know I haven't been one of those since dinosaurs roamed the earth. Did you have a nice time?"

"For the most part, it was pretty spectacular," I admitted.

"That's wonderful. Well, I'm going to bed, and you should, too, if you're going to be making donuts in the morning. Good night, Suzanne."

"Good night, Momma."

I couldn't believe she hadn't pumped me for details

about my evening. As a matter of fact, I was kind of disappointed. Normally she'd never let something as momentous as me going out on a date slip past like that, but tonight, when I was perfectly willing to talk about what had happened, my mother decided to go to bed.

I went to my room, and on the spur of the moment, I called Grace.

"Hey, are we okay?" I asked when she picked up.

"Of course we are," she said. "I'm sorry if I was being a little too overprotective. I just don't want to see you get mixed up with Max again."

"Would it help if I told you I just got home from a date?"

Her voice frosted over. "Don't tell me you're seeing him again."

"No, you don't understand. I went out with Jake Bishop, the state policeman."

Her shriek nearly deafened me. "Are you serious? That's outstanding. Now tell me what happened, from the second he picked you up to the moment he dropped you off. Don't leave out a thing."

I laughed softly. This was exactly the reaction I'd been hoping for. As I started telling her about my evening, I mentioned running into Deb. "You should have seen her, Grace. She's a knockout. That mousy little girl was replaced by a real looker. She was absolutely gorgeous."

"Who was she with?" Grace asked.

"I don't know. I've never seen him before, but they looked awfully close. She didn't exactly convey the image of a woman mourning her boyfriend's murder."

"We need to find out who she was with," Grace said. "This could have something to do with Blaine's murder."

"Short of a police lineup, I don't know how."

"Okay, let's drop that for now. I can't wait to hear, so let's fast-forward to the good-night kiss."

"There wasn't one," I said.

"Suzanne, what am I going to do with you? You're not exactly a teenager anymore. You have to keep him interested, and I doubt playing coy is going to do it. He's a grown man."

"Believe me, I wanted to. Max got in the way, though."

Grace sighed. "You're going to have to bury that part of your life, or his ghost is going to interfere with your chance at happiness. Forget about him, especially when you're out on a date with another man."

"No, you don't get it. My ex-husband was on my porch, waiting in the shadows for me to get home."

"Please tell me Jake shot him by mistake," Grace said.

"Don't sound so pleased, he nearly did."

"Really?" She sounded absolutely tickled by the idea.

"It was tense for a few minutes, but I sent Jake on his way so I could deal with Max myself."

There was a hitch in Grace's voice as she asked, "You didn't let him off the hook again, did you? He doesn't deserve you, Suzanne."

"That's pretty much what I told him. By the time he left, I think it was finally starting to sink in that I was serious about him staying out of my life."

"But you missed out on your good-night kiss."

I said, "Tonight, anyway, but I have high hopes for another shot at it the next time."

"You're going out again? When, tomorrow night? Don't hold out on me, woman, I said I needed details."

"We haven't made specific plans yet, but he seemed agreeable to the idea of going out with me again."

"If Max didn't ruin it," she said.

I stifled a yawn. "He's not going to, because I won't let him."

"That's the spirit," Grace said. "Suzanne, I'm so proud of you."

"I didn't win the spelling bee," I said. "I just went out on a date."

"Hey, don't blow this off. Tonight was a big step forward for you."

"And a giant leap for womankind, right?" I was feeling silly, and relishing every moment of it.

As I fought back another yawn, I realized that it was nearly nine o'clock, a normal enough time for most folks, at least ones who didn't have to get up in four hours.

Grace saved me from making excuses when she said, "Suzanne, go to bed, you sound beat."

"I am," I admitted, "but I just had to call you and tell you about my evening."

"I'm so glad you did."

"So am I."

After we hung up, I realized I didn't care how much sleep I'd be missing. Things had been tense between Grace and me, and I couldn't deal with my best friend being mad at me.

As I drifted off to sleep, I found myself editing out all of the bad parts of the evening, and focusing instead on Jake's eyes, and the way he really listened when I talked. I wasn't sure what kind of long-term prospects we had, but for now, I was giddy from a fresh encounter, a new person to look forward to seeing.

Grace and my mother had been right about one thing. I'd been in mourning for a broken marriage too long.

It was time to open my life up again and start living, whether Jake was a part of it or not.

And I was surprised when I realized that I was ready to see what was out there for me again.

SPICED BUTTERMILK DONUTS

These spiced buttermilk donuts are a nice treat on a rainy day! They are light enough to snack on, and we like ours fresh out of the fryer and dusted with powdered sugar.

INGREDIENTS
1 cup granulated sugar
½ stick butter (¼ cup)
2 eggs, beaten
4 cups flour
2 teaspoons baking powder
1 teaspoon baking soda
¼ teaspoon salt
¼ teaspoon nutmeg
1 cup buttermilk

DIRECTIONS
Add the sugar gradually to the beaten eggs, making sure to mix thoroughly as you go. Beat in the butter, and set aside. Next, add the dry ingredients and sift together.

Alternate adding the dry ingredients to the mix with the buttermilk, making sure to mix thoroughly at each step.

Chill the dough for about 1 hour, then turn it out onto a floured surface, knead it into a ball, and roll the dough out to about ½-inch to ¼-inch thickness. Use your donut cutter and cut the rounds and holes, then fry them for about 2 minutes on each side in 375-degree oil or until they're done. Turn out onto paper towels. Enjoy plain or add a topping.

Makes 1 dozen donuts, plus holes.

CHAPTER 9

"Tell me again," Emma said the next morning as we finished making our yeast donuts and got ready to open for business.

"We've been over it half a dozen times already," I said. "It was just a date."

"Come on, between going to night school and working here, I don't have time for a social life of my own, and I never realized that you did, either. Can I help it if I'm living vicariously through you?"

I laughed. "Oh, that's just sad. You need to do something about that."

"I know, but for now, I'll just listen to you. When do you think you'll see him again?"

"We didn't make any definite plans," I said.

"But it's going to be soon, right?"

I flicked a towel at Emma. "You're driving me nuts. Finish putting the trays in the display so I can touch up our list of specials."

Our donut production changed from day to day, partly because of what had sold well the day before, but mostly according to my capricious whims. It was one of the things I loved about owning my shop. There were certain donuts I made every day, and I didn't mind that one bit, just as long as I got to play with new recipes, as well. I was finally happy with my pumpkin recipe, so it was time to start trolling for another idea. I'd been toying with the idea of making an apple pie donut, but wasn't sure how I was going to pull off the crust. If things ever settled down at Donut Hearts, I would have time to start experimenting again.

When I unlocked the front door, I was surprised to see a patrol car sitting out in front of the shop.

Peering through the dim light cast by the shop window, I could see that it was Chief Martin, and I felt my heart sink. It wasn't that I liked talking to Officer Moore, a cop who had appeared to take an interest in the case, but he was better than the chief. Officer Grant would have been nice, too; I saw him often enough as a customer not to be intimidated by him.

I waved to the chief and tried to smile anyway, but he held a hand up in my direction and went on talking on his radio.

Sometimes it seemed as if the man was going out of his way to be rude to me.

I decided to ignore him and go about the business of selling donuts. If the chief wanted to speak with me, he knew how to find me. In the meantime, I had things to do myself.

Ten minutes later, he was still sitting there when George walked in. "Did you know the chief's out there?"

"I spotted him when I opened for business," I said.

"I keep expecting him to come in, but he's spending so much time on the radio, I'm beginning to wonder if he ever will. Who on earth could he be talking to this early in the morning?"

George smiled, but didn't comment.

"What is it?" I asked. "Do you know something I don't?"

Turning his back to the door, George said, "I could be wrong, but I think he's trying to shake you up a little. The longer he sits out there, the jumpier he thinks you're going to get. At least I'm willing to bet that's what he's counting on. By the time he actually comes in, he's going to think you'll be willing to tell him anything he wants to hear."

"He can think whatever he wants to," I said as I topped off George's coffee. "I'm not about to let him rattle me."

"That's the spirit," he said as he winked at me.

After taking another sip, George said, "I keep waiting for you to say something about last night, but if you're not going to bring it up, it looks like I'm going to have to."

I slapped the towel down on the counter. "For goodness' sake, would folks around here get lives of their own so they don't have to borrow mine for their thrills?"

George held his hands up, his palms showing. "I was talking about Max stalking you, not your date with Jake Bishop."

"He wasn't stalking me," I snapped.

"Don't be so quick to defend him. You don't know what he's been doing. I see him outside your shop all the time. As a matter of fact, he could have been watching you ever since the divorce."

That wasn't something I even wanted to consider. The thought of my ex looming around every corner was more than I could take.

"Let's change the subject, shall we? I'll talk about anything but my love life. Is that a deal?"

"It's fine with me," George said.

"I never even asked you why you showed up first thing this morning. What brings you by so early?"

George grinned. "I'm doing a little police work of my own today," he said.

"Is there anything you'd like to share with me?"

He stood and put a five on the counter. "Not yet, I don't want to jinx it. Take my word for it, don't trust anybody. Until I have something more concrete, you should watch your back, okay?"

"I will if you will," I said.

As George started out the door, I saw that the chief had finally decided it was time to come in. If he thought that by making me stand there stewing in curiosity about why he was parked in front of my shop for so long, he was going to get to me, he was wrong. Hanging around George had taught me that much. The more I played things close to the vest, the more the chief would be forced to disclose to get me to talk.

And I was ready for any errant clues he was ready to throw my way.

"Have you decided on what you'd like, Chief?"

He frowned at me. "Give me a second. I just walked in the door. Besides, I'm not here for donuts."

"I figured since you were outside in your patrol car so long, you were having trouble making up your mind."

He ran a hand through his hair. "I actually came by to do you a favor."

"I'm listening," I said.

He looked at me a second, then said, "I just wanted to give you a little advice. You shouldn't be going out with Inspector Bishop," he said, spitting the words out like they tasted bad.

"What?" I was sure he'd planned to talk about my impromptu investigation into Patrick Blaine's murder. Was he seriously giving me advice about my love life? "You're kidding me. How did you even find out about it?"

"It's a small town; you should know that more than most."

"Chief, if I want to date the governor, it would still be none of your business."

He frowned. "This didn't come out the way I was hoping," he said.

"Somehow, that doesn't surprise me. Why don't you want me dating him?" I couldn't help myself. I was just too curious about what could possibly motivate him to try to interfere with my dating.

His face clouded up. "All I'm saying is, don't give him a reason to hang around here. I've got this case covered, and he knows it. But if he's seeing you on the side, then he might drag things out, and I want this wrapped up."

"I appreciate your input," I said.

"Which means you're going to ignore my advice," the chief said.

I just gave him a smile, and he left the shop empty-handed. I wasn't all that sorry I was inconveniencing Chief Martin with my love life, and I certainly wasn't going to stop seeing Jake just because the police chief wanted me to. In fact, if anything, it gave me more incentive to make things work with Jake.

After Donut Hearts was closed for the day, I picked up the telephone and called Grace. "Hey, I know you're working today, but I was wondering if you could skip out a little early today."

"Sure, I'd be delighted to," she said.

"Don't you even want to know why?"

Grace's laughter caught fire. "All I need is a reason to skip work, and I'm there. I'll be by at two. Is that soon enough?"

"That would be great. I'll be at the house, so come over there."

"See you then."

After we hung up, I started thinking of ways to get on the inside of Allied Construction using subterfuge instead of donuts.

And then it hit me.

When Grace and I walked in, the results would be completely different than they had when I'd visited the place alone.

I called Grace back. "What are you wearing?"

Pretending not to know that it was me, she said, "Nothing but my shoes and a smile. Is this an obscene telephone call, by any chance? I've never gotten one before, so I hope I'll hold up my end of the bargain. Why, what are you wearing?"

"This is Suzanne."

Grace chuckled. "I know it is, you nit." In a lower voice, she added, "You should see the man sitting near me in the restaurant. He's turned twelve shades of red. I wonder if I can get his face to catch on fire from the heat."

"You're bad. Seriously, though, I need you to pull out all the stops. Wear the best thing you've got."

"Business, pleasure, or somewhere in between? I need a range here."

"We're going to impersonate two high-powered businesswomen."

Grace paused, then asked, "Should I bring something for you to wear as well, then?"

"I couldn't fit into your clothes with a shoehorn and a bucket of Crisco. I'm going to go by Gabby's on the way home." We both knew my wardrobe was definitely on the shabby side of shabby chic.

"Good, I just love to play dress up. What's our cover going to be?"

"We're going to be representing an eccentric millionaire who wants to commission a new home," I said.

"Oh, that sounds lovely. I can't wait."

After we hung up, I marveled that I had such a friend. She was up for whatever insanity I could create, and would play the role better than I could. It was a cherished thing, having her in my corner.

Grace picked me up at three minutes to two. I was standing by the door waiting for her, praying that she got to the house sooner than my mother did. I doubted my dear momma would approve of what we were up to.

On my way home, I'd stopped in at the second-hand clothing store next door for something to wear. Gabby had been curious enough about my strange request, but she'd found a suit on her racks that not only fit me, but made me look just right for the role I was about to play.

Grace got out of her car, looking like she owned the world. From her high-priced pumps to her tailored suit, I had no trouble believing she was exactly who we were going to pretend to be.

I said, "I'd give you a wolf whistle, if I could. You look fabulous."

She twirled there on the sidewalk, then said, "So do you."

"It will do, but you really look the part."

"It's my interview suit, so I spared no expense," she said.

"You're looking for a new job?"

Grace laughed. "Sweetheart, I'm in sales. I'm always looking for a new job. Shall we?"

"We shall," I said.

As we drove toward Allied Construction, I realized we'd go right past BR Investments.

"Would you mind a stop along the way?" I asked.

"I'm all yours. What did you have in mind?"

"I'd like to get another look at the investment brokerage Patrick Blaine was doing business with just before he was murdered."

"That sounds like fun," Grace said, and I wondered if she was taking all of this seriously enough.

"This isn't entertainment," I chided her lightly.

"We're looking for incriminating evidence involving a murder, not going out to have fun."

"Why can't we do both?" Grace asked.

"You're hopeless, but I couldn't do it without you," I said.

"Are you kidding? This is the most fun I've had in ages. Can I be an heiress with a brand-new fortune, looking for someone to manage it for me?"

"That's fine. I'll be your personal secretary."

Grace bit her lip. "No offense, but won't he recognize you? For that matter, you've been at the construction company before, too."

"You're giving them too much credit. I had a box of donuts in my hand the last time I was at their offices, and I was dressed in jeans and an old shirt, with my hair in a ponytail. This tight little bun and my suit will be the perfect disguise. If anyone looks like they know who I am, I'll tell them they're mistaking me with my cousin, but I'll bet you ten dozen donuts no one makes the connection."

"You sound pretty sure of yourself."

"Grace, it's all about context. If one of them walked into Donut Hearts and I was wearing this suit, they might put it together, but I'd still be surprised."

"I'll bet you, but not for donuts. How about lunch at Napoli's, or do you only go there with handsome state investigators?"

"I was waiting for the first shot," I said. "You almost disappointed me, you took so long. Go ahead. Give me grief about dating a cop. I know you wanted to last night when we talked on the phone, so let's get it over with."

She shook her head. "Are you serious? I thought it

was great when you told me on the phone, and I haven't changed my mind. It's time you got back on that particular horse, don't you think?"

"I suppose so, but it wasn't easy."

"Suzanne, is anything worthwhile ever painless? Don't worry, it's all going to work out. I have a good feeling about it."

"I hope you're right."

She parked her car in front of the brokerage, and said, "It's not much, is it?"

"If anything, the inside is even less impressive."

Grace shrugged. "So, it will call for more acting than I thought. That's fine, I can do that."

"Do you want to come up with more background story before we go in?" I asked, suddenly nervous about this new game we were playing.

"Now what fun would that be? Just follow my lead and you'll be fine."

Before I could stop her, Grace was out the door and walking toward the office. Whether I liked it or not, it was showtime.

Donald Rand, though in different clothes, was as rumpled as ever. I saw Grace's eyebrows go up when she saw the shoddy, barely furnished office, and I was proud of her when she kept from commenting.

"Ladies, how can I help you?" There was something greasy about the way he spoke, as if the simplest sentence could carry smutty innuendo.

Grace said a bit dramatically, "Mr. Rand, I'm afraid I've inherited an obscene amount of money, and I don't know what to do with it all. My personal assistant"—she nodded to me, and I looked as grave as I could—"received a recommendation for your services, so I thought a preliminary visit might be in order."

"Excellent," he said, barely able to keep from licking his lips as he spoke. "Won't you have a seat?"

I wondered how he was going to manage that, since there were only two chairs in the entire place. To my surprise, he seated me in his visitor's chair, then retrieved the better desk chair for Grace. In a move that looked too practiced to be spur-of-the-moment, Rand leaned against his desk for support.

"Might I ask who recommended me?"

No doubt there was a kickback involved somewhere. "I spoke with a dear friend, Patrick Blaine. You know him quite well, don't you?"

He flinched, but if I hadn't been watching for it, I would have missed it. Quickly regaining his composure, Rand asked, "When exactly did you speak with him?"

I pretended to think about it, then said, "Just before we left for Europe. We've been gone two weeks, and returned late last night. I plan to call Patrick later to tell him how the meeting went."

He was definitely feeling the stress now. "Ma'am, I'm sorry, but I didn't catch your name."

"It's Dewberry," I said. "Cynthia Dewberry."

"Miss Dewberry, I don't know how to tell you this, but I'm afraid something's happened to Pat."

This was the first person I'd encountered who'd called Blaine by any kind of nickname.

"I hope he's all right," I said, trying to keep from telegraphing my foreknowledge.

"I'm afraid that he's gone."

I said, "Where did he go? Surely Patrick wouldn't just leave. He has so many ties to the community."

Rand shook his head. "No, that's not it. I'm sorry, but I'll have to be blunt. Someone murdered him."

"What?" I asked. "I can't believe it."

He nodded slightly. "Apparently, it was a random act of violence," he said.

I wasn't quite sure how he classified a bullet wound as random.

"This is horrid," I said.

"I hope we can still do business," Rand said, looking intently at Grace.

"I'm not sure now," she said. "How well did you know Mr. Blaine?"

"We were drinking buddies," he said, before realizing how that made him sound. "Not that we were alcoholics, but every Friday night, we'd meet for a beer and spend a little time together."

"So, you never did business with him at the bank?" Grace asked.

He shrugged. "There were a few occasions when we worked together on different projects."

"Anything lately?" I asked.

"You two seem to be more interested in Pat than in doing business with me," Rand said suspiciously.

I didn't know how to respond, but Grace obviously had been waiting for the question. "Mr. Rand, you've just lost your single reference. How else can I determine if you are suitable to handle my funds if I don't determine the true relationship you had with Mr. Blaine. Surely you can see that it's a reasonable line of inquiry."

"I see your point," he said. "Pat and I were friends

who happened to do business together occasionally. That's about all I can tell you."

"And he never showed you any favorable treatment in his capacity at the bank?" I asked.

Rand stood upright. "Sure he did. Half the business that's done in this town is handled on the golf course. But we never did anything wrong."

"I've heard enough," Grace said.

"So, what kind of numbers are we talking about here? If you'd rather talk about it over dinner, I'm sure we could work something out. Just the two of us," he said, ignoring me completely.

"I'm afraid I never go anywhere without my assistant," Grace said.

As she started to get up, he said, "Listen, I didn't mean anything by it. If you don't want to have dinner, how about a drink at my place? I mix a mean martini."

"Cynthia, we're leaving," Grace said with the perfect amount of frost in her voice.

"At least let me give you my card." There was a puzzled look on his face. No doubt he was wondering how things had gone so badly so fast.

I stared at the offering a second, then took it and shoved it into my purse. The poor man was trying to follow us out into the street, and it was a relief to get into the car and drive away.

Grace and I waited until we turned the corner, and then burst out laughing. "Did you see his tongue hanging out? It was all he could do not to make a move right there in front of me," I said.

Grace shook her head. "Don't kid yourself. I could have looked like Eleanor Roosevelt and he would have acted the same way. The temptation of money was all it took to get his motor racing. Interesting stuff, wasn't it? Did you get the feeling he was a bit too defensive when he talked about doing business with Patrick Blaine?"

"He did protest just a little too much," I said. "But does that make him a killer?"

"No, but it doesn't take him off our list, either. There's something about that man that I don't like."

"Just one thing?" I asked.

"Well, at least one. Now to the construction company."

As we drove, Grace said, "Don't look now, but I think we're being followed."

Of course I turned around and looked, just in time to see a patrol car duck between two buildings. "Is it the chief?"

"I couldn't tell, but it's pretty clear that someone on the force is keeping watch on us."

"Lovely. So, what should we do?"

She bit her lip, then said, "I'm not sure."

I thought about it a few seconds, then said, "There's really only one thing we can do, isn't there? We keep digging into this until somebody stops us. I won't be intimidated by a police escort."

"Neither will I, then," she said.

As we neared the construction company, I turned around and looked, then said, "It looks they finally gave up."

Grace said, "Good, they were making me nervous." She parked in the building's lot, then said, "Now, should we stick to the same story, or come up with something new? I've got it. Why don't I play a wealthy debutante with money to burn on a new house, and you're there to push the wheelbarrow full of cash around."

"No, I think we should stick to our original idea. We're two executive assistants to a multimillionaire interested in building a custom house."

Grace glanced over at me. "Why? Don't you think I could pull off being a debutante?"

"Please, you should have won an Oscar for that performance at the investment office. I just have a feeling the construction company is going to be a little harder to fool, and if we keep it as vague as possible, we might have a better chance of learning something."

Grace nodded her agreement, and we walked into Allied Construction together.

The receptionist in front was as frosty as ever. "I'm sorry, but without an appointment, no one sees Mr. Klein," she told us after we requested a meeting.

I turned to Grace. "Our employer will not be pleased. He wants an estimate to the closest hundred thousand by 5 P.M."

She said, "He asked for three quotes, and we've already gotten two. Let's just average them and tell him Allied bid three million four, and be done with it. You know he never accepts the middle bid on any project. The low bid is a hundred thousand below that, so there's no danger in him choosing it, either."

I could see the secretary had been in a whispered conversation on the phone as we'd batted numbers around, and after a few moments, she hung up.

I signaled to Grace, and we were starting to leave

when the secretary called out, "Ladies, could you hold on one moment please? Mr. Klein just had a cancellation, and I'm sure he'd be happy to speak with you."

I looked at Grace, then glanced at my watch. "Do we have time for this? You know how impatient *he* can be."

"Yes, but *he* also demands accuracy."

"I'm just not certain this establishment meets his basic requirements," I said.

The door to the back offices opened, and a man walked out to greet us. He was tall, and at one time in his life, he must have been fit, but he was carrying around an extra fifty pounds he didn't need. He looked familiar, no doubt from visiting me at Donut Hearts. He didn't get that girth eating oatmeal and bran for breakfast in the mornings.

"I'm Lincoln Klein," he said as he offered his hand. "Won't you come back to my office, ladies?"

We looked at each other, then reluctantly accepted. As we walked through the doors into the inner sanctum, I noticed a scale model propped against the wall for some kind of development. Someone had smashed a few of the houses, and it was clearly waiting for the trash.

Mr. Klein kept walking, but I held my ground. "What happened here? Did this model fall off the table?"

He shook his head. "No, it was a project we had to drop suddenly. Our investors backed out at the last second." Realizing how that must sound, he quickly added, "It happens in this business. People's dreams exceed their bank accounts."

Grace said, "I can assure you, our employer's well is quite deep."

That certainly got his attention. "Who exactly do you work for, if you don't mind me asking?"

I said, "Our employer wishes to remain anonymous while gathering preliminary information. It keeps things on an even keel that way, and stops bids from being overly inflated once his name is attached to the project."

As Klein led us into his office, I looked around. The place was huge, and it needed to be. There were mounted trophies on the walls of boars and bears and deer, and I wondered if he'd ever seen an animal he didn't shoot. The place gave me the creeps from the moment we walked in, and it was all I could do not to run right back out again screaming.

He said, "I understand his desire for anonymity completely. I hope you convey to him that I'm extremely discreet." Klein rubbed his hands together, then said, "I don't see any plans with you, so I'm not sure how I can give you a fair bid."

That rascal had us. I could see Grace start to panic, her careful mask beginning to slip, when I said, "Mr. Klein, for the purposes of this discussion, let's assume something quite like Miranda Gentry's home, doubled. We are looking for a general estimate, just to see how serious the builders we are interviewing are about winning the bid."

He tented his fingers behind his desk, a monstrous mahogany slab, and pretended to consider it. "Without being too specific, I believe I could build something like it for three million two."

What a surprise, his secretary had fed him the exact number he had to beat to secure the job.

I nodded. "That would be acceptable."

"Nothing's certain, though," Grace said.

Now it was time for me to move in for the information that had brought us here. "Our employer was a little concerned about something else."

"Ask me anything. I'm sure I'll have an answer to it," he said.

I was sure he would. "He understands you've been doing business with Patrick Blaine recently."

Klein looked surprised to hear the news, but managed to keep it to himself. "We were discussing some possibilities, but nothing came of it."

"So, you deny you were working together?" I made it sound like we had prior information, and if you counted Blaine's secretary Vicki's declarations, I suppose we did.

"No, I thought you meant future projects. We've done business in the past. What does this have to do with the bid?"

"Our employer is thorough," Grace said. "He likes to know who he's doing business with."

"Then he should come by and meet with me himself. I'll be able to allay any fears or misgivings he might have."

I didn't doubt that. This man was slick enough to sell saltwater to a mermaid. "Perhaps he'll do that after we've submitted the bids."

I stood, and Grace followed my lead.

Klein wasn't about to give up that easily, though. As he followed us out, he said, "Do you have a card?"

"They tend to say too much, don't they? Don't worry. We'll be in touch," I said.

We were back in the car heading toward Donut Hearts when I realized where I'd seen him before. "That was the man I saw with Deb Jenkins last night," I said.

"The mistress? Was he her dinner companion?"

"I think so. I just saw him for a second, and I have to admit, I was so taken by her transformation that I barely looked at him, but yeah, I'm pretty sure it was the same man."

"What was Blaine's mistress doing going out with one of his business partners?"

I bit my lower lip, then said, "They looked pretty cozy together, so I doubt they just started dating after the murder."

"Jealousy is a motive for murder as much as greed."

I nodded. "That's the problem. We have two different motives going here, with too many suspects. Instead of narrowing the field, we seem to be adding to it."

Grace frowned. "I hate to say this, but if it's too much, we could always let Jake handle it."

"I'm in too deep now, wouldn't you say?"

"I don't know," Grace replied. "I'm just starting to get a little worried about the whole thing."

"So am I," I admitted.

My phone rang at that moment. I said, "Hello?"

"Suzanne? It's George. I just learned something that might be valuable information, and I wanted you to have it as soon as possible."

"What is it?"

"It's about Patrick Blaine's insurance. I started

wondering about Rita's claims, so I called in a few favors to see whose name is really on that policy."

"It's Deb Jenkins, isn't it?"

"No, that's why I thought you should know. No matter what she might have told you, it appears that Rita Blaine is going to inherit everything after all."

"So she lied to us," I said, thinking about the ramifications.

"I don't see why. It's really not all that much a motive for murder, is it?"

I stared at the phone a second before replying. "George, I don't know what kind of circles you're running around in, but a million dollars is enough of a motive for just about anybody I know."

He paused, then asked, "Suzanne, who told you the policy was worth a million dollars?"

"Rita did," I admitted.

"I wonder if she was lying about that, too, or if she didn't know."

"Know what?"

"The main insurance policy had lapsed, and Blaine didn't renew it. That left what he got from the bank, a little over fourteen thousand dollars. Hardly enough to kill him for, wouldn't you say?"

I thought about that for a few moments, then asked, "What if Rita didn't know the main policy had lapsed?"

"Then she was in for a rather unpleasant surprise if she killed him for fourteen grand. These days, that's probably just enough to bury him, and the poor grieving ex-wife gets nothing."

"That's a reason to stay drunk, isn't it?" I asked. "Thanks for the information."

"You're welcome. I'm glad I could help."

I hung up, and Grace whistled softly. "I caught enough of that to get what's going on. It makes you wonder why Rita really went on a bender, doesn't it?"

"Enough to go ask her. Are you up for it?"

"Are you kidding? Let's go."

THE EASIEST DONUT RECIPE IN THE WORLD

I hesitate to call this a recipe, it's so simple, but the results are spectacular, and the process is the easiest I've ever come across. Try them when you've got hot oil for a different batch of donuts, and I think you'll agree.

INGREDIENTS
1 can, biscuit dough (I like the sourdough recipe)

DIRECTIONS
Take the biscuit rounds from the can, then use your hole cutter only to cut out the center. Add the rounds and holes to 375-degree oil, and turn after 2 minutes on each side. A trick here is that the centers often turn over in the oil on their own when they're done.

After draining them on a rack or on paper towels, you can eat these plain, or dust with powdered sugar. It's amazing how pretty they turn out, and they taste good, too. What more could you ask for?

Makes 4 to 8 donuts.

CHAPTER 10

The door was locked when we got to Rita's place, and no amount of banging would bring her to answer.

"Maybe she's gone," Grace said.

"More likely, she's passed out on the floor," I said.

We were walking back to the car, though, and something made me turn around. I saw a face duck away from a window in the living room, and just before it vanished, I recognized it as Rita's.

"She's watching us," I said.

Grace asked, "How do you know that?"

"I just saw her."

"Then we're going back."

I grabbed her arm. "Grace, she obviously doesn't want to see us."

My friend had a determined look on her face. "If she's in there, and she's awake, I'm going to make her come to the door."

"Grace, we can't make her talk to us. It's not like we have badges or anything."

"That doesn't mean she can just ignore us."

I shook my head. "Sorry, but that's exactly what it means. Let's just go. We'll figure out something else."

"Fine, but I think we're giving up too easily."

"Maybe, but it's been a long day. I'm tired and hungry, and in a few hours, I've got to get up to make donuts again."

"Do you want to grab a bite while we're out?" she asked.

"No, I just want to get home and forget about the world tonight. Do you mind dropping me off at my Jeep?"

"Not a problem," she said. As we drove, Grace asked, "So, what do you make of all we saw today?"

"It's going to take some time to digest it all, but one thing's certain."

"What's that?"

"Nobody recognized me," I said, smiling. "I won our bet. I can't wait to have lunch at Napoli's."

"You were right, so I'll pay up. I can't believe nobody knew who you were."

"Like I said, it's all about context," I said.

We arrived at my Jeep back in April Springs, and I got out of Grace's car. "Thanks for helping out this afternoon. I couldn't have done it without you."

"Are you kidding? I had a blast. Suzanne, I know you're sick of the entire town worrying about you, but be careful, okay? I've got a feeling somebody we've talked to in the last few days is a murderer."

I would have loved to be able to disagree, but I couldn't. "I think you're right. I just wish we knew which one."

"That would make life easier, wouldn't it?"

After she drove off, I noticed something tucked under my windshield wiper. It couldn't be a parking ticket. I was in front of my own shop.

Instead of a ticket, I found a note.

"Sorry I missed you. I'll catch up with you later. Jake."

He wasn't the only one who was sorry. Though we'd just had one date—and it had ended less than perfectly—I found myself becoming attached, something I hadn't planned on, or been expecting.

I was still smiling when Max, my ex, walked up, with a dozen long-stemmed red roses in his hand.

And suddenly, the lightness of my good mood was gone.

"There's my Suzie girl. These are for you."

I made no move to take them. "You should have saved yourself the money," I said. "I don't want them."

Max frowned gently. "Hey, I'm trying to apologize here. The least you could do is let me." His words were a little slurred, not enough for most folks to be able to tell that he had been drinking, but I'd been around him a long time.

"How much have you had to drink?"

He held up his thumb and index finger about two inches apart. "A little, I admit it. So, how about it? You wanna go out with me tonight?"

"You must be out of your mind," I said. "Right now I wouldn't go out with you again on a bet, and that doesn't even have anything to do with the fact that you wrecked my date last night."

"Are you seriously telling me you'd rather date that cop than me? Suzanne, we had something special."

"I thought so, too. I wonder what Darlene would say?"

"Would you drop that once and forever?" Without realizing he was doing it, Max swung the roses down, smacking them on the hood of the Jeep. Petals flew off onto the asphalt, and I took a step backward.

Keeping my voice calm, I said, "Your temper has gotten a lot worse since we split up, hasn't it?"

"I'm going crazy trying to get you to forgive me," he said. I could swear he looked like he wanted to cry.

"I'm sorry, but I can't." This was a scene I'd been dreading since we ended our marriage. Max almost never drank, because when he did, his emotions dictated his actions, and he hated losing control.

"I want you back in my life," he said, after he'd managed to compose himself. "I'm not giving up."

He started to try to hand me the flowers again, then noticed their beaten appearance. After flipping them into a trash can, Max walked away, and I finally started breathing again.

What was I going to do about him? I thought we'd worked out a way to be around each other without scenes like this, but evidently, I'd been wrong. At one time, he'd been the most important part of my life, and he'd thrown it away with one stupid, thoughtless indiscretion.

But it was all I could think about when I saw him, and I wondered if the image of him and Darlene together would ever go away.

* * *

Momma was waiting for me by the door.

"Don't you look all grown-up," she said.

"I just picked it up today. I got it at Gabby's."

She brushed a bit of lint off one shoulder. "It suits you. Did you have another date with Jake Bishop tonight?"

I looked down at my outfit. "Dressed like this? I don't think so."

"Then why were you wearing it?"

"I had an appointment I wanted to look nice for," I admitted. "Momma, it's been a long, hard day. Can we leave it at that?"

"Fine," she said, surprising me with her instant capitulation. "I made some cheesy chicken for dinner."

That was one of my favorites. "Did I do something special? It's not even my birthday."

Momma smiled. "I know you've been having a hard time lately, so I thought you could use a treat."

I kissed her cheek.

She asked, "What was that for? I've fixed dinner for you before."

"For understanding what I'm going through," I said. "Do I have time to change?"

"Absolutely. You'll have the suit dry-cleaned before you put it in your closet, won't you?"

"First thing tomorrow morning," I said.

I changed into some jeans and an old sweater, clothes I was much more comfortable in. Momma had the table set, and we enjoyed a quiet meal, filled with small talk and skirting my recent activities.

After we had some brownies she'd just made, it was time for her attack.

"Suzanne, we need to talk."

"I've never liked that particular phrase," I said. "I thought we had been."

"This is serious. I'm not sure you realize how dangerous your behavior has been lately. You're taking far too many chances."

"Who have you been talking to? Not Grace, I know that much."

"I have my sources," she said. "Don't try to deny that you are meddling in police affairs. Let the chief handle this. And if you don't trust him, surely you must feel Jake is competent."

"Momma. I can't just leave this alone. If I don't figure out who killed Patrick Blaine, I'm afraid nobody's going to. He wasn't some stranger; he was my friend."

She reached for the telephone.

"Who are you calling?" I asked.

"I'm going to speak with the chief and see if he can come by here and talk some sense into you. Clearly, I can't."

I couldn't believe I was hearing this from my own mother. I grabbed a heavy jacket by the door. "Call whoever you like, but don't expect me to just sit here. I'm going out."

"It's dark," she said. "Where exactly do you think you're going?"

"I'm going to take a walk in the park. I need some fresh air."

"There you go again, taking chances that aren't necessary. I'm calling the chief this instant."

I had to get out of there before we both said things we'd regret.

The park was my happy place, somewhere I could go to get away from the world. There was more to it than most folks saw. It had a distinct personality; it was a place with a soul. I found myself walking directly to my thinking tree, a gnarled old oak whose trunk was twisted into a saddle where I could sit comfortably off the cold ground.

As I stared into the night sky, stars ablaze with wintry fire, I thought about who might have killed Patrick Blaine. His ex-wife, Rita, was a candidate, especially if she hadn't known he'd let his insurance lapse to nearly nothing. That seemed to let Deb Jenkins off the hook, but then again, I'd seen her being awfully cozy with Lincoln Klein, the builder who was also a suspect on my list. Had she simply moved on to another man after hers had been killed, or was there more to it than that? And what about the builder himself? That model we'd found destroyed was a sign that all was not well there. But was it because of Blaine's death, or was the banker's murder a direct result of a failed project? And then there was the sleazy investor, Mr. Rand. I didn't like him, but I tried not to let that cloud my judgment. If I was being honest with myself, I had to admit that particular lead had petered out. I wouldn't have invested money I found under a seat cushion with him, but that didn't make him a murderer. Was that it, then? Did my entire list of suspects include the ex-wife, Rita Blaine, the ex-mistress, Deb Jenkins, the ex-business partner Lincoln Klein, or another party I wasn't aware of yet? Was there someone else lurking in the background, someone I'd spoken to, but not been aware of their stake in the murder? Could Vicki Houser have more motive than I'd found? Was her leaving town simply a ruse to divert suspicion? I had to admit it was possible if I was being fair about it. In fact, it might not even be anyone I'd talked to. Chief Martin and Jake might very well be on the killer's heels, and I'd just been going around annoying people for nothing. It wasn't a possibility I was ready to accept.

I wasn't sure where to turn next, but I did know it was time to go back home. My fit of pique had dissipated with the cold, and I knew my mother's intentions—no matter how much they frustrated me—were well meaning. She loved me, and I couldn't fault her for that.

I was a hundred yards from home, and could see the soft glow of the lights inside, when someone jumped out of the bushes and grabbed me from behind.

I struggled against the attacker's grip, determined to go down swinging. The assailant might get the better of me, but I was going to make sure whoever had me knew they'd been in a fight. One of the attacker's forearms covered my mouth, while the other hand pinned my right arm behind my back. I could feel the rough texture of some kind of ski mask on my cheek, and the heat from their breath sent cold chills through me. I was alone in the darkness with someone who wanted to harm me, and I didn't even have a house key on me to jab at them with. If I ever lived through this, I promised myself I'd be better prepared the next time.

I had enough to deal with at the moment, though. I tried to struggle free, but it was useless. I was

strong—or at least I liked to think so—but my attacker was stronger.

"Stop fighting me, or I'll really have to hurt you,"
the voice whispered in my ear.

"You're going to hurt me anyway," I said as I tried
to kick backward.

The assailant's grip tightened on my arm, forcing
it higher up my back, and I stopped struggling, at
least until I could get some kind of advantage.

A rough voice whispered, "If you don't butt out of
this and mind your own business, I'm going to do
more than hurt you, and that's a promise."

There was more of a threat in the voice than I
could imagine, not because of the intensity of the
words, but from the lack of it. If the tone of voice was
real, the attacker would have no more compunction
hurting me than swatting an annoying fly.

I had to do something.

I took a deep breath, then drove the fingernails of
my free hand into the arm that covered my mouth. I
don't have much in the way of nails, since they interfere with working the dough at my shop, but they
were long enough to make the attacker's grip ease as
I jabbed them downward into the arm. I hoped I'd
drawn blood with the attack, but I couldn't be sure.
All I knew was that I was suddenly free.

I had no fight instinct left in me. It was time to
run. With everything I had, I raced for my momma's
front porch, hoping the attacker wasn't going to follow me and finish the job.

As I stumbled inside the door of my house, I said,
"Did you call Chief Martin yet?"

"No, I didn't want to make you any angrier than you already were."

"You'd better call him after all. Somebody just attacked me in the park. He'd better get over here." I dead-bolted the door as soon I got inside, then went into the closet for a baseball bat we kept there for protection. It wouldn't stop a bullet, but I'd put my swing up against just about anything else. I had been a pretty mean softball player in high school, and I still knew how to swing for the fences.

All of my mother's defiance left her as she rushed to me. "Are you all right? I'm so sorry."

"Why? You didn't grab me from behind out there."

"No, but you ran off because of me. Tell me what happened, Suzanne," she said.

"Momma, you know I love you, but I just want to do this one time, okay? Get the chief over here, and you can hear all about it when I tell him what happened."

She nodded, and reached for the phone as I slumped down on the couch. The threat had been all too real, and I wondered who I'd spooked enough to make them come after me.

In a way, I guess it was progress, but not the kind I'd been hoping for.

"So let me get this straight," the chief said after he'd heard my story twice in our living room. "You didn't see who attacked you, and after he grabbed you from behind and threatened you, he just ran off. Is that it?"

My mother snapped, "Phillip Martin, I expect you take my daughter's complaint seriously."

The chief of police for April Springs was a large man, carrying thirty pounds more than he should have. He was my mother's age, but still had a full head of ginger hair, though it was starting to go white at the temples.

"I'm interviewing her, aren't I? Dorothy, I've got three officers I can't spare investigating the park even as we speak. What more can I do?"

"You can believe her when she tells you that she was mugged," my mother said.

He nodded. "I believe that's exactly what happened."

"Hey, wait a second," I protested. "This wasn't just some random act of violence. It had something to do with Patrick Blaine's murder. And you keep saying it was a man. I can't be sure that's true. It could have been a woman."

"So now you're changing your story?"

I had to bite back my temper. "I never said it was a man. But whoever it was, I know it was because of what I've been doing."

The chief shook his head. "You have no proof of that, Suzanne." He frowned, then added, "From what I've been hearing around town, you're under the impression that you're better at my job than I am. Now you're saying that you're so good, the killer is afraid of your investigation, but not mine?"

He stared at me, no doubt waiting for me to deny what I'd been up to, but I wasn't going to give him the satisfaction of admitting I was exploring the crime, as well.

"Let's get back to the mugging," my mother said.

I interrupted her. "I wasn't mugged, Momma. The

voice told me to butt out or I'd be next. Does that sound like a random attack to you?"

"I'm sorry, Suzanne," my mother said, obviously a little flustered by my retort. "I misspoke."

The chief's cell phone rang, and he moved over by the window to take the call out of our hearing.

As he was talking, Momma said, "I'm trying to support you here, you know that, don't you?"

I patted her shoulder gently. "I know. I guess I'm just a little jumpy."

"With the week you've had, you've got every right to be," she said.

Chief Martin hung up, then said, "They swept the park twice, and nobody's there."

"Not now," I said. "Why on earth would they stick around after they attacked me?"

The chief blew out a huff of air. "Suzanne, there's nothing I can do about it if I can't find anyone to question. But it might not be a bad idea to take his advice."

I couldn't believe he was suggesting it. "So, you're taking this bully's side over mine? I should just crawl into a hole and pull it in after me, is that what you think?"

"What I think is that you should let me do my job," he said, not even trying to hide the aggravation in his voice.

"I'm disappointed in you, Phillip," my mother said.

"Dorothy, you know I hate like fire going against you, but Suzanne's going to get herself into trouble if she keeps trying to do my job for me."

My mother just shook her head. "It appears she has

to, since you're not making any progress. Thank you for coming by, Phillip. You may see yourself out."

"Yes, ma'am," he said, obviously hurt by her curt tone. Perhaps he was finally beginning to learn that no matter what he did, he'd never have her for his own.

After he was gone, Momma said, "Suzanne, you need to stop this, and I mean this instant."

"You're taking everybody else's side? What happened to loving and supporting me?"

She shook her head. "Don't do that, child. I love you, and I can't bear to see you get hurt. You're all the family that I have left. Don't you understand that?"

A trail of tears slowly slid down her cheek, and I hugged her before I wiped it away.

After a few moments, she said, "Do you promise?"

"No, ma'am, I'm sorry, but I can't. This isn't something I want to do. I have to, or I might be next."

"Not if you stop right now."

I shrugged. "I can't take that chance."

This was getting us nowhere.

There was a knock at the door, and I found myself hoping it was Jake Bishop.

It was Officer Grant, one of my regular customers, instead.

"Sorry to bother you, but I just wanted to make sure you were all right. I was out sweeping the park with everyone else, and I thought you should know for your own peace of mind, there's nobody's out there."

"Thanks, I appreciate that."

After he left, I started for my room, and Momma asked, "Where are you going?"

"To bed."

She said, "Do you honestly think you can sleep with all that's happened?"

I glanced at the clock. "It's nearly nine o'clock, and I have to be up at one. When do you suggest I go to bed? If I don't get some sleep, I'll never make it through tomorrow."

"Good night, then."

I made it into my room and collapsed on the bed. I worried over what had happened for thirty seconds, then I let it all slip away. I'd learned early on that the only way to function with my crazy schedule was to sleep whenever I could, for however long I could manage.

My problems would still be there come morning, or what passed for it in my life, and I needed to be fresh if I was going to handle things without getting myself killed.

The next morning, George was waiting for me when I opened at five-thirty.

"Why didn't you call me last night? I could have helped when you were attacked."

I shook my head. "I didn't call you because I didn't want to worry you. How'd you find out, anyway?"

"I talked to one of the men searching the park for the attacker last night. You know him, don't you? The kid's name is Grant."

"He's a customer of mine," I admitted.

"Well, I'm glad he said something. Suzanne, from now on, you need to come clean with me and keep me in the loop, do you understand? It's serious business."

"Hang on a second," I said. "I called Chief Martin, and he thought it was just a random mugging."

George got close enough to me so I could feel the heat coming off him. "You know better, though, don't you? You were warned to butt out. What do you think this guy's going to do when he realizes you're still digging into the murder? Do you honestly think you're going to be so lucky next time? One man has died, Suzanne."

It was clear I'd hurt George's feelings by not calling him, and that just wasn't right. "Listen, I'm sorry, I didn't mean to exclude you."

He accepted my apology. "I'm just saying, I can't help you if you don't tell me everything. What did Bishop say when you told him?"

"I never called him," I admitted. "It was so late when it happened, and all I wanted to do was go to bed."

George handed me his cell phone. "Call him."

"It's too early," I said.

"Would you do it as a favor to me?"

I shrugged. "I will, but I'll use my own telephone." I didn't want George hitting redial later and calling the state investigator himself.

I expected to get his voice mail, but to my surprise, he answered on the first ring.

"Bishop here."

"Hi, it's Suzanne."

"Hey, did you get my note yesterday?"

"Thanks, it was sweet of you." I took a deep breath, then said, "I'm guessing you haven't talked to Chief Martin yet."

"Not since yesterday afternoon. Why, what's up?"

I rubbed my forehead for a second, then said, "There was an incident in the park last night, and I thought you should know about it."

"What happened? Are you all right? Where are you?"

"I'm at the shop," I said. "Somebody grabbed me while I was out walking, but I managed to get away."

"Did they say anything to you?" Bishop asked after a moment's pause.

"They warned me to butt out, or I'd be next," I admitted, hating to repeat the chilling words over the phone.

Jake's voice went cold. "Don't go anywhere. I'll be there in twenty minutes."

"I've got nowhere else to be," I said. "I've got a shop to run."

"I'll see you soon," he said, then hung up.

I turned to George. "There, are you happy?"

"Not until he shows up. Until then, I'll be at a table up front watching out for you. Don't go out the back way, and don't let Emma go there, either."

"I'd say no if I could, but the advice is too good to pass up." On impulse, I reached back into the case and grabbed a pumpkin donut and a small carton of milk. "These are on the house. Thanks for caring."

"Sure," he said gruffly. George fought hard to keep up a rough exterior, but I had an idea how soft he was on the inside.

Jake came in fourteen minutes later, and from his expression, it was clear that this morning, he was unhappy with me.

"You should have called me, Suzanne," he said.

"Everything happened so fast," I replied. "By the time I thought about it, I was nearly asleep."

He looked around the shop, which was starting to fill up in the predawn rush. "Is there somewhere we could talk?"

"The only place with any privacy at all is my office."

"Then let's go there."

I nodded. I didn't care to broadcast our conversation for the world to hear any more than he did.

Jake followed me through the door to the kitchen, and I could see a few frowns on the faces of my patrons. They'd obviously been hoping for a show, but I wasn't in any mood to give them one.

His presence intensified in the close proximity of my office. I took the main chair, and he leaned against the wall, looming over me.

"Now, tell me exactly what happened," he said, giving me his full attention.

"Like I told you over the phone, somebody grabbed me, I fought back, and then I called Chief Martin."

"Do you remember his exact words when he threatened you?"

"I'm not likely to forget," I said as I felt his phantom grasp. "He said if I didn't butt out, he was going to do more than hurt me. That's when I got away."

"How'd you manage to do that?"

"I dug my nails into his arm, and he let go. He

had a heavy jacket on, so I doubt I made any marks on him."

Jake took my hands in his. "That's not going to help, is it? Your nails are really short."

"Try making donut dough with a manicure," I said.

He dropped my hands. "So, there's not much chance you wounded him."

"Probably not. I broke a nail, but I doubt it did any good. I got away, though. That's all that counts. He won't forget me soon."

Jake studied me a moment, then asked, "Suzanne, are you sure it was a man?"

"No, I can't be positive about anything," I admitted. "To be honest with you, I was scared, and all I could think of was to try to get away. I tried to tell the chief that it could have been a woman, but he wasn't interested in hearing any of my theories. I'm just glad I escaped."

"You're right. That's really all that matters," he said. There was a hint of softness in his voice when he said it.

He stood there a second, then asked, "Is there any chance that you're going to stop digging into this?"

"I can't," I said softly.

He looked as though he wanted to cry. "Listen, you've got to let us handle this. It's too dangerous for you."

I thought about lying, I swear I did, but something made me tell him the truth. "He was my friend, and besides, my neck's on the line, and no one else's. I'm motivated."

"To do what, get yourself killed?"

"Don't you understand? I don't have a choice."

He shook his head. "I'm not getting through to you, am I? You're putting your life in jeopardy."

"I'm being as careful as I can, but I'm not going to sit around here waiting for the killer to come after me next."

I wasn't sure what he said; it was spoken softly and nearly under his breath.

"What was that?" I asked, seeing if he had the guts to repeat it.

"I said that stubborn streak of yours is going to get you in trouble one of these days."

He started for the kitchen, and his escape, as I called out, "Jake, I'm not trying to drive you away."

"You surely could have fooled me."

"Jake?"

He stopped. "What?"

"I'm sorry. I should have called you last night."

"Yes, you should have." He smiled as he said it, and I felt my heart flutter again. At least we were back on good terms, something that had become surprisingly important to me.

After Jake was gone, I sat there a second, trying to catch my breath before I rejoined my customers out front. The worst part was, he made perfect sense. If I had a lick of brains, I'd do what everyone was advising me to do.

But there wasn't a hole in all of April Springs big enough to hide me, and even if there were, I wouldn't use it.

I had donuts to make, and a killer to catch, and I wasn't going to be able to do either one if I was in hiding.

MOMMA'S CHEESY CHICKEN

INGREDIENTS
4 chicken breasts; skinned, deboned, and
pounded thin
4 oz. sharp cheddar cheese, cut into long rectangles
4 oz. mozzarella cheese, cut into long rectangles

Coating
4 oz. Parmesan cheese, grated and divided in half
4 oz. Italian bread crumbs
1 tablespoon Italian seasoning

And
1 tablespoon Italian seasoning
Cooking spray

DIRECTIONS
Lay the chicken breasts on a sheet of foil, then spray
each with the cooking spray just enough to coat.

Lightly sprinkle the Italian seasoning over each breast,
then take ½ oz. of Parmesan mixed with ½ oz. Italian
bread crumbs and spread out over each breast. Then,
to each breast, add on one of the narrow ends 1 oz.
cheddar rectangle and 1 oz. mozzarella rectangle.

Roll each chicken breast into a cylinder, being sure
to keep the cheese inside. Lightly coat the outside of
the rolled breasts with cooking spray, then sprinkle
each with the ½ oz. of Parmesan and ½ oz. Italian
bread crumbs mix.

Cover and refrigerate for 2 to 4 hours.

Preheat oven to 425 degrees, and cook the chicken breasts until they are no longer pink inside, approximately 30 minutes.

This cheesy chicken is great together with a salad, cooked baby green peas, and a fancy rice dish.

Serves 4.

CHAPTER 11

When I walked back out front, George motioned for me to join him. I wasn't in any mood to rehash my conversation with Jake, but I owed him that much, since he'd gone to so much trouble to help me.

"What's up?" I said as I refilled George's coffee cup.

"I've got an idea how to find out who attacked you last night," George said. "I think you must have scratched him. Or her."

"I appreciate the offer, but he was wearing a coat, and my nails aren't that long to begin with. I broke one, but I doubt there was any skin under it."

"But you could have bruised his arm," George said. "Isn't it worth trying to figure out who might have done it to you?"

"If you can come up with a way to look at some forearms without causing suspicion, I'm all for it, but I'm afraid it's hopeless."

George took a sip of coffee, then he said, "Don't

worry, I'll come up with something plausible, or I won't do it."

"I should hope not," I said.

George stared outside for a minute, then asked, "Suzanne, do you still have that parking ticket you found in Patrick Blaine's house?"

"Sure, it's at the house. Why do you want to see it?"

"I keep thinking that it might be significant. I'd like to see if it's the same kind of ticket used in April Springs, or if it's some kind of novelty blank meant to be a joke."

"I've never had a parking ticket, so I couldn't say," I said. "Would you like to swing by and get it this afternoon? It's at home, on the desk in my room."

"Is your mother there?" George asked. "I'd rather find out now if it's another dead end, or if it might actually be a real lead."

"Okay, let me call her."

"Don't wake her on our account," George said.

"Are you kidding? She gets up at five because she likes to, if you can believe it."

I made the call, then hung up and turned to George. "She'll put it in our mailbox, since she's going out in a few minutes."

George stood. "I'll be right back, then."

I put a hand on his arm. "Do you really think it's important?" I was starting to feel guilty about how dismissive I'd been of my discovery.

"Probably not, but I'd rather know, one way or the other."

After he was gone, a rash of customers came into

the shop, and Emma and I were busy filling orders long after George returned.

When things finally slowed down again, I approached him. "Was I right? Was it just a gag?"

"No, it's real enough," George said. "I think somebody on the April Springs police force was meeting with Blaine, and they didn't want anyone else to know about it."

"I don't get it," I said. "Why go to so much trouble? Wouldn't it have just been easier to call him and set up an appointment?"

George studied the ticket. "You can't be sure who's listening on the other end, can you? Here's the thing. If you saw someone slipping a note under a driver's windshield, you'd think something was going on, but if it was a cop putting a ticket there, nobody would pay the least amount of attention to it. It's really pretty clever."

"I guess. But I'm still not sure what it means."

George stood. "I keep wondering if it has something to do with the dirty cop I keep hearing about. I'm just not sure how it's tied to Blaine, but I'm going to find out. Let me do more digging, and I'll get back to you later."

After he was gone, I grabbed my jacket and told Emma, "I'll be back in an hour. Can you handle things until I get back?"

"You know I hate running the shop without you," she said.

"Come on, it'll be good practice for you when I go on vacation this summer."

Emma frowned. "You haven't taken a vacation in two years."

"Don't you think it's time, then?"

I swear she looked like she was going to cry. I quickly said, "Take it easy. I was just kidding."

"The thought of making all of those donuts by myself is just too much," she said. "I don't mind helping you, but I can't imagine doing it all alone. How do you do it on my day off?"

"I know it's hard to believe, but somehow I manage. See you in an hour."

"I'm setting one of the alarms in back the second you walk out that door," Emma said.

I walked out onto the sidewalk, wondering where to look next, when my neighbor Gabby spotted me. She was putting out a sandwich sign near the sidewalk proclaiming special deals, something she trumpeted every day. Honestly, how special could it be if she never missed a day?

"Suzanne, where are you off to this morning?"

I hadn't planned it, but seeing her gave me an idea. "Actually, I came over to talk to you. Do you have a minute?"

"For you? Always."

I followed her inside, realizing that if I wanted the scoop on what was going on in April Springs, I didn't have to go farther than next door.

"Do you have time for tea?" she asked.

"I'm sorry, but I shouldn't leave Emma alone any longer than I have to. If it weren't so important, I never would have left her."

"She's a sweet child," Gabby said, "but the young lack our stability and dedication, don't you think?"

I wasn't about to get into Emma's personality and character description with my gossiping neighbor. "I need your in-depth knowledge of April Springs," I said. "Only someone with your keen sense of what's happening can help me."

Gabby looked at me with a stony glance. "Honestly, do you think idle flattery will get you information that a simple request would not? Suzanne, were you under the impression that I wasn't aware that the entire town thinks I'm nothing but a gossiping fishwife?"

I didn't even know how to sidestep that one. "I wouldn't put it like that."

"No, of course you wouldn't. You're kinder than that, but you'd be in the minority, and we both know it. I'm nosy," she said, "and I don't mind who knows it. I don't have much of a life of my own, and watching the twists and turns people's lives take keeps me interested in getting up every day. Is that honestly such a bad thing?"

I thought about all of the times I'd heard Gabby say something malicious and intended to draw blood, making it a bad thing, indeed, but it wasn't the most prudent time to bring that up now. I decided to ignore the question completely, on the grounds that I didn't want to get struck by an errant thunderbolt for lying. "As I said, I need your help."

She nodded. "I will, if I can, and you know it."

"I'm looking into a possible connection between Patrick Blaine and anyone on the April Springs police force. Have you ever seen him chatting with any of them around town?"

She thought about it a moment, then nodded. "As a matter of fact, I did see him speaking with an officer once after dark in the park here in town. I thought it looked odd at the time, but I'm afraid I just dismissed it out of hand."

"When did this happen?"

She stared at the ceiling of her shop for a full minute. "Unless I'm mistaken, which I highly doubt, it was two nights before the man was murdered. Do you think that's significant?"

"It might be," I admitted. "You didn't happen to see who it was, did you?"

"All the officers on the force look alike, the way they're dressed in uniforms. It wasn't the chief, but that's about all I can say for sure." She paused, then added, "I can ask around, if you'd like."

"Don't do anything too obvious," I said. "I'd hate for you to get the wrong kind of attention."

She patted my arm. "Dear child, I've been snooping so long, I've got it down to an art form. No one will even realize they are being grilled. Give me an hour, and I'll come find you next door."

I nodded. "Thanks, Gabby. I mean it."

She took my hands in hers. "Yes, I can see that you do."

When I left her shop, she was already on the telephone. Could it be that I'd been underutilizing a deep source of information about the activities of the residents of April Springs?

I glanced at my watch and saw that I had forty-one minutes of freedom left. How should I use it? Then I noticed a school bus parked in front of Donut Hearts. One look inside, and I saw that Emma was swamped behind the counter, a gaggle of elementary school students all vying for her attention at the same time.

"Okay, settle down," I said as I waded through

the crowd of kids in the shop. "I need you all to line up in an orderly fashion, or no one will be getting any donuts today."

A harried-looking teacher came out of the restroom in back. "What happened to my line, children? Do as the nice lady asks. Now."

They hadn't listened to me, or Emma, either, but this woman had managed to whip them into shape without raising her voice.

"How do you do that?" I asked her.

"They've learned to read me pretty well," she said. "When I stop smiling, they know it's time to straighten up. I'm Missy Dunbar."

I took her hand. "I'm Suzanne Hart. I own the donut shop."

She lowered her voice, and said, "Listen, I'm really sorry about barging in on you without any warning, but we were going to take the Krispy Kreme tour in Hickory, and the bus broke down. We missed our slot, so I was wondering if you'd mind stepping in."

It wasn't the most sincere compliment I'd ever gotten in my life, but she was in a jam, and I hated to disappoint all those little faces. "Sure, we can show them how we make donuts here."

I turned to Emma. "If you watch the front, I'll give the tour."

"That's a deal," she said. "Hey, Suzanne."

"Yes?"

"Thanks for coming back in, even after you saw the bus."

"You'd have done the same thing for me," I said.

"Don't be so sure," Emma said with a grin.

I took a deep breath, then clapped my hands.

"Listen up. Welcome to Donut Hearts, a place where we put a part of ourselves in every donut."

A little girl up front said, "That's gross. What part do you use?"

"Fingernails and belly fuzz," a little boy next to her said.

"Yuchhhh. I'm not eating that."

"And frog's legs," the little boy added with a malicious grin.

I knelt down in front of the little girl and said, "We use the same things your momma uses in her kitchen every day."

"My mommy's dead," the little girl said.

Great. I'd managed to put my foot into it again. "Then your daddy."

She giggled. "Daddy doesn't cook. We eat out a lot."

"Okay, so the folks who make your meals use the same ingredients I do." I saw that the little boy was about to say something, when I added, "Every boy and girl who listens and doesn't talk will get a special donut hole after we're finished. Okay?"

They cheered, and I saw the teacher nod her thanks. There was no comment from junior, and I hoped the lure of a donut hole was enough to keep him silent.

I led the group back into the kitchen, and said, "The first rule here is not to touch anything, okay?"

They nodded, and Miss Dunbar added, "If anyone misbehaves, there will be no snacktime for a week."

It was as if she'd instituted martial law. I wanted them quiet, not petrified, but it was her class, not mine.

I put on a tall chef's hat, though I usually just wore a hairnet when I worked. "Now, here is where we store the flour we use. Can anyone guess what's inside a donut?"

The little boy who'd mentioned belly fuzz shot his hand into air. Did I dare call on him?

I looked toward the teacher for a clue, and she nodded.

Taking a deep breath, I said, "Yes."

"Flour and sugar and yeast and other stuff," he said proudly.

"Very good," I said. "That's right. How on earth did you know that?"

"My mom makes donuts for me, and they're better than yours."

"Andy," Miss Dunbar said with a snap in her voice. "You need to apologize. You're being rude."

"It's true," Andy said stubbornly.

"Apologize."

He took a deep breath, then said, "I'm sorry my mother's donuts are better than yours are."

"Andy," the teacher snapped.

I couldn't hold back my laughter. "It's fine. I'm glad he likes his mother's food. Now, let's look at the bags of flour. They weigh more than any of you do."

"Even Stinky?" a little girl asked.

I looked around for an overweight child with an olfactory deficiency when the teacher said, "Stinky is her pet pig."

"Well, it depends on how big Stinky is. These bags weigh fifty pounds each."

"Stinky weighs a hundred times more than that," she said proudly.

"Good for him," I said, trying to move the conversation past Stinky and his eating habits.

"Here's where we mix the dough," I said as I pointed to the cutting board, "and here's where we proof it. Does anyone know what proofing is?"

One little girl raised her hand and said, "It's when you say something is true, and then you say why."

"That's proving, Jenny," Miss Dunbar said.

I stepped in and said, "Proofing is the second rising of the dough. It normally lasts about half an hour. After the dough is mixed, it rests the first time, then it's cut out into different shapes before it goes into the proofing cabinet."

"What's that thing hanging up there?" a little girl asked.

"That's a donut cutter," I said.

She looked at the aluminum wheel with a circle of round cutouts. "Could we see it work?"

I shrugged. "We don't have any dough at the moment, but when we do, we roll it out on the board, and then I roll this over it, just like this." I took both handles and rolled the cutter across the table.

"Ugh, what's that?" a boy asked as he pointed to the fryer. The grease had already started coalescing, and there was a skim coat of yellow on top.

"That's where we fry the donuts," I said.

"Gross," he said.

"Jimmie, that's enough."

"Well, it is," he said.

"Don't worry, once it's heated up, it's clear," I said.

"But that junk goes somewhere, doesn't it?"

Miss Dunbar said, "Class, we're getting off track. Let's let Mrs. Hart finish."

I wrapped up the tour and hustled the kids back out into the dining area before something happened to one of the little darlings. I thought about having kids of my own from time to time, but certainly not in such massive quantities. They were a bit overwhelming.

Missy Dunbar said, "Thanks so much for pitching in."

A little boy tugged at her pants. "Miss Dunbar, aren't we getting hats? My dad took me on the Krispy Kreme tour, and we all got hats."

"How about those donut holes?" I asked.

Fortunately, the hats were quickly forgotten.

As I was collecting enough donut holes to feed the miniarmy of kids, a gruff man came in, wiping his hands on a rag. "Okay, Miss Dunbar, you're all set. I'm afraid you missed the tour, though."

"That's fine. We had a lovely time here," she said.

"Let me box these up for you, and you can have them on your way back to school," I said, shoveling donut holes into the box as fast as I could.

"You just want them hopped up on sugar as revenge, don't you?" she whispered.

I returned her smile. "It's the least I could do. Seriously, that was fun. Thanks for stopping by."

"Thanks for accommodating us," she said. "Next year, we're going to schedule a tour here first."

"I should be recovered by then," I said with a laugh.

Once they were gone, Emma said, "That was a nightmare."

"I thought it was fun," I said.

"You would," she replied as she ducked into the back, no doubt to see how much carnage they'd created on their visit.

Emma popped her head back out a minute later. "It looks fine back here. What happened?"

"You just have to know how to talk to them," I said, trying not to laugh. Miss Dunbar had my undying respect, being able to handle all of those kids as well as she did, and making an abrupt change in plans at a moment's notice.

I found myself wishing I'd had a teacher like that at some point on my own way through school.

I was just getting ready to close up for the day when Gabby walked in. "Suzanne, do you have a second?"

"What did you find out?" I asked. I was alone in the donut shop, having sent Emma home half an hour earlier. It had been quiet, and I didn't want to pay her for standing around, especially when there were a thousand other places she'd rather be. She'd also been complaining of feeling drained and worn out, like she was starting to get sick, and I couldn't afford losing her on the early shift when I needed her help making donuts.

"There was indeed one police officer who had a special relationship with Patrick Blaine."

"Who was it?" I asked. Gabby wasn't making it easy on me. She knew something I wanted to hear, and it was against her nature to just blurt it out without making me beg for it.

"His name is Grant," she said proudly.

"Not Moore? Are you sure about that?" As soon as I'd heard a police officer had been involved, I'd automatically assumed it had been Officer Moore. After all, he'd kept coming by the donut shop to check on my memory of events since the murder.

"I was told it was Officer Grant," she said severely.

"Okay. Thanks for checking into it for me."

"Are you going to confront him? I could come with you," Gabby said.

"I'm not ready for that, but I'll call you when I am," I lied.

After she was gone, I kept staring off into space, wondering if I could have been so wrong about Stephen Grant. Had I assumed he was one of the good guys, since he'd been a regular customer of mine for years? Could I be that blind? Did that mean that Officer Moore was clean in all of this? When I thought about it, I really had no reason to suspect him of anything. Maybe he'd just been checking up on me as part of his job. I was starting to feel really bad about the way I'd been treating him when I saw a squad car pull up in front of the shop.

It was Moore himself, and I was surprised when I realized I was glad he'd come by, instead of the chief or Officer Grant. I didn't want to see Chief Martin, and I wasn't sure I could face Stephen Grant, at least not until I knew more about his meeting with Patrick Blaine.

"Am I too late for a cup of coffee?" Officer Moore asked as he came in.

"It's not that fresh, but it's on the house, if you'd like some. I was just getting ready to close up."

He looked at the donuts still in the display case behind me, then glanced at the window. "In that case, I'll take a glazed donut, too."

I'd been talking about the coffee and not the donuts, but why not? It couldn't hurt to get a little good will out of something I was just going to give away anyway.

I put the donut and coffee in front of him, and as

he took a sip, I said, "I have a question that's going to sound a little crazy."

"That's fine with me," he said as he took a bite.

"Does anyone on the force have a bandage on his forearm?"

He nearly choked on his coffee. "Why in the world do you want to know that? And don't tell me it's idle speculation. What are you after? Is there someone in particular you're asking about?"

Why not? Now was as good a time as any to try out my theory. "I was wondering about Officer Grant."

"Steve?" he asked. "Let me think. Yeah, he does have a scratch on one arm. Claims he was cutting a tree limb, and part of it snagged on his shirt and cut him through the skin. It's not much, but he's got a bandage on it. Do you mind telling me how you knew about that? I didn't think you'd be able to see it, since we're all wearing our long-sleeved uniforms right now because of the cold weather."

"I thought I saw him favoring it the last time he was in, and I was worried he'd hurt himself," I said.

"He's fine. From what I hear, it's not that big a scratch." He finished his donut, then asked, "Is there anyone else you were curious about? Hurley has a trick knee, but he's doing okay, too."

"It's good to hear the police force is ready to serve and protect," I said.

Moore must have thought I was crazy, but I didn't care. I'd found some possible evidence that Officer Grant might have been the one who'd attacked me in the park.

But what was I going to do with my newfound information? I couldn't ask Chief Martin about it—he wasn't all that inclined to care about my theories—and Jake was still mad I hadn't called him after the attack. Anyway, I'd need something a lot more concrete than I had at the moment before I accused a cop of any wrongdoing.

It was time to see what I could find out about Officer Stephen Grant.

But I still had three dozen donuts to deal with. I'd made too many again, and was starting to wonder if April Springs was growing tired of what I had to offer. Was it time to come up with some new recipes, or should I try something more drastic? I'd experiment with the recipes first, since that was the least expensive way to generate new business. I really should box up the extras and take them around to a few businesses in town, but I just wasn't in the mood. Instead, I'd drop them off with Father Pete and let him deal with them.

The rector wasn't in his office at the church, and I thought about just leaving the boxed donuts on his desk, but I'd done that once before, and he hadn't found them until the next day. He liked to roam around his parish, and I wanted to be sure he knew I'd been there.

I found him in the hallway outside the youth rec room of the church.

"What are you doing out here?" I asked.

He put a finger to his lips. "I'm eavesdropping on the rehearsal," he said.

I looked inside, and saw Max and his troupe of seniors working on *West Side Story*. It was amusing, watching them figure out the choreography for the big fight scene. I'd have to buy a ticket to see it myself when they went on sale.

"They're really good," Father Pete said. "Once you get over the premise that they're supposed to be a bunch of teenagers. It was a bold choice for Max to make."

"He's been known for his bold choices over the years," I said.

Max was demonstrating a move when I caught sight of his right forearm. There was a bandage on it, and I felt the blood drain from my face.

Father Pete noticed it, too. "Suzanne? Are you all right? You look as if you've just seen a ghost."

"I wish that's all it was," I said. Could Max have been my attacker? It was hard for me to believe, but he had reacted violently when he'd brought me those roses. Was the park confrontation a way for him to get back at me anonymously?

"Tell me what happened," he said calmly, and I knew why so many folks in April Springs came to Father Pete with their problems, regardless of their faith.

"It's nothing," I said as I thrust the donuts into his hands.

He took them, then said, "You know I'm here if you ever need me."

"I know. Thanks, Father."

I left the church, and had to try putting my key into the door lock of the Jeep four times before I could steady it enough to get it in. I had two new suspects, two men who hadn't even been on my list a day earlier. But could I really see Max, or Officer Grant, attacking me in the park?

I had trouble visualizing it, but I had to admit that I'd been wrong before.

It was time to do a little more digging into the lives of the suspects I'd been considering all along. I might not be able to eliminate any of my new suspects yet, but maybe I'd be able to knock Rita or Deb or Lincoln Klein off the list.

Rita answered her door when I knocked, and to my great surprise, she was stone-cold sober. "Yes?" It appeared that she didn't recognize me.

"I need to talk to you."

She started to slam the door in my face, then hesitated. "I know you, don't I? You came by here and demanded to see me."

"More than once," I admitted. "The first time we had the most charming chat, and the second time you hid inside and refused to even answer your door."

Rita's face melted into a frown. "I was afraid of that. Whatever I told you before, it's not true. I can't be held responsible for anything I might have said. I was taking a prescription that didn't agree with me."

"That's funny, I don't know any doctors who prescribe vodka. We need to talk, or I can come back with a state police investigator, if you'd rather."

I could see the wheels turning in her mind. Finally, she said, "You might as well come in."

I walked inside, and was surprised to find the living room clean, as well as being devoid of empty liquor bottles.

"For the record, I wasn't hiding from you the other day. I'd had a bad conversation with one of my friends, a former friend, I should say, and I wasn't in the mood to speak with anyone. Please don't take it personally."

"How could I?" I asked. "It's your right not to answer your own door."

She seemed to accept that. "Coffee?" she offered. "I'm drinking it by the gallon, so you might as well join me."

"That would be nice," I said, amazed at the woman's transformation since I'd seen her drunk. She was now polished and elegant, though no doubt still hungover from her bender.

After she poured me a cup, she said, "I hate surprises. What exactly did we talk about when you visited earlier?"

"Your husband's beneficiary was the main topic of conversation," I said.

She nodded. "That's what I thought. And he was my ex-husband, I vaguely remember telling you that before."

"But you lied to me about who got his money."

She raised an eyebrow. "I didn't lie to you, at least not knowingly. I had been under the impression that tart Deb Jenkins had been listed as his sole beneficiary, but I was wrong. It all comes to me," she said, and it was easy to catch the sadness in her voice. She added, "I also discovered that it was just enough to bury him, not even close to the million I'd been expecting. The poor, unfortunate man let his policy lapse three days before he was murdered."

"You were pretty angry with him when we spoke."

"My, I must go on when I'm drinking. That must be why I so rarely imbibe."

"But you're not denying you were expecting a big payoff, are you?"

She laughed ruefully. "No, I'm not denying it. I've taken the money provided by the insurance company and paid for his funeral. With what's left—though it's not much—I plan to buy a karaoke machine in his honor."

"Did he like to sing?"

"No, he was dreadful at it. Patrick once claimed the only thing worse than his singing was mine, and I plan on serenading him at the service. Quite a gesture, wouldn't you say?"

"I'd say it shows you aren't ready to let go," I said. "That's another motive for murder, isn't it?"

"Just who are you?" she asked as she put her coffee cup down.

"I'm working on a story for the newspaper," I said.

"We'll just see about that," she said as she reached for the telephone. "I know Ray quite well."

It was time to lie to her yet again. "It's not for the *April Springs Sentinel*. It's for the *Observer*."

She put the phone down. "I don't know anyone there. Why are you so curious about me, though?"

"You must admit, you weren't the model of decorum the other day."

"No, but I've already apologized for that, haven't I?"

I took a deep breath, then said, "So you won't mind if I ask where you were the night of the murder, would you?"

"I could tell you, but it's nothing I want plastered all over a newspaper."

I said, "You can tell me off the record, if you'd like."

She frowned at me. "Does that really work? I thought it was some kind of twist the movie people came up with."

I didn't know if it was or not, but I needed to convince her that it was true. "If you tell me something in confidence, I can't print it, or you could sue me for everything I own, plus get me fired. Do you think I'd be willing to risk that?"

She shrugged. "I assume not." Rita bit her lower lip, then said, "At any rate, I don't suppose there's any reason to keep it a secret. I've already told the police, and they've cleared me of all suspicion."

That would have been good to know, but since the chief wasn't keeping me in the loop—and neither was Jake Bishop, for that matter—I had to find out these things on my own. "I'm listening," I said.

"I was at Murphy's Diner in Union Square, milking a cup of coffee and a slice of pie all night long while I waited for my husband's mistress at a hotel room across the street with her other boyfriend. I was going to prove to Patrick that she wasn't worth dumping me for. Pathetic, isn't it, the scorned ex-wife fighting to get her husband back." She stood, then said, "Hang on a second, let me get the photos."

I watched her dig into her purse, and for a second, for some irrational reason, I thought she was looking for a gun.

It was with great relief that I saw her pull out a blue and yellow packet of photographs instead.

The first photograph showed Deb Jenkins going into a hotel room across the street with Lincoln Klein. There was a clock that showed clearly in the picture on the wall of the diner, and it read 10:15. From the darkness outside, it was obvious it had been taken at night.

"This could have been taken any night," I said.

"Look at the next shot."

I flipped to the next photo and saw Lincoln disappearing into the room, but the focus was on the newspaper sitting on the table in the foreground. It was a copy of the *April Springs Sentinel,* and it had the date of the day before someone had dumped Patrick Blaine's body in front of my donut shop.

"Go to the next shot," Rita coaxed me.

I did, and found the next photo showed Deb and Lincoln leaving the hotel. The clock now read 2:45. Not only had Rita offered an alibi for herself, she'd also eliminated two of my other suspects.

"These could have been doctored," I said.

"They could have been, but the police were satisfied, so I think you should be, too. Since there's nothing else to discuss, I'm afraid I need to ask you to leave. Unless you feel like singing a little karaoke with me so I can practice. The memorial service starts in an hour, and I need to get warmed up."

"Sorry. I've got other plans."

"I only wish I did," she said.

I went back to my Jeep with a new perspective. Without realizing it, Rita had given me the key to figuring out what had really happened. With the list of my suspects so drastically narrowed down, I had a very good idea who had killed one of my favorite customers. I knew in my heart that it couldn't have been my ex-husband, and I'd probably known it all along. While I had to admit that it was dramatic enough for Max to have approached me in the park with no more intent than to keep me safe by scaring me half to death, there was no real reason he would kill Patrick Blaine, at least none that I was aware of.

That left one of two cops who had to have done it.

But I still wasn't sure which one.

ORANGE SPICE CAKE DONUTS

These donuts sport a subtle orange touch, something I'm always game for. They can be glazed with a topping flavored with orange extract, dusted with powdered sugar, or eaten while they're still warm.

INGREDIENTS
2 tablespoons canola oil
1 cup granulated sugar
½ stick butter (¼ cup)
3 egg yolks, beaten
1 tablespoon orange extract
Zest of one orange, fine
1 teaspoon cinnamon
1 cup milk (2% or whole)
1 tablespoon baking powder
3–4 cups flour

DIRECTIONS
Mix the oil, sugar, milk, egg yolks, cinnamon, orange extract, and orange zest until combined well. Sift the flour and baking powder together, then add to the liquid, stirring well. This will make a stiff dough.

Chill the dough for about 1 hour, then turn it out onto a floured surface, knead it into a ball, then roll the dough out to about ½-inch to ¼-inch thickness. Use your donut cutter and cut the rounds and holes, then fry them for about 2 minutes on each side in

375-degree oil until they're done. Turn out onto paper towels to drain, then enjoy plain or add a topping.

Makes 1 dozen donuts.

CHAPTER 12

I dialed Jake's telephone number, trying to figure out what I was going to say to him, when the call went straight to his voice mail.

"Hi, you're reached Officer Jacob Bishop. Leave your name and number, and I'll get back to you as soon as I can."

"Jake, this is Suzanne. Call me as soon as you get this. We need to talk."

I was getting ready to add my suspicions when the machine cut off. My hesitation must have come across as the end of the message, and I thought about calling Jake back, but did I really want my suspicions recorded on his telephone? What if I was wrong? Did I really want there to be concrete evidence that I'd accused a cop of murder?

I got into my Jeep and tried to figure out what my next move was. I must have driven around for an hour, because I still hadn't come up with anything by five, and my rumbling stomach demanded to be fed.

It was a better idea than any I'd had so far, so I

pulled into the Boxcar for a quick bite to eat. Maybe I'd find inspiration there, but at the very least, I'd get fed.

I walked into the narrow boxcar, hoping to find a seat by myself. Trish tried to get my attention, but I wasn't in the mood to chat with the owner, so I kept walking, offering her a wave as I passed the grill.

"Suzanne," she called out. "I need to talk to you."

I moved to the counter, and before I could ask her what was going on, the restroom door opened and Max walked out.

"Sorry, that was it," she said.

"Thanks for trying." I was in no mood to see Max, especially after spotting that bandage on his arm earlier, but I wasn't going to let him run me out of my favorite diner, either.

I took a booth as far away as I could from where Max was sitting, but he approached me anyway.

As he slid onto the seat beside me, I said, "Sorry. That seat's taken."

"I don't see anyone sitting there," he said.

"That's because he's not here yet."

"Then I'll move when he gets here," Max said. "We need to talk."

I couldn't believe how obstinate he was being. "Trust me, Max, you don't want to talk to me right now."

"What's gotten into you?" he asked. "You're not acting like yourself."

That was enough. "Who should I be acting like, Max? You? One second it's roses in front of my shop, and the next you're attacking me."

I don't think he could have been any more surprised if I'd proposed to him.

"What are you talking about?"

I jabbed his covered forearm. "How'd you get hurt, Max? Care to tell me that?"

"One of the props fell on me, and I had to block it from crushing my skull."

"Prove it."

He shook his head. "How could I possibly do that? I was working by myself when it happened." He paused, then his eyes grew cold. "Wait a second. Are you talking about what happened at the park? You can't be serious."

"I stabbed my attacker with a fingernail. Is that what you're covering up?"

He pulled back his shirtsleeve and ripped off the bandage. I saw in an instant that it was far more damage than I ever could have done.

"I didn't attack you. Satisfied?"

"You could have made it worse on purpose, in case someone demanded to see it," I said. "It's exactly that kind of melodramatic thing you'd do, scaring the life out of me to get me to back off my investigation."

"You've lost your mind completely, haven't you?" Max stood, then stormed out of the diner.

Trish came over. "I was about ready to call the cops. What was that all about?"

"Sorry, but I had to make it clear where we stood."

Trish whistled, then said, "I think you took care of that. I've never seen him so mad."

"Stick around, I bet I can make him even madder."

She shook her head. "I'm not going to mess with you tonight, woman. You're dangerous."

"Not to my friends," I said.

"Then I'm glad I'm counted among them. What will you have?"

"Let's go crazy. How about a hamburger, fries, and a chocolate shake?"

"Sounds good. Why don't I have Hilda make two, and I'll join you."

"I'm fine," I said. "Honestly, you don't need to babysit me."

"Are you kidding? I haven't had a bite all day. I've been looking for an excuse to get off my feet for a bit."

"Then that sounds good."

Ten minutes later, she came back with a tray brimming with food. "Let's dig in while it's slow. Hilda's got the register, and Gladys came in early to cook for the dinner shift."

Trish stabbed a French fry into a pile of ketchup, then pointed it at me like a finger. "Now, what's going on with you? I heard you got mugged in the park."

"There's not much to tell," I said, sick of recounting the tale yet again.

"From the way I hear it, you were surrounded, but you fought your way out, and three of them are in the hospital."

I shook my head. "One guy grabbed me from behind. I jabbed him with a fingernail and he let me go. End of story."

Trish frowned. "I like the other version better. It made you sound like some kind of Wonder Woman or something."

"Okay, but I'm not wearing the outfit."

Trish sipped her shake, then said, "I can't blame

you there. I'd have to diet for a year to fit into those shorts, and what fun would that be?"

"If I got an invisible plane and a magic lasso, it might be worth it," I said. "But probably not."

We both laughed at that, and soon enough, our meals were finished.

As I pulled a ten from my purse, I said, "Trish, I can't tell you how much I needed that."

"I was pretty hungry myself," she said.

"That's not what I'm talking about, and you know it," I said.

"I'm here any time you need someone to talk to," she said.

I touched her hand lightly. "I know, and I appreciate it."

As I headed for the door, she asked, "So, off to fight more crime?"

I stifled a yawn, then said, "To tell you the truth, I'm beat. I think I'm going home so I can go to bed."

"I don't know how you do it. Your schedule would kill me," she said.

"It's trying," I answered as I walked down the iron steps, over the old train track, and toward my Jeep. Jake hadn't called me back, and I was a little miffed about that, but when I thought about calling him back, I just grew wearier. I didn't have much fight left in me, and I didn't want to waste it on him.

I drove home, made my excuses to Momma, turned off my phone, then curled up with a good book and fell asleep before seven o'clock. I'd been missing too much sleep lately, and it was time to start catching up.

* * *

I felt good when my alarm went off a little after one A.M. As I dressed, I thought about what the day would bring, and how I could find out more about Officer Grant. I needed something more than a rumor to take to Jake. But proof was tougher to get than I'd ever realized.

I left the house, warmed up the Jeep, then headed to the donut shop. I used to love the short drive there, when I had the world all to myself, but lately, all I saw were shadows and wondered what they were hiding. It was amazing how much my perspective had changed since Patrick Blaine's body had been dumped in front of Donut Hearts.

I went through my new, expedited routine of using my headlights to illuminate the storefront as I raced inside to turn on every light in the place. After that, it was a quick dash back outside to park the Jeep in front of the shop, then dead-bolt myself back inside.

My heart was racing by the time I finished my checklist, but at least I was safe.

I turned the deep fryer on as I passed it on my way to my office to check any messages I might have gotten overnight.

There was a neon numeral 2 illuminated.

"Hey, Suzanne. Sorry to do this to you at the last minute, but I feel awful, and I won't be able to make it in. Hopefully I'll see you tomorrow. Bye." Emma was sick, and I'd known it was a possibility, given the way we'd left things the day before. It meant a longer morning with a great deal more work, but there wasn't anybody I could call, especially at two in the morning. I'd have to cut back on a couple of the experiments I'd been planning to try, but I should be fine.

The next call was from Jake. He sounded clearly aggravated as he said, "Your cell phone is off, and your ringer at home must not be working, either. I'm returning your call. Sorry it's taken me so long, but I finally have a lead in the case. I should have this wrapped up soon. Behave yourself until I do, Suzanne."

I had to laugh at that. Jake hadn't known me long, but from the amused tone in his voice, it was clear he knew better than to think I'd take that last bit of advice.

I was measuring out the different portions of flour for the morning batch of cake donuts when I replayed everything I'd learned about Patrick Blaine's life over the last several days. I went into kind of a Zen thing when I worked alone, having done it so much that I didn't really need to focus all that much on the process.

I replayed past conversations I'd had with both Officer Moore and Officer Grant, and thought about the times I'd interacted with them in the course of my investigation. While Officer Grant's inquiries had been routine, I suddenly realized that Officer Moore was the one who had been pressing me about what I'd seen the night of Patrick Blaine's murder well past the time he should have dropped it and moved on.

There was something else that had been nagging at me.

Who was the first person on the scene after I'd reported the crime to the police?

Officer Moore.

Who had pointed my suspicions away from himself by claiming other suspects had wounds to their arms?

Officer Moore.

And who had bragged about being a Carolina Panthers fan right in front of me? I suddenly realized that had been the symbol I'd seen on the faded sweatshirt of the killer.

I was right the first time; it had been a cat, or more accurately, a panther.

Officer Moore.

I dug into the top drawer in my office and took out my copy of the statement I'd given him on the night of the murder, something I hadn't even glanced at since he'd given it to me. Then I took out the parking ticket with the time and date printed on the back.

The sevens were identical with their slashes across the middle. Officer Moore had been the one who'd demanded a meeting with Patrick Blaine. But why?

And then I remembered the rumor George had heard about dirty cops on the April Springs police force. Maybe Patrick had uncovered something on a dirty cop. Was it dangerous enough information to get him killed?

I really had to talk to Jake now.

I was dialing his cell phone, regardless of the hour, and just as the call went straight to his voice mail, there was a banging at the front door. Grabbing the knife I'd used before, I came out of the kitchen and looked outside into the darkness.

Jake was leaning against the front door.

Then on the glass I saw the smeared blood coming from his chest.

I dropped the knife in my hand and struggled to open the door.

As I did, Jake collapsed in my arms.

I had to get him some help.

And then someone else came rushing in.

I wasn't at all surprised to see that it was the man I'd just realized was a cold-blooded killer.

"Why did you do it?" I asked Moore as I held Jake in my arms on the floor. I put my fingers on his throat and found a slight, whispering pulse, and he was taking short, shallow breaths. He wasn't in very good shape, but at least he was still alive.

"He was getting too close," Moore said as he stepped over Jake's body. "Tonight, I'm taking care of loose ends, and you're next on my list."

I shook my head in anger. "I knew you were the one who killed Patrick Blaine," I said as I kept staring at Jake. I had to help him if I could, even if it meant taking a chance with my own life. From the look in Moore's eyes, I knew in the end it didn't matter.

He clearly had no plans to leave me alive.

"Get away from him," he snapped. "I'm going to drag him back into the kitchen, and you're going to lead the way. If you do anything stupid, I'll go take care of your mother after I'm done with you. If you cooperate, though, I'll leave her alone. You wouldn't want to be the cause of her death too, now, would you?"

He was just the sort of maniac to do it, too.

"I won't give you any trouble," I said.

He dragged Jake's body back into the kitchen, and I followed them in. I positioned myself by the heavy maple rolling pin, but I knew I couldn't swing it before he put a bullet or a blade in me. Still, if I got the opportunity, I was going to take it. I didn't have any other choice.

Moore let Jake fall again as soon as they were through the kitchen door, and as the rogue cop turned to me, I said, "I always wondered how you managed to drop Patrick Blaine's body so fast, and still be the first one on the scene. What did you do with the car you were driving?"

Moore almost smiled as he said, "I parked it in the garage behind Newberry's. Nobody thought to look there, especially since that was *my* part of the search area for the abandoned vehicle. It's still back there, covered with a tarp. I'll move it after I'm through here."

"Why dump him in front of the donut shop? You could have put the body anywhere, but you did it where someone might see you."

"Think about it, Suzanne. I needed a perfect alibi, and I knew you were the only one who could give it to me at that time of the morning. I could dump him in the darkness, then drive back to where my squad car was parked. I made sure I was the only one patrolling in town, so I figured you'd be the only witness. I just didn't expect you to flip your lights on when you did."

"It took me a while to put it all together," I admitted.

"From everything I've heard about you around town, I knew you wouldn't give up until you found out who killed Blaine."

Was Jake starting to stir? I had to keep Moore's attention. Maybe then Jake would have a chance to distract him, and I could use the rolling pin to help. "If it's any consolation, I just now managed to figure it out," I said quickly. "Patrick knew you were on the take, didn't he? Was it the investment firm or the construction company that was paying you to look the other way? That's the only thing I haven't figured out yet."

"You're pretty smart, but not that smart. If you don't know, I'm not going to tell you."

"I still can't believe you killed him over money."

He said, "The money was never the issue. Blaine caught me taking a payoff he never should have witnessed, and I had to get rid of him before he went to the chief with it. I tried to buy him off, but he wouldn't budge. Can you believe it? The man made dirty deals on paper all day long, he gambled away every cent he had, but he witnessed one little collection and decided he owed it to his conscience to turn me in. I couldn't let him do that, now, could I? He backed me into a corner, and I couldn't see any other way out."

I heard Jake mutter something, and then there was a clatter behind us. He'd managed to pull a few pans off the shelf. It wasn't much, but it was enough to distract Moore. I grabbed the rolling pin, but instead of swinging it at his head, I suddenly realized I was too far away.

I could throw it, though.

But not directly at Moore's head.

There was a better target right next to him.

I tossed the rolling pin into the scalding hot oil in

the fryer, and it made a terrific splash of boiling liquid. Moore caught it in the face, and he slumped to the floor, clawing at his eyes.

It had been a direct hit.

I grabbed the phone and dialed 911, then picked up a knife to cover the downed cop, but he wasn't a threat to anyone anymore.

I unlocked the front door and propped it open, then went to Jake's side. He was slumped over, and I felt for a pulse, afraid of what I might find.

Was that a heartbeat, or was it just wishful thinking? I took a clean towel and pressed it against his chest wound, whispering to him gently as I waited for the ambulance to arrive.

A paramedic brushed me aside and started working on him as Chief Martin came in behind them.

"What happened here?" he asked gruffly.

"Your officer just tried to kill me, and he almost took out Jake, too. It was all because he was on the take."

The chief looked down in disbelief. Moore wasn't in any shape to answer as he lay there writhing on the floor.

Another paramedic started to tend to him when the chief put a hand on his shoulder. "Take care of him first," he said, nodding toward Jake. "This one can wait."

"He'll be on his way to the hospital in thirty seconds," the paramedic said.

"Then that's how long you're going to wait." I half expected the chief to pull his gun when the paramedic refused and started to treat Moore, but he just turned his back.

"You and I need to talk," Martin said.

"I need to go to the hospital with Jake," I insisted.

"You can't ride with them; they're busy trying to save his life. Come on, I'll give you a lift. What about the shop? Should we wait and lock it up?"

"I don't care if somebody steals everything in it," I said, and I meant it.

We rode to the hospital in relative silence. It was pretty clear that the chief was just as shaken by having a bad cop on his force as I was. "It answers a lot of questions," he finally said. "I've heard rumors that one of my men was taking bribes to look the other way, but I just couldn't bring myself to believe it."

"You mean Moore was one of your suspects, too?"

The chief shook his head. "No, I guess I was blinded by loyalty to my men. I owe you an apology."

In better days, I might have reveled at the admission, but the words were dead to me at the moment. "I just hope Jake is going to be all right."

"Believe me, I do, too."

We made it to the emergency room as they wheeled Jake by on a cart. A doctor was working on him as they moved, and I worried about the flurry of activity around him.

Chief Martin said softly, "It's going to be a while. Why don't I grab us both some coffee, and we can wait together."

I nodded, and he guided me to a chair in the waiting room before going off in search of coffee. I barely noticed him when he got back.

"I said, take it," he repeated, and I realized there was a cup almost under my nose.

"Thanks," I said as I took a gulp. My hands were shaking so badly I could barely hold the cup. "I don't know what's wrong with my nerves."

"I've seen a lot of good people go through that," he said. "You were calm when it counted, that's all that matters. Did you actually throw a rolling pin at him?"

"No. I knew it would be hit or miss if I aimed for him, and I had to stop him fast. The rolling pin was the heaviest thing around, so I tossed it into the oil. I wonder if I blinded him."

"If you did, it was no less than he deserved," Martin said.

An attendant came out a few minutes later, then said, "It was close, and there's going to be some scarring, but I think his eyes will be fine."

I asked, "His eyes? What are you talking about?"

The attendant said, "Naturally I assumed you were here with the police officer. I thought you'd want to know."

"He's not fit to wear the uniform," the chief said, his voice full of disgust. "How's the state policeman?"

"Not as lucky," the attendant said, before he was called away.

"What did he mean by that?" I asked the chief.

"It's too soon to worry yet," he said.

"Don't you have somewhere else you should be?" I asked. "There's a crime scene you need to take care of. Chief, you don't have to babysit me."

He shook his head. "My best man's on it right now. There's nowhere else I need to be at the moment."

I couldn't believe how nice he was being to me. The ER doors burst open, and my mother came in. "Thank you for calling me, Phillip."

"You're most welcome, Dorothy. Now, if you two will excuse me, I'd better get back to the donut shop."

"Thanks for everything," I said.

He tipped his hat. "Just doing my job."

George arrived shortly afterwards, but by the time dawn broke, we still hadn't heard anything about Jake's condition. There would be no donuts today, but that didn't seem to matter.

All I cared about was Jake pulling through.

A doctor in scrubs finally walked out, and approached us. I wasn't sure what the chief had told them, but it was clear someone had instructed him to keep me informed.

"Ma'am, you're with Officer Bishop, aren't you?"

"I am," I said. "How is he?"

"He was lucky, if you can ever call getting knifed in the chest a matter of luck. We were able to take care of most of the muscle damage. He's going to be off his feet for a while, but I don't see any reason he shouldn't make a full recovery."

"Can I see him?" I asked. I had a thousand questions for him, but none more important than to find out if I'd been the cause of him getting stabbed.

"Not until later today. After three, I think he might be able to have one visitor, but that's the soonest possible."

"Thank you, Doctor."

"Don't thank me. You should thank whoever got him in here in time. He'd lost a lot of blood, and in another ten minutes, he would have been gone."

After he left, I turned to Momma and said, "Let's go."

"You're right. Home is where you should be."

"That's not where I'm headed," I said. "If the chief is finished with the crime scene, I'm going to make donuts."

She looked at me as if I'd lost my mind. "Suzanne, be reasonable. Nobody expects you to provide donuts today. You're being ridiculous."

I grabbed my mother's hands in mine. "You don't understand. I have to make donuts right now, or I'll never be able to go back into that shop again. I've got to wipe out the memories of what happened, and replace them with good ones."

George overheard me, and said, "I'll give you a ride. Come on."

"My daughter will come with me," she said, still trying to protect her cub.

"Let's all go," I said. "If we can get in there, the donuts will be on me."

We formed a little caravan and drove back to Donut Hearts. There was only one squad car parked there, and I was surprised to find Chief Martin on his hands and knees scrubbing the floor. The splashed oil had already been cleaned up, and he was nearly finished with the dining area.

"Chief, you didn't have to do this," I said. "What about your crime scene?"

"We expedited it," he said as he stood. "I couldn't let you come back to what was here, not after what my force put you through, so everyone off duty came by to help clean up. It should be ready for you tomorrow, if you're up to coming back so soon."

I was sure the disappointment showed on my face. "Does that mean I can't make donuts today?"

Momma said, "Please, Phillip, it's important."

The chief nodded. "The place is yours. I just thought . . ."

My mother took the pail from him, and the rag he'd been using. "We appreciate this more than we can express."

He was clearly tongue-tied by my mother's praise.

"Sorry about everything," he mumbled.

My mother kissed him lightly on the cheek. "Nonsense. It's not how you start something, it's how you finish."

They walked out together, and I looked through the open door at my kitchen, the scene of so much distress. Could I ever work there again? Was it time to sell the place and move on to something else?

No, I couldn't bring myself to do that. Making donuts wasn't just what I did, it was a part of who I was.

George came back in from my office, wearing the tall chef's hat I'd gotten as a gag gift from Emma and trying to tie an apron that barely covered his girth.

"I'm ready to get started. What's first?"

"We'll measure the flour, just as soon as I top off the oil in the fryer," I said.

I was back, and it felt good making a batch of donuts, almost as if things were back to normal. George and I made a batch of cake donuts with Momma watching us, giving us tips I didn't need as we worked. There wasn't time to make the yeast ones, but the cooking was symbolic, and the donuts tasted especially good when we ate them.

After we cleaned up, I boxed up a dozen donuts, and headed back to the hospital.

"I can't believe you brought me donuts," Jake said when I walked into his room.

"I'm sorry, but they won't let you have any. Not until at least tomorrow."

"That's just cruel," he said. "If I can't have any, why did you bring them?"

I smiled down at him, trying to ignore the bandage covering most of his chest and the drip tube in his arm. "I wasn't taunting you," I said. "I didn't know. I'm going to leave them at the nurses' station. I figure they'll need a treat after putting up with you."

I leaned forward and kissed him lightly, being careful not to disturb anything.

"What was that for?"

"For protecting me," I said.

"Are you kidding? From what the chief told me, you're the one who took care of me. That was quick thinking, chucking the rolling pin into the oil."

"It was natural for me; I've been working with that fryer for years. I had a good idea what kind of impact it would make when it hit. I couldn't have done it without you, though. You pulled those pans off the shelf, and that gave me the time I needed to grab the pin and toss it."

He smiled. "So we're both heroes."

"Not quite. I need to ask you something. Are you lying here with a hole in your chest because of something I did? I'll never be able to forgive myself if it is."

He shook his head. "I did that all on my own. I

was worried about you, so I decided to stake out the donut shop in case somebody dropped by. Moore tried to tell me the story about Grant attacking you, but I didn't believe it for a second. I talked to Grant about his arm, and he told me that he was cutting a tree branch when it snapped. It scratched him up pretty badly, and I guess Moore decided to use it divert the suspicion away from himself. I've got to admit that while I was sitting out there in the darkness watching your back, I'd decided I needed to focus on Moore. To be honest with you, he got me before I could do anything about it. I don't know why he dragged me from my car to your shop. Showing off, I guess. He wanted someone to see how clever he'd been taking out a state cop, and since he was . . . you know."

"I know what you're going to say, so I'll finish it for you."

"You don't need to," he said softly.

I ignored him and said, "Since he was going to kill me anyway, what harm could it do? Only you were too stubborn to die, and that's what saved us both."

"I guess we were both lucky this morning," he said.

"I'm just glad it turned out all right."

He frowned. "Hey, are those donuts fresh?"

"Would I ever bring you stale donuts, even if you can't eat them?"

"That's what I mean," he said. "I can't believe you made donuts today."

I started to stammer. "I knew you weren't going to be able to see me until later, and I had to get back on the horse again, you know?" I looked down at him and saw that he was smiling. "What are you grinning about?"

"I'm just glad you're not giving up the shop after what happened."

I smiled at him. "Don't worry, it will take more than that."

A nurse came by and said, "I'm sorry, but you'll have to leave."

I handed her the boxed donuts. "Could I bribe you with these for one more minute with him?"

She took the offering, then grinned. "I suppose we can make an exception, just this once."

After she was gone, I said, "Where does this leave us?"

"I think the case is pretty well wrapped up."

"I'm not talking about what happened today, and you know it."

He shrugged, and I saw him wince from the pain. "Let's just take it a day at time and see, okay?"

I kissed him again, then said, "Okay, I get the hint. I'll be back tomorrow."

"Bring chocolate sprinkles next time. I love chocolate sprinkles."

I laughed at him as I left his room.

It would be good having someone in my life again, if that's what Jake was becoming. There were a thousand reasons why we shouldn't even try to work out some kind of relationship, I knew that better than anyone else, but there was one factor that overruled all of the rest.

I felt better about myself when I was with him than I did when we were apart.

And really, what other reason did I need?

Tomorrow's delivery would be overflowing with chocolate-sprinkle donuts.

I couldn't think of a better way to let him know that I cared.

INDEX OF RECIPES

Here's an exciting sneak peek at

FATALLY FROSTED,

the next Donut Shop Mystery from Jessica Beck,
also available from
St. Martin's / Minotaur Paperbacks!

I thought getting away from my business—Donut Hearts—for a few days might be fun, but when I agreed to make gourmet donuts for one of my friends, I had no idea it would put me right in the middle of a homicide investigation where one of my donuts would actually be used as a murder weapon.

Just about everyone I knew in April Springs, North Carolina—population 5,001—was looking forward to the September Kitchens Extraordinaire home tour ever since it had first been announced in *The April Springs Sentinel*—including me. When my friend, Marge Rankin, suggested I demonstrate how to make something special in her newly remodeled kitchen for the tour, I'd jumped at the chance to show off just what I could do with some dough and a portable fryer. There wouldn't be a yeast donut or an apple fritter on the menu; I was going to pull out all of the stops and make something unforgettable.

"Jake, do you really want to learn how to make beignets?"

My boyfriend—a state police inspector named Jake Bishop I'd been seeing since March—smiled at me as we stood in the kitchen of Donut Hearts. He looked cute wearing one of our aprons, but I knew better than to tell him that. Jake was tall and thin, with a healthy head of sandy blond hair, and there was something about the man's presence that made me smile.

"Not as much as I like being around you," he admitted. I didn't get to see him nearly enough, since his casework took him all over the state of North Carolina. I had to give him points for honesty, but I still had a job to do.

"I've got an idea," I said. "Why don't you sit over there and keep me company, and I'll let you sample the beignets I make? You can be my official taster."

He took off the apron as though he'd been pardoned for a crime he'd never committed. "That's the best deal I've had in weeks."

"You don't have to look so relieved when you say it," I said with a grin.

"What can I tell you? I'm all about leaving tough stuff to the experts."

I frowned at the finished dough. It was close to the consistency I'd been hoping for, but the true test would be in the taste. "I'm not sure I qualify."

"Come on, you're the best donut maker in the

world. You told me yourself beignets are just fancy donuts, and no one's better at making those than you. I'm a cop; trust me, I know donuts."

"I appreciate the sentiment, but I don't have time on the tour to make these with yeast, so I'm going to have to substitute baking powder instead. It's more chemistry than you'd imagine." It was true. While cooking recipes could usually be slightly modified with impunity, baking was another matter altogether. I needed enough baking powder to make the dough rise when it hit the hot oil, but not too much, or it would be a disaster, and if there was one thing I couldn't afford, it was to wreck my demonstration.

He laughed. "Don't sell yourself short. I know I couldn't do it."

I lightly floured the counter and rolled out the dough until it was somewhere between a quarter- and an eighth-inch thick, and then cut it into squares. For the demonstration, I'd be using my ravioli cutter, a scallop-edged tool that left perfectly shaped circles, but this test-run was more about taste than appearance.

I dropped the first rounds into the oil and held my breath. After cooking two minutes on a side, I flipped them, and then pulled them out after another two. I had a plate ready, and dusted them with confectioner's sugar while they were still hot.

"Man, those smell fantastic," Jake said as I slid the plate in front of him.

"Tell me how they taste," I said.

We both reached for the same one, and I laughed. "There's plenty for both of us."

"That's what you think." He took a bite, and I

watched his expression. If the look of joy meant anything, I might have a winning recipe after all.

"Outstanding," he said as he reached for another one.

I was happy with his reaction, but I was a harsher judge than he was.

I bit into the treat, and felt the texture of the beignet in my mouth. The flavor was spot-on, a hint of airy lightness that tasted something like a sophisticated funnel cake from the fair. I had to agree that it was good—there was no doubt about that—but was it as good as my yeast beignets?

"Are you sure?"

"Well, maybe I'd better eat the rest of these so I can be sure." He had a hint of powdered sugar on his nose, and I reached over and wiped it off.

We were about to have a moment when his cell phone rang.

"Bishop here," he said as he answered, his voice becoming instantly serious. I didn't have any idea how he could turn it off and on like he did.

"Yes, sir. I understand. I'm on my way."

After he hung up, I asked, "Bad news?"

"I've got a case. It's on the Outer Banks, Suzanne. Looks like I'm going to have to miss the tour. Sorry."

"You've got a job to do," I said, a little sad that he wouldn't be there for my demonstration.

He shrugged, and then wrapped me in his arms. "I'll call you later."

"Liar," I said with a grin. When he was on a case, I knew how focused he could get, so I didn't expect daily, or even weekly telephone calls.

"You caught me," he said, and then to make up for it, he kissed me.

After he was gone, I could swear I could still taste the beignets on his breath.

The day before the tour, Marge stopped by Donut Hearts half an hour before we were set to close, to go over my menu one more time. She was a petite woman in her early sixties, and her smile was always a little crooked, shifting slightly to the left whenever she grinned. You couldn't see it at the moment though, since Marge wasn't anywhere close to smiling.

"Suzanne, are you certain you're ready for the big day? I don't mean to put any extra pressure on you, but this is important."

I nodded and did my best to reassure her. "Marge, I've got everything under control. I've been staying late an hour every day for a week to test my recipes and polish my cooking techniques with the portable fryer, and I've got it all down cold. Don't worry. It's going to be fabulous."

Marge Rankin had inherited a great deal of money from her father when he'd passed away a few years earlier. Rumors around town put her net worth at two million dollars on the conservative side, and all the way up to ten million on those hot summer days when no one had anything else to talk about. It was impossible to tell that Marge had money by the way she dressed, though; she bought her clothes from Gabby Williams's shop next door to the converted train depot that now housed my donut shop. ReNEWed

was a clothing store that offered some of the best re-
cycled clothing in our part of North Carolina, and
Marge wasn't afraid who knew she shopped for her
apparel second-hand.

"It just has to be perfect," Marge said, wringing
her hands together with such force they were white.
"I've dreamed about this kitchen for twenty years,
and I can hardly believe I finally have it. I want everyone to know it, too."

I'd had the grand tour of her remodeled place the
day before, and she had every right to be proud. From
the Viking stove to the deluxe six-burner industrial
cook-top, the lustrous marble countertops to the elegant hardwood floors, it was truly a thing of beauty.

"It's going to be the star of the show," I said. "Everyone will be talking about it when we're through."

Marge smiled. "I certainly hope so. Thanks again
for making donuts for me."

The underlying theme of the exhibition was Working Kitchens, and everyone with a stop on the tour had
hired a professional chef to show off their creations. I
was the lone demonstrator who hadn't gone to culi-
nary school, and I was beginning to feel the pinging of
my nerves, something I couldn't let Marge see.

I tried to match her smile as I said, "Are you kidding? How often do I get the chance to work in such
elegant surroundings? I'm looking forward to it."

She looked around the shop, then frowned softly.
"I think your place is quaint. Who doesn't love an
old train depot?"

I glanced at the painted burgundy floor, the large
windows overlooking Springs Drive from one view
and the abandoned railroad tracks from the other,

and saw Donut Hearts in a different light. Sometimes I took it for granted, but it really was a welcoming place to spend my days, even if they did begin at one-thirty in the morning and end a little after noon.

"Don't get me wrong," I said. "I'm a huge fan of my shop. After all, it's named after me, isn't it?"

Marge nodded. "That was so clever, adding an E to your last name. Hart for Heart, it's perfect."

"I like it," I admitted. "Now, don't you have a thousand things to do to get ready for tomorrow? Do you have the list of ingredients I asked you to get for me?" Marge had insisted on supplying everything I'd need for the day's donut-making, and I hadn't fought her on it. After all, it freed me to try some things that I'd only read about in books before, and I wasn't going to scrimp or substitute on second-class ingredients.

"I've got three of everything you requested, so we'll be fine. I *do* have to see about the china, though. I'd better go check to see if it's arrived at the house yet."

As she started for the door, Marge hesitated, then asked, "Have I thanked you recently for doing this for me?"

"Just a thousand times," I said with a grin. "Just remember to relax and have fun with it. Our stop is going to be the talk of the town. Now shoo."

CPSIA information can be obtained
at www.ICGtesting.com
Printed in the USA
BVHW042222020523
663442BV00003B/73

9 781250 250476